Little Red Flags Endorsements

"An urgently told story of a woman's hope and self-deception in the midst of a destructive relationship. Jeanette Settembre writes about the blissful yet agonizing experience of first love with startling sensitivity and keen observation."

—Hanna Halperin, author of *I Could Live Here Forever*

"In *Little Red Flags*, Jeanette Settembre offers a heartfelt exploration of what it means to fall deeply in love with a deeply flawed man and lose yourself in the process. It will leave readers asking themselves what they would do every step of the way."

—Jill Santopolo, author of *The Light We Lost* and *The Love We Found*

"An emotionally gripping debut about love, sacrifice, and finding the strength to choose yourself. Jeanette Settembre writes with a terrific sense of tension and suspense."

—Jo Piazza, author of *Everyone Is Lying To You*

LITTLE RED FLAGS

Jeanette Settembre

A REGALO PRESS BOOK
ISBN: 979-8-89565-379-1
ISBN (eBook): 979-8-89565-380-7

Cover Design by Cody Corcoran

Publishing Team:
Founder and Publisher – Gretchen Young
Editor—Adriana Senior
Managing Editor – Caitlin Burdette
Production Manager – Morgan Simpson
Production Editor – Rachel Paul

As part of the mission of Regalo Press, a donation is being made to The Jed Foundation, as chosen by the author. Find out more about this organization at https://jedfoundation.org/.

This book, as well as any other Regalo Press publications, may be purchased in bulk quantities at a special discounted rate. Contact orders@regalopress.com for more information.

Regalo Press
New York • Nashville
regalopress.com

Published in the United States of America
3 4 5 6 7 8 9 10

For my mother—
Everything I am is because of you.

He's standing in the ocean, up to his knees. It's low tide. The waves are steady. I'm standing at the shore, afraid to go in. Ben is out of reach, but he's smiling back at me in a blue tank top and shorts, the sun beaming off his mirrored sunglasses. His skin is golden, the Boston skyline rising through the clouds. He's so handsome, my mind registers calm. He's standing sideways.

Parts of him were good. I believed that.

Chemistry

CHAPTER 1

THIS TRAFFIC JAM IS MADDENING. We should have known better than to leave during rush hour on Friday. But I was stuck in the office working late on a deadline. I'm still working, toggling for an internet hotspot. We inch closer and closer to a green minivan with a "No Bad Days" bumper sticker. Bumper to bumper. Stop and go, stop and go. The dizzying back and forth as I look down at my laptop and up at the windshield and back at the WordPress screen. I obsessively reread my words.

"All right, give it up already!" Lauren says, closing my laptop with her Big Apple Red nails as I push the screen back up. Sometimes I need that aggression to snap me back. It's a story weighing whether New York City pizza crust should be charred. Debates are clickbait. I picture Pat Kiernan holding up the piece on the "In the Papers" section of the NY1 morning show, so much more validating than monitoring the lifeless analytics.

"You're right. It's not that serious. How much longer?" I say, surrendering to the Sunrise Highway traffic.

"Okay, that's it."

She veers out from behind "No Bad Days" onto the shoulder. A car swerves in front of us. My sister catches my jolted body with her arm, my seat belt cinched at the waist. She holds her hand down on the horn, cursing at the driver. "Put on a fucking blinker!" she shouts, as he speeds off toward the exit with the same impatient entitlement, her middle finger waving out the sunroof.

"How the hell did you not see him?" I ask.

"He cut in front of me, sweetie." Lauren rolls her eyes and lowers the window, unfazed. I haven't driven in years, and before that, never more than forty minutes away, or without having a panic attack on the Tappan Zee Bridge—let alone this nearly four-hour drive to Long Island. Lauren's three years younger, but somehow, she became the adult after our parents' divorce. We're both hot and starving. The August humidity is making everything worse.

"Where are we?" I just want to get there.

"Relax, honey. We're almost there," she says as we inch by a golf course, a P.C. Richard & Son, a Sunoco gas station, and a McDonald's.

"Shouldn't the Hamptons look more rich? I don't get it," she says.

"It will. Wait until you see the houses," I say.

Jones Beach was the only part of Long Island we ever saw growing up. "Where do you summer?" was a foreign question until I graduated from college and moved to the city.

"I hope it doesn't rain this weekend," I say, glaring out from Lauren's used gunmetal BMW.

"It's the beach. It'll clear up," Lauren says. "I can't believe my sissy is turning twenty-five." She grabs my cheek.

"Neither can I. Wow, I'm old."

It just feels like another year to me, but I'm happy to be spending it with my sister. She is half of me, even though we are polar opposites.

We turn into the parking lot of Hotel Sole, a tall white house with yellow striped shutters and royal blue stairs leading up to glass doors. Rays of sunlight pour through the floor-to-ceiling windows, illuminating the foyer. It looks more like a boutique art gallery than a hotel, with white walls dressed in portraits of Marilyn Monroe over red and yellow canvases tagged in spray-painted hearts. Orange and blue books that say *Capri* and *Saint-Tropez* and *Hamptons Private* and *Chic Stays* are stacked on a coffee table.

There's a party happening on the pool deck with waiters carrying trays of hors d'oeuvres. The DJ in a white V-neck T-shirt is playing a Whitney Houston remix of the song "Higher Love" under a black-and-white striped awning near the outdoor bar. This could be a beach club in Positano.

It's embarrassing that I'm Italian American and still haven't been to the Amalfi Coast. I think about the summer everyone studied abroad in Italy. I worked as a school RA for free rent in an ancient apartment building in the Bronx. I lived vicariously through *The Talented Mr. Ripley*, ordering margherita pizzas at Goodfellas. The one thing Tom Ripley and I have in common? We're good at acting like we belong.

It smells like sunscreen and citronella candles. A procession of Hermès sandals taps against the pebbled gravel. The outdoor restaurant connects to the gated pool deck. There's a group of svelte girls in low-rise bikinis, a trend I thought was gone for good after I graduated high school, and one I never felt thin enough to partake in.

"This looks like fun," I say, rolling my suitcase up to our room.

Lauren kicks off her sandals, tossing her sunglasses on one of the beds punctuated with an "ahoy" pillow. She paces in bare feet around the cheap vinyl flooring, pursing her lips as she looks at a toilet paper roll hanging on a knotted rope. Not quite the "finest amenities" the website described.

"I can't believe we spent almost $1,000 on this," she says. She thinks I'm a sucker for handing over my money so easily for a zip code with hype.

Lauren squints at the empty mini-fridge, then fills it with the turkey sandwiches packed from the restaurant.

"Lauren, we're paying for the location. We have a pool outside, and the beach is minutes away."

She narrows her eyes at me, not convinced.

"I'm excited for tonight," I say, looking at my reflection in the mirror, pleased that my black, flowy maxi dress conceals my curves.

"Looks like there are some hot guys out there. I saw a daddy who looked beautiful," Lauren says, with a Sebastian Maniscalco accent, our favorite comedian.

Being raised by immigrant parents, I learned to love his dad jokes—his impressions of his father are hysterical.

Lauren is putting on her bathing suit. Her body is made for bikinis. I wish I had those genes. I glance at my flat chest, my pear-shaped body, envious that Lauren's weight magically distributes to all the right places—ass and boobs. She puts on a knit cover-up.

I flash a press credential, and we get access to the day party happening on the pool deck. We make our way to the raw bar, piling on pieces of shrimp, oysters, sushi, and mini quiche. Our plates are too full to belong. I savor a bump of black caviar pearls over raw oysters, the salt washed away with Chablis waves. Another sip. Another.

My buzz slowly settles in. Shrimp drowning in cocktail sauce. I smile at a waiter, exchanging my empty wineglass for a champagne flute, the calm I need to tread this social scene. Another shrimp. Another sip. I reach for a piece of pink toro sweating over rice. The sky is rosé. A Kelly bag left open, dangling on the wrist of a contoured arm, brushes past us. My shoulders are sheltered in a jean jacket. I dab my forehead, staining a napkin with bronzer, and turn the label on my tiny black Gucci bag to face out, an early birthday gift from Lauren from the tips she earned working fifty-five-hour weeks at the hair salon.

"Is my lipstick okay?" I turn to Lauren, who is chewing on a pig in a blanket, mouthing to a cocktail waitress for another.

"I'm starving. There better be more food," she says, gripping the slender bulb of her champagne glass.

I glide her hand down the stem. "That's not how you hold it," I whisper.

She bats my hand away, rolling her eyes. "Thank you so much," Lauren says, reaching for another tiny hot dog—one of the few foods she ate when we were kids—from the ponytailed waitress who looks our age.

"Actually, can you just leave the tray?" she asks, sliding a twenty-dollar bill into her apron pocket.

I'm grateful for Lauren taking charge of the canapés. "You're welcome," she says, cheers-ing me with her glass half-full.

We're eating off the silver tray. My lipstick is textured with crumbs. I picture Lauren and me scooping Italian ices into paper cups summers ago. Cherry. Lemon. Pistachio. "Thank you" written in cursive with a smiley face on the plastic tip jar atop a freezer cart outside of our family's red sauce restaurant. She smartly saved her tips. I'd spend mine on little luxuries, like charm bracelets and Juicy Couture tracksuits.

I got a taste of this world covering entertainment for the newspaper. I started building up contacts by interviewing celebrities at parties and on red carpets. Those interviews sell newspapers, but my favorites have always been about food. I'm a food columnist covering Michelin-starred kitchens, hole-in-the-wall mom-and-pop shops, and viral sensations. The Cronut. Mini-croissant cereal. A rainbow cookie crumb cake. Chicken parm pizza.

I eat, drink, and travel like a celebrity, but my paycheck is far from private jets and vacations in the Maldives. I overhear a woman ask the ponytailed waitress if anything here is gluten- and dairy-free. The privilege here is infuriating—and addictive. The fifty-dollar workout classes and twenty-dollar green juices. I've been living this aspirational lifestyle since I can remember—watching *The O.C.* in our tiny apartment growing up, a pile of *Teen Vogue* magazines stacked like Bibles. I've worked my whole life to eat off these silver spoons, a luxury I will never take for granted.

It's fun to be part of this world sometimes, even if I can't pay my student loans and live in a one-bedroom with Bob's Discount Furniture and a roommate. One minute, I'm scrambling to pay rent; the next, I'm on a Jitney, eating oysters and caviar on some wealthy real estate mogul's dime. It's like a Carrie Bradshaw cliché, only I leave the tags on my red-carpet dresses and don't have nearly enough sex. We have no real friends here, just publicists who offer to make dinner reservations with "xx" email sign-offs I will pay for in word-count currency.

My sister elbows her way between two spray-tanned blondes to get us cocktails. She gives me an eye roll, unamused by our tony surroundings.

"These bitches are too much," she says, handing me another drink.

We find two empty chairs by the pool. There's a clan of girls in matching pink bathing suits with "Bride Tribe" painted across their slender stomachs. The bride is wearing a skimpy white bikini, showing off her Tracy Anderson abs, a reminder that I am moving into the phase of life where all my friends are getting engaged or pregnant. I couldn't be less ready for that—I'm turning twenty-five tomorrow, and I want to enjoy the last five years of my twenties without a husband or child. My career is just getting started. I can't get sidetracked, and the idea of moving back to a suburb with three restaurants and no culture feels like a death sentence.

Still, I'm determined to at least give someone my number on this trip. I suggest we do a shot at the bar. Lauren hates shots—she doesn't even drink that much—but agrees. She's trying to be fun for my birthday weekend.

We down two shots of tequila. A blond-haired, blue-eyed, preppy-looking guy in a light pink bathing suit, wearing a Rolex Day-Date, is walking toward us. He's handsome in a rich, Polo, White privilege kind of way. I can tell he's already eyeing my sister. He must be in his late twenties or early thirties, which, Lauren will say, is too young for her.

"Can I join in?" he asks, lifting his sunglasses.

"I don't know, can you?" My sister's arms are crossed.

"I'm James," he says, shaking our hands. "I'm throwing this little pool party. My brokerage sponsors it."

"Oh, are you?" My sister pretends to sound impressed.

"Yeah, it's my real estate—my mother's real estate—company. We're launching a new luxury magazine, and I'm helping promote it. We invited a few influencers. I'm glad you two ladies could make it."

Sounds like he's charming us. I also hate the entitlement that hangs over the word *influencer*, a vanity title competing with my word counts and reader attention spans for superficial likes and followers. I do admire his confidence—convincing us we were invited and that he's important.

"You both from the city?"

"I'm in Westchester, but my sister lives there," Lauren says.

"I live on the Upper East Side." By that, I mean a sliver of space in a walk-up. He nods his head.

"We're here for her birthday." Lauren puts her arm around my shoulders. I smile shyly.

"Well, this most definitely calls for some Casamigos-sponsored birthday shots." James eyes the bartender.

"These are on me," he quips, his back muscles flexing as he leans in for two more shots.

"Have you met my buddy, Ben?" he says, pointing across the bar to a brunette with his back turned. He's talking to the two spray-tanned blonde girls we saw earlier.

"Ben!" he shouts.

Ben is tan, with a scruffy beard and deep-set, piercing green eyes. He gives James a cool nod, holding up his finger to signal he'll join us in a minute. He looks like he hasn't shaved in about a week, but it suits him. He walks over, his arms chiseled with definition. He is exactly my type—if I have one—and I can feel myself blushing. I put on my sunglasses so I can look at him more discreetly. He could be of Israeli or Italian background. His drink is empty, and he gives the bartender an "I'll have another" thumbs-up. I'm waiting for him to make an introduction, but he looks past us, like he could get any girl he wanted without saying a word.

"Bro, come join us," James shouts again. Ben breaks away from the blondes and walks toward us. I pretend to scroll on my phone.

"There he is. This is…" He reaches his hand out to Lauren.

"Lauren," she says, looking him up and down.

"They're sisters."

"I can tell. I'm Ben."

"Mia," I manage as James cuts in, raising a shot glass.

"Well, cheers to our new friends, eh?"

Lauren can barely finish hers, and James gives her shit. She pours her shot into his glass, and he takes it.

"So, how did you two meet?" I ask, making shy eye contact with Ben.

"Back at UTampa," James cuts in. "My day-one wingman. The legend!" He goes in for a high five.

"The guy couldn't keep up with my game, ladies," Ben brushes off.

"Okay, I'll give you that. He was the man, that's for sure. I wish you didn't leave me hanging junior year, bro."

"Had to, man," he says, tucking his hand into his pocket.

"It was a blessing in disguise, because I got my baby girl, Terry, that year. She's a Jack Russell terrier—and an actual terror sometimes," Ben says, holding up his phone with a picture of the white dog with black blotches on a beach.

"She gets it from his zaddy," James says, visibly regretting the word choice.

"Ew. Don't ever say that," Lauren scoffs.

James brushes off the secondhand embarrassment.

"Dude, you should have let me bring her! You would love her. She's a softie, like you. Mary Anne would love her too. Almost as much as she loves me. Why do you think she let me stay with you in that guesthouse for weeks last summer?"

"Leave my mom out of this. You're way out of her league," James jokes.

"She says she loves me because I'm not a nepo baby like her spoiled son," Ben quips.

"You got me there, man." James doesn't seem to mind being a punch line. I want to know more about Ben.

"What was this guy like in college?" I ask James.

"Oh, this guy? Aside from being the world's best wingman? Let me think."

"That is quite a compliment. What did the ladies like?" Lauren asks with a hint of sarcasm.

"I mean, have you seen this face?" Ben deadpans.

"I could have been a Calvin Klein model. Maybe there's still time. But enough about me. You girls are the real models," he says. I can feel myself blushing again.

"Guess who's older!" Lauren interrupts. We've been playing this game since we were teenagers. She loves it when people guess that she's the older sister.

"She is," Ben says, pointing at me, so sure. "She is the *sophisticated* older sister. A little more reserved. I can tell."

"No way," James says, his head tilted sideways, looking at us up and down.

"She can actually be the wild one," Lauren tells Ben.

Ben takes another sip of his drink, looking straight at me. I lower my eyes.

"Can she?" Ben takes another sip.

"Never." I roll my eyes.

Lauren is wide-eyed, her narrative growing more theatrical. She puts her drink down to talk with her hands. "This girl threw a drink at a concert in Vegas for my twenty-first birthday, then fell asleep standing up. This was all in the same night."

"Lauren!" I slap her arm. She always blows up my spot. "That was one time!"

"Mhm," she hums, raising her eyebrows at me.

"It happens to the best of us," James fawns. He's growing on me.

"Well, let's see if we can get her to come out of her shell tonight," Ben toasts, holding his glass up to mine.

"Let's see." I smile, staring back at him.

James interrupts our moment, boasting that he threw this party to celebrate his sales team, even though he's carrying the quarter after closing a deal on a multimillion-dollar home in Noyack.

He lives in Sag Harbor year-round, mostly selling summer homes to one-percenters. At some point, the conversation splits between James and my sister and me and Ben. We leave the pool deck and find two Adirondack chairs on the hotel porch.

"I really want a cigarette. I love to smoke when I drink. Bad habit, I know," I say, my eyes scanning the desolate porch for anyone to ask.

"Don't judge me. You don't have one, do you?"

"Actually, smoking is a deal breaker for me. You're cute and all, but that's a gross habit," Ben says, reaching into his back pocket and making a pack of Marlboros appear.

"I only have one more left." He dangles it in front of me, an exposed V-cut ab peeking out from his shorts.

"Lucky for you, I am a gentleman," he says, leaning in with a Nick & Toni's matchbook.

"A waiter gave me these. I don't have a lighter."

I huddle in closer to him, inhaling.

"You are a lifesaver. Thank you, thank you." I exhale, more aware that we're the only ones outside.

"Having fun at the party?" I ask.

"Oh, yeah. Glad to be out here for a minute, though. A lot of sensory overload in there, and I can only tolerate James for so long."

Ben glances at his phone, a screensaver of his dog Terry eclipsed by a text from someone named Julia that he ignores. I wonder if it's his girlfriend.

"Guess which one of these cars is mine?" He points to a row of crayon-colored Ferraris lining the parking lot.

"Um, the red one?"

"No, but close—may I?" He leans in for a pull of my cigarette. I nod, buzzing with nicotine.

"The orange," he exhales.

"Subtle. I like your style."

"James has the keys to one of them. He said we can test-drive it later."

"That's fun. I'm not really a sports car girl—I hate driving, but it would be cool to take a Ferrari for a spin at least once."

"I can make that happen," he says. "Let me guess, you're from the city?" He takes another puff, saving the rest for me.

"Yes, how did you know?"

"You're wearing all black, and you said you hate driving."

I roll my eyes.

"Okay, fair. Where in the city are you?"

"A suburb just outside of Boston," he says. I'm surprised by the out-of-town revelation.

"I'm just here for the weekend. I come down here every summer to visit James. I drove in and took the ferry."

"Oh, that's nice," I say.

"What do you do?"

"I work in customer support for a lottery app," he says, opening the app on his phone. "It's the digital way for young people to buy Mega Millions and Powerball tickets," he continues, scrolling through.

"Wow, I never thought that was an actual thing. I used to love buying scratch-offs," I say, thinking of Lauren and me ripping them off birthday cards from our aunts as kids.

"It's kind of cool. I mean, I needed a job, and they hired me in, like, a month when they were in startup mode. You definitely read stories about, like, winners blowing all their money and ending up in massive debt, which is kind of nuts!" His eyes get wider as he trails off on a tangent about how we make our own luck.

"Ironically, I'm not actually allowed to play the lotto anymore since I work for the app. It's a conflict of interest. But I still go into stores and buy tickets all the time. Who is really going to find out? Sometimes I do it just for the thrill of thinking I could win. In the rare chance I do, I could always make my mom cash it in, or, like, James. Don't tell my boss," he says.

I nod, still trying to get a read on Ben. He doesn't feel like the corporate type. I'm not surprised he'd defy a company policy.

"Well, that sounds like a lucky job." I laugh, pleased by my own bad joke.

"When I win big one day, maybe we'll go on a fancy date. Or before then, if you're lucky," he says, and smiles.

I can feel myself blushing. I love that he's already thinking about taking me out. I wonder if he's just being polite.

"Yeah, I get a few work perks. I can work from home some days, which is great because I live right by the beach. It's a private beach. Only people in our town can use it. I ride my bike there almost every night."

"That's so nice," I say, picturing it. "I would love to live near the beach."

"What about you? What do you do besides crash parties in the Hamptons?" he asks me.

I give him side-eye. Taking another sip of my tequila club.

"I write," I say.

"What do you write about?" He's intrigued. And I get a rush of confidence talking about working at a major newspaper at twenty-five, wearing success like a security blanket.

"A lot of things," I say coyly. "Entertainment, mostly. Sometimes I cover red carpets. Sometimes I write profiles. But I love writing about food the most. Restaurants. Chefs. I really want to be a food critic. I once flew to Girona in Spain to cover the Roca brothers. Have you heard of them?"

I know he hasn't, and I get great satisfaction in knowing something he doesn't.

"Who?"

"The three brothers? Joan, Josep, and Jordi. They're like, the Spanish holy trinity of culinary. They own El Celler de Can Roca. It's a three-Michelin-star restaurant in Spain, just outside Barcelona."

I can still taste the piercing acidity of two-hundred-year-old red wine held captive on my tongue; see the cathedral-like wine cellar, the "World's Best" glass globes on display in the kitchen, a reminder of the near-maniacal level of perfectionism it took them to get it.

"Oh, I've never heard of them. Or that restaurant. My fanciest Boston meal is at the Legal Sea Foods or Outback Steakhouse."

Restaurants are the most familiar to me. I think about being in the pizzeria my parents owned before Lauren was born. I'd scribble in a Guest Check pad and watch my parents at work. My mom's red lipstick and Maybelline lashes. Her olive skin. Her kind way with the customers she seated and how she asked about their families. I picture my dad tossing up pizza dough and teaching me how to tie garlic knots into perfect bows. The sweet smell of confectioners' sugar from fried zeppoles I'd devour from a red vinyl chair. Sometimes a babysitter would let me scribble on the paper placemats. Other nights, I'd stay with my mom until the dishwasher took a mop bucket of bleach to the floors.

They worked seven days a week and eventually put away enough money to have Barney and a pony show up at my third birthday. My mom beaming with pride, able to afford little luxuries for everyone in our family.

A wrecking ball changed everything when the town we lived in up north had plans to widen the road. The pizzeria my parents worked tirelessly to build was destroyed. They had to start from scratch, opening a new location in a less busy part of town.

Money was tight, and my dad's temper from the stress of it all made everything more chaotic. Their marriage ended shortly after Lauren was born. We lost our house. Then it was the three of us in a bedroom that felt bigger than it was. My dad went to work at another restaurant, while my mom got a job in a school cafeteria cooking. I relished the giant churros and cookies the size of my face she'd bring home to us. Sweets to soothe the aftermath of my fractured family. We were just making ends meet. I hid the star on my free lunch card at school.

Dinner was a drive-through at Burger King, the Number 8 Grilled Chicken sandwich or an El Paso No-Fuss Fajita kit when my mom was too overwhelmed to cook. I loved folding the flour tortilla and piling handfuls of processed, shredded Kraft cheese filler from the one pack of C-Town brand chicken that miraculously went a long way. I would fold up the leftover flour tortillas and bite into them to make a snowflake. I always ate more than my sister and usually tricked her into letting me have her leftovers.

I started shopping in the juniors section of the department store when I was seven or eight, by the time Dad had his own red sauce restaurant. We were always at my grandparents, who fed us pasta almost every night, chicken cutlets and pasta e fagioli, something none of my classmates had ever heard of. Cannellini beans and broken up spaghetti with heaping spoonfuls of cheese, what my grandfather's family cooked in southern Italy. I lied to my friends that my grandparents' house was our real address because it was an actual house, but really, my mom used the address so we could go to the better school district.

But when friends came over, they must have found it bizarre. A house filled with relics from Italy, ancient pink lamps draped in rosary beads, antique furniture, and a Jesus portrait by the bathroom that scared the shit out of us.

"Those are good chains!" I fawn, overcompensating for Ben's lack of taste. I wonder where we'd go on a first date. God, I'm already picturing him as my boyfriend.

"So, who are these Roca brothers?" he asks. I love a follow-up question. Now I know he's engaged. Or at least, interested.

"They are incredible. It started as a family-owned, rustic restaurant in Spain. Then they each carved out their own specialties," I say, my voice growing more and more excited. "Joan is the chef, Josep is a sommelier, and Jordi is this incredible pastry chef. He made this 'cigar' dessert. It's a dark chocolate cigar filled with ice cream and infused with actual cigar smoke," I say, talking with my hands, sparing him the specifics about gastronomy.

The menu opened as a 3D cutout of their family's old restaurant, with photos of the three chefs as boys and Catalan tapas—minced chicken cannoli, sweet pork sausage over a salted wafer, a love bomb of salmon and Beluga caviar beads. Then we traveled through time as waiters carried globes with croquettes with hints of different countries. Japan, two blissful bites of panko-fried kimchi kissed with sesame oil. Morocco, sweet almond-honey seduced by saffron and tangy goat yogurt. Turkey, a marriage of smoky lentil and eggplant purée.

It was dinner theater, a different kind of emotional eating. I savored the privilege. The excitement of not knowing what was coming next. Eating, this time with feeling. Not to suppress my own. I am addicted to flavor. Or fullness.

"Wow, I've never heard of anything like that," Ben says, snapping me out of my food fantasy.

"So, you sometimes get to travel for work and write about it? Sounds like you're the lucky one. How did you land that?" he asks.

I respond casually, like I haven't worked tirelessly. The killer deadlines, the late-night networking, the never-ending emails. It will all be worth it one day.

"I've been writing since high school," I say, taking another sip. "Then I was the editor in chief of my college newspaper, and I've been writing ever since. I got an internship at the newspaper I'm working at now as a senior, and the editor hired me on full-time a few years ago," I say, a flashback of my boss and our two-minute conversation that came with a salary I could make working as a barista. My bylines would be currency enough, I told myself. I got a small raise recently and can finally pay my bills without overdrafting.

He seems eager to know more, like he'd never met a woman with an actual career before.

"That's cool," he says. "Very cool. I've always wanted to write, but I suck at it, I think."

"I'm sure you're not as bad as you think," I say.

"What's your favorite story?" he asks.

"My favorite story? God, that's hard. That's like asking to pick my favorite child."

"You don't have any, do you?" he asks. I can't tell if he's being serious.

"God, no!" I can barely parent myself.

"So, tell me what you like to write about, other than obscure chefs?" he smiles, leaning in slightly.

"I like profiles about people. Getting to know them and then portraying them in a way that nobody has before. My favorite part is the interviews: that's when you really get to know someone. I did a story about a group of refugee women who escaped terrorism and abuse from countries like Nepal and Iraq and got jobs working as chefs in New York. They cooked for me. It was incredible."

"That sounds interesting. It's cool you get to cover all these stories," Ben says.

"Thanks." I smile.

Our conversation lulls, and I look at my phone to break up the silence. I can feel Ben's stare.

"Whoa. Is that an iPod?" he says, making fun of my old iPhone.

"Yeah, it is actually," I say, playing along. "They remade one just for me. It's vintage."

"I didn't realize they still make those," he says. "You must get that appraised."

"Oh yeah, I did. It's going to be worth millions one day. Especially with the cracked screen." I'm so clumsy I drop it every second when I'm doing interviews, but I just don't care enough to get it fixed.

I shake my head, but I'm attracted to his sarcasm.

"Want to see if there are any more oysters?" he asks, reaching for my hand.

I can feel myself blushing. The intimacy of his hand in mine makes my whole body relax.

"Sure," I follow him back out to the raw bar.

James is laughing with Lauren back at the bar. She must have made another joke at his expense. I'm grateful they're staying busy so I can keep getting to know Ben.

He comes back with a plate of six oysters.

"I'm no food critic like you, but I do know that these are definitely, maybe, I think, Wellfleet oysters," he says, raising the shell to my lips.

"And I only know this because I grew up going to the Cape. My mom has a boat passed down from my grandparents, and we sail from Boston Harbor to Hyannis Port. I take it out on my own sometimes, late at night. That reminds me, I need to pay her back for a speeding ticket I got a few weekends ago. Let's just say I like to make waves."

I force a laugh at his joke, wondering about the speeding ticket.

"Anyway, it's really peaceful being out on the water," he says.

"I'm sure of it. I love Cape Cod. I've only been once, but I obviously love the seafood. What are you doing?"

He pours a handful of salt on a cocktail table, balancing the shaker on its side.

"Look," he says. "Magic."

"The wait staff is going to want to make you disappear next! That's going to be so annoying for them to clean."

"This is a no-waste magic trick. I'm getting us more tequila."

He comes back with two shots and sprinkles the table salt on our inner palms.

"See, no waste," he brushes off the rest.

"Cheers, Mia," he says. "I like your name. Short and sweet. I've never met a Mia before." He's smiling. I notice a gap that's almost invisible in his perfectly white front teeth. I notice a dimple on Ben's left cheek when he smiles at me.

Before I know it, we're doing another tequila shot.

"Come on, you've got to finish it," Ben encourages. He gets in closer and puts a lime to my lips.

I toss it back and bite down on the lime, making eye contact with him. My lips sting from the tequila.

"What was that? Two?" I'm starting to lose track.

"Not sure. Hey, what is your toxic trait?" I ask, more confident with my buzz, craving more unfiltered conversation.

"My toxic trait? Hm. That's a good question. I have a few. Obsessive dog dad is one. Very proud dog dad, as you know. And I, weirdly, like reality TV to decompress. *Below Deck*, because, I mean, shallowly, the girls on that show are hot. My ex used to make us watch it. And then I watched, like, fifty episodes of *Love Island.*"

He crosses a hand under his arm, talking in a British accent mimicking one of the contestants.

"I was up until like 4 a.m. watching," he says.

"Wow, I did not peg you for a reality TV show guy, but I can get on board with it."

"Yeah, oh, and maybe not toxic, but probably embarrassing. My mom still does my laundry. Sometimes she'll come over with dinner she made, and my laundry is magically also done. I trained her well. It's an added amenity of living nearby," he says.

"Another lucky perk for you," I say.

"Okay, your turn."

"My toxic trait is that I love—well, you already know I like smoking when I drink."

"That doesn't count. Come on, Mia, you can do better."

I love hearing him say my name.

"Okay, hm. Oh. Obviously when I'm drunk, I get McDonald's delivered. Sometimes I fall asleep. Then I'll wake up with a twenty-piece chicken nugget meal and soggy fries on my doorstep. Not proud of that. I truly hate to waste food," I say, realizing how unsexy all this sounds.

"There's a TMI but FYI for ya." I smile.

"How does Lauren stay so fit?" Ben changes the subject, taking a sip of his drink. I'm taken aback that he's thinking about Lauren's body. I wonder if he heard anything I just said.

"I'm sure you could have her body if you worked out together," he says.

I'm stunned by how forward he's being. I wonder if he means to compare us. It makes me feel embarrassed. But I just laugh it off.

"She must work out non-stop," he says.

"I do love me some McDonald's, though. You're a girl after my own heart," Ben says, raising his glass to mine.

I cross my arms and keep drinking. I still want him to find me funny and sexy despite the weird remark. I feel my confidence build with my buzz.

"What else can you tell me about you?" I ask.

"Well. Let's see. I actually got kicked out of college my sophomore year," he says, scratching his face like he's embarrassed.

"Kicked out?" That gives me a little pause.

"What'd you do?"

"I failed a few too many of my classes. It's not because I couldn't do the work. I'm actually really smart without trying. I just didn't take it seriously. Partied too much. James did too, but his dad paid someone at the school to get him out of it. Very *Varsity Blues* scandal of him, I know. I selfishly wished he had done the same for me. So, there's that, and then…" He pauses for a moment, brushing his hands through his hair.

"I got caught hooking up with a girl at the gym on a Saturday while they were giving school tours. I know. I keep it classy. And then the last straw was getting busted at a party underage. It's embarrassing, but yeah, between that and skipping classes, my mom was like, 'Not paying for your free ride here,' so I transferred to a community college back home. It was for the best, I guess. Somehow, I landed that job at the startup."

I find it a little off-putting that he could be so reckless with his schooling. I think about how my grandfather had to co-sign one of my student loans and all the scholarships I had to maintain just so I could graduate. I couldn't get below a 3.5 GPA, let alone be so careless. I don't blame his mom for making him leave.

"I wish I was passionate about work like you are. For me, it's just a job. I'm not really an office guy. I like working out, so that helps. I thought about getting my personal training license, but my job now pays way more. I'm crushing it there, for the most part. I'm trying to get a job with James's mom in real estate. I'd be open to moving. And who knows, maybe I'll win the lottery."

So, he may lack some ambition or still not know what he's meant to do in life. I guess that's normal. I know careers don't just fall into people's laps. His realness makes him convincing. Like he'll figure it out. He seems so sure of himself, like he's been worshipped his whole life. Or maybe he's gotten away with everything, so he needs to push the limits.

I change the subject.

"So, did you always live in Boston?"

"I was actually born in Boca Raton, and we lived there for a few years until my parents got divorced. Then we moved up to Boston."

I uncross my arms when he says that, recognizing common ground. I wonder what happened with his parents. He tells me he went to boarding school as a teen because he was acting out. How he wished he had a better relationship with his dad.

"I've only been to Boston once, but it reminded me of, like, a cleaner New York."

"Yeah, that's what they say. It's not nearly as dirty as New York, with all those rats. Those pizza rats."

"So, then you went back to Tampa for school?"

"Yeah, James and I went to school there together, and I've stayed in touch with him ever since. He's a good guy, and I like crashing his parties out here. It's a nice escape. I give him shit for being a spoiled rich kid, but I mean, it has its perks. He's a generous host."

"Well, that sounds like a really good deal," I say.

Ben pulls out a joint.

"Want a hit?" He struggles to light the end with a match.

I become aware of my shoulders rising; my body is always tense. I usually hate smoking. It makes me anxious and paranoid. But I remind myself this trip is about letting loose a little.

"Sure," I say, taking a puff.

"Want to see something fun?"

He shows me a video on his phone of his dog howling.

"She's saying, 'I love you!'" He plays it again.

"Wow, that's insane. I can hear it!"

"She's a good girl," he says again.

I love that this Boston stranger has a soft side.

"Okay, dog dad!" I say, my voice more playful. "When did you get her?"

"I co-parent with my ex, but she can't have pets in her new apartment, so I got to keep her. The one good thing to come of the breakup."

"Oh, that's fun," I neutralize. My blanket response when I don't know what to say. I'm suddenly curious to know when his last relationship ended. I wonder who Julia is.

"It looks like your sister is hitting it off with James," Ben says, shifting the topic. Lauren is sitting close to James on the patio outside our room. He seems to be making her laugh, which is surprising because she usually doesn't go for white-collar white boys, as she would call them.

"Yeah, it seems that way," I say.

I can feel my mind shedding my usual layers of overthinking. I feel free and so present. I picture what will happen next. I wonder if Ben will try to kiss me.

"You want to go in the pool?" he asks, putting out the joint.

"I think it's closed," I say, pointing over at the gate.

"So? Haven't you ever hopped a fence before?" Honestly, no, I hadn't.

"Okay," I say. "Let's go."

Ben carries over a glass end table from the lawn and positions it in front of the gate, strategically making sure he's out of the camera's view. He's done this before, I can tell. He shakes it to make sure it's sturdy enough for us to climb onto.

"Okay, come on. Let's go," he says.

James and my sister are still occupied talking, but Lauren always has one eye on me. She knows I can get…a little unlike myself when I'm drinking around men.

The calls to her in panic at 6 a.m. after waking up with a stranger in my bed. The refrain, "should I buy the morning after pill?" Sometimes, I get carried away with the feeling of letting go. My mind is always in overdrive. I long for autopilot. So, I lose sight of my limits every once in a while. Not often.

Lauren never judges me. I can tell her anything. She'll tell me I'm stupid for making the same mistakes, but she always calms me down. She tells me to act like nothing happened, to move on. It doesn't make it less embarrassing. I wish I could be as stable as she is, putting out my fires, comforting me like a parent. She's the safest person I've ever known.

"Um, excuse me. Where do you guys think you're going?" Lauren calls out.

"We're just going in the pool, sis," I shout back. She knew it had been a long summer for me. She wanted me to have fun, so she was playing distant chaperone. What a good sister, talking to a guy for hours just so I could have fun with mine.

"She's in good hands!" Ben loudly whispers back. I can hear James faintly say, "I bet she is."

"Will you join me for a night swim?" he asks, holding his hand out. "I'm dying to know what is underneath all those layers," he says, gently sliding the jean jacket off my shoulders.

"It really is your lucky day. I actually do have my bathing suit on," I say.

Ben strips down to a mint-green bathing suit. His bare feet in the grass, his scruffy beard. He's so sexy, like he really could be a Calvin Klein model. He reminds me of a mix between Gerard Butler and Eric Bana. There's something mysterious about him, too.

I dip my feet in the water. I contemplate whether I want to get my hair wet or not when Ben throws me in, flooding my lungs.

"Oh my god! Asshole! Are you kidding me?" I call out. "What the fuck?"

Ben laughs mischievously, like a high school boy who just pulled a prank.

"I'm sorry," he says. "I couldn't resist. It was just too easy. You were going in anyway, right?"

I cup the top of my bathing suit, readjusting the straps that must have fallen off. I could barely fill the top out.

"I'm going to get you back," I say in my loudest whisper.

"No, you won't," Ben says, diving in.

There is a sense of an immature, impulsive boy, but he's so endearing and attractive. Like he's not afraid to hide his flaws—for better, or worse.

I sigh.

"Never do that again." I think he interprets it as flirting because he swims over and splashes me again.

"Oh yeah?" he says. "What are you going to do about it?" He inches closer.

We're so close now I can see the pores of his skin. He has thick dark-brown eyebrows and a small patch of lighter hair above his right ear. His feet can touch the ground, but he's still treading water, like he can't stay still. We've both had a lot to drink, but I can't tell how drunk he is.

"You know you want to kiss me," he says. I can see the hair on his defined biceps standing up, the goose bumps on his shoulders. I look at his lips, perfectly defined with a cupid's bow that women would pay for. He's so handsome, but there's something weird about him too. Something stunted or a bit juvenile. I can't tell if he's been with a million girls or very few. Then I remember the ex he kept referencing.

He reframes the question. "What if I kissed you right now?" It's straight out of a high school rom-com and a slight turn-off. I love a confident man who can take charge. I'm taken aback by this suddenly shyer side of Ben.

"The suspense is killing me," I say, playing it cool. I fix my wet hair, a nervous tic, and I wonder if he'll perceive it as such. I'm insecure at the thought of my mascara dripping under my eyes. I wipe the imagined dark spots. I feel like the ball is in my court, and I'm the prize Ben is trying to pursue.

Ben leans in and presses himself against me. I can feel his lips, his tongue on mine. I kiss with tight lips. Just another physical barrier; my body clenches up because I have a problem letting people in. I kiss him back again shyly. I can feel his tongue brush up against mine, sobering my entire body. I know where this could go, and I know I shouldn't let it go there. His body clenches against mine. I wrap my legs around him, floating against the buoyant water. His soft lips taste like salt and cigarettes. I like it when he bites down on my lower lip. My nails brush against his coarse hair. I can feel him getting hard.

"Wow, someone is getting excited," I say in a playful whisper.

"Yeah, you seem to be having that effect on me," Ben says, pulling my body in closer. I can feel the fog of his breath on my wet cheek.

Our hands are interlaced underwater. He continues to kiss down my neck as we rock against one another. Nothing is more intoxicating for me than being wanted, especially by a stranger. I'm shivering. I can tell Ben is craving more of me. I don't feel so drunk, but I know I'd never act this playful sober. Ben keeps kissing me, and I'm incredibly turned on.

Snapping back for a moment, I get nervous that people will see us in the pool. I hope my sister can't hear us. She's out of our line of sight. The patio is suddenly dark; Lauren and James must have gone to the bar again.

Ben starts feeling down my bare stomach, massaging me through my bathing suit bottom. I put my hand over his, guiding him. I don't want to stop, but I hesitate to go further when Ben tries to take off my suit.

"Hey, hey," I say pulling back. "Slow down."

"What? Sorry," he says. "How is this?" He gently kisses my neck. "Is this better?" he asks. It is.

"We're okay," he says. I can see the bulge in his bathing suit.

"We have to be good," I say, pulling back. I worry that if I sleep with Ben tonight, he'll see me only as a one-night stand, and I desperately want something more serious. I want to be in a relationship. We've known each other for a few hours, and I can already tell he has no trouble making up his mind and going for what he wants.

"Okay," Ben says. "I'll just keep kissing you here then." He's teasing me now, his tongue massaging mine.

He moves back down my neck. I don't stop him. He traces his hand down the front of my bathing suit, cupping my bare breast. I bite down on his bottom lip. He's getting harder. I grind my body into his, my mind calming down as I go with it. He's pulling the bottom half of my bathing suit to the side.

"Not here!" It comes out as a nervous laugh.

"It's totally fine," he says. Ben is very convincing with his toned arms and tan skin. He might be one of the most gorgeous guys I have ever kissed. And the most irresistible.

"I know you can be spontaneous. We could have so much fun together."

He looks at me, his head slightly tilted.

"Plus, I mean. It goes without saying. You are beautiful. And maybe the wittiest girl I've ever met. I'm so attracted to you."

He moves his hand slowly on my hips again.

"I won't be able to stop thinking about you, Mia," he says.

I can feel goose bumps on my skin. I'm overcome with the thought of being so close to Ben.

"We can go to my room if you want?" he suggests. "For a little more privacy."

He leans in again to kiss me, reaching for my hand as we climb out of the pool, our bodies dripping wet. Ben wraps a towel around me, kissing me.

He searches for the room key in his pocket, then turns on the lights. There are clothes everywhere. Suit jackets, belts, boat shoes—evidence that two twenty-something men are staying here. There's an empty bottle of vodka on the nightstand next to a contact case, and a bag of weed on the dresser. Ben dries his hands on my towel and reaches for another joint.

"You want a little more?" he asks.

"No, I'm good," I say. He takes another hit. Then another.

I wonder if he's been high this whole time. He seems so cool and laid back. I sit on the bed looking up at Ben as he jabs the joint out onto a pristine cover of *Hamptons Magazine*, letting the ashes dirty the print as they float onto the wooden dresser. I think about how hard the writers worked on those articles, all that work abused and thrown away. Sentenced to deadlines.

The digital alarm on the nightstand is glaring 11:30 in neon red. Thirty minutes until I've been alive for a quarter of a century. How fun would it be to have birthday sex with this attractive stranger? I try to block out any negative thoughts.

"Hey, come here," he says coyly, snapping me back to the present.

"Hi," I say, pouring another shot of warm tequila. I need to get on his level. I can feel his damp body on mine; we're both shivering from the blasting AC.

"Wet bathing suits aren't a good idea," he says, smiling. "We better take these off."

I roll my eyes, but I really want him to continue where he left off in the pool. He kisses me again. We make our way into the bathroom. Ben first strips off my suit, then his. He looks way bigger below the belt than I could feel in the pool. We are both naked now, and I watch him play with the shower knob until steam fills the bathroom. He presses himself against me, kissing down my neck again, then takes my hand and leads me into the shower.

I can feel the water on my eyelids as we kiss. Ben's hand moves to the inside of my legs. It's been so long since I've had sex this lucid. My mind is flooded with self-conscious thoughts, and I have a hard time being fully myself with someone else, especially during sex. Ben is good at finding the exact rhythm that unclenches my tense body. It feels so good. Our faces are wet as he kisses me harder and harder, biting my lower lip, a handful of my hair in his palm. Things are getting more intense, and one of my intrusive thoughts guilts me back to reality. I told myself I'd stop doing this, hooking up with strangers, but this feels spontaneous. I want to go with the flow.

Ben gets down on his knees, positioning me over his face as he massages me with his tongue. My knees unlock as he plunges his tongue deeper inside me.

"You're. So. Good. At. This," I say, punctuating every word.

Ben glides his tongue back inside me. I could come right now, but I'm trying so hard not to. I can feel myself getting wetter until I'm about to.

"Oh my god. Don't stop," I say. "Don't stop. Don't stop. Don't. Stop."

I can't hold back any longer. I try locking my knees to hold myself up. Ben's mouth is still against me. He slides behind me and bends me over. The shower water pours onto the white subway tile floor. I couldn't care less that my hair is completely wet. I'm still reeling. My feet slip as I get on my knees and arch my back. I want him so bad. He knows I do.

I can feel his wet body behind me as he strokes my back. Then, suddenly, I feel him plunge inside of me. Is he wearing a condom? I'm not sure. It's too late to ask. It feels so, so good. He's going harder and harder, maneuvering my back into a sharper arch.

"Come for me," I say, in a low voice.

I can tell he thinks it's hot because he fucks me harder and harder. I can feel his leg muscles tense up. I can feel myself starting to come again. The water is still running on our naked bodies. Moments later, he finishes. We're both breathless.

"That was so good," I say, filling the silence to reassure him.

"Happy birthday," he says.

Ben finds me a towel to dry off, and I'm already strategizing how I can leave the room without blaring "one-night stand."

My body is shaking with that nervous post-sex excitement. I don't want it to end after this.

"Hey, what's your number?" he asks, giving me his phone. I can't tell if this is just a polite gesture. I desperately hope he'll want to hang out for the rest of the weekend. Maybe even after.

I store my first and last name. Something I only do if I absolutely want someone to find me. I want him to look me up. I don't want him to forget about me.

"Text me," I say, hoping that I don't sound too eager.

We walk outside to find my sister and James sitting on the patio again. Lauren found a cigarette. The older sister in me has the urge to police her, but I'm too insecure about my behavior. I walk out with raised shoulders, my body cringing in embarrassment.

"Well, hello." I can hear my sister calling. I know she knows. I'm slightly mortified. How sobering. "So nice of you both to join us."

"Hi there. What have you guys been up to?" I say, draping my jacket over my shoulders, trying to act like nothing happened.

"What have we been up to? What have *you two* been doing?" James calls out.

"Oh, Mia just wanted to see my room," Ben says, clearly blowing our cover.

"Just wanted a tour!" I roll my eyes at Ben.

"Hey, man. You want to go get some party favors?" Ben asks James.

I wonder if he means booze or a cocktail of other drugs.

"Do you ladies want to join?" James asks.

"It's getting late. I think we're good," I say.

"Yeah, we're going to go to bed," my sister chimes in, leaving me alone to say goodnight to Ben.

"Are you sure? It is your birthday," Ben says.

"Yes, I'm old now and need my beauty rest," I insist.

"Okay, birthday girl. Let's hang tomorrow," he says. I get a full-body high at the thought of us together again.

"You have my number."

He gives me a quick kiss. I can still taste the tequila on his breath. I watch him walk to James' car. The headlights beam over the empty hotel parking lot. I hear wheels on the gravel as he speeds out, and I stand between the gate, heart racing.

CHAPTER 2

IT'S OVERCAST AT HAVENS BEACH, but I can still feel the sun warming my skin. Lauren's reclined in her beach chair, determined to soak up every ounce of sun she can on this trip.

"Saw your neck," she says, her eyes still closed.

"What?" I pull up my phone camera and see the reflection of a red bite mark. "Oh that." I trace my hand over my neck. "Ben was a little aggressive."

"Yeah, his friend is a little frisky as well," Lauren says, telling me how she let James make out with her.

I planned on having a productive beach day, finishing the unread articles left in my *New York* mag and working up to my summer reading list, but all I can think about is being on all fours in the shower with Ben. His lips. His body. My inability to practice any restraint. I daydream about what will happen next, checking my phone obsessively for a text.

"Do you think he'll text me?" I ask Lauren. She's always so self-assured and never judges me for being insecure.

"I don't know—I'm sure he will. They'll be here for another night. Plus, I'm sure he had fun with you." She gives me a knowing look.

"Yeah, I'm sure we'll hear from them," I say, trying to convince myself.

The salty ocean air mingles with the smell of Ben's skin lingering on mine. I still haven't showered. We got up early for the beach before the crowds. I'm surprised that I'm not hungover from the tequila and an empty stomach, but the adrenaline of last night is still coursing through me like an electric current. I try to focus, but I keep re-reading the same sentence over and over. I want to know more about Ben, but I don't even know his last name. Google and Instagram are useless. I type in "Ben" and "University of Tampa" and find tons of guys. No sign of him. He's not leaving until Monday morning. We still have a full day and a half. I try to distract myself by people watching, imagining what life is like for passing strangers.

The beach starts pulsing with energy as people trickle in. Families, solo walkers, and a pack of blonde women in biker shorts and sports bras. I spot a young couple running in sync through the sand. I wonder if they live here, or if they're renting a summer home. The woman must be in her late twenties. She has dirty blonde hair, and her abs peek out from her shirt. Her boyfriend/fiancé/husband is very handsome, shirtless, with a fit physique and dark brown hair. It's like they were made for each other. I fantasize about finding my person, having someone to be in sync with all the time. I've never been in a relationship where I felt fully myself. I think about how I contorted my personality to like sports and drink beer for my first boyfriend, who love-bombed me and then became emotionally unavailable. The hot and cold were familiar. I gave him an E.E. Cummings poem about how much I liked his body with mine.

He never reciprocated my feelings. But I couldn't let go. I resented him for not loving me back. For not liking poetry or having an appetite for anything other than diner food. Until one night, I got drunk and made out with a friend of his sister's. When he matched my infidelity, Lauren slapped him so hard across the face that the entire town bar stopped and stared. I realize now the only thing we had in common was sadness.

I want to know what it feels like to be loved. I've never been truly in love.

The thought brings me back to Ben and last night. The anxiety that comes with the aftermath of alcohol. I hope we were safe.

Lauren wakes from her nap and sifts through the cooler for a sandwich. Minutes later, I hear the ping of my phone. Of course, I turned up the ringer. It's a text from Ben, and I nearly jump out of my seat.

"Hey, last night was fun. James and I are getting sushi later and maybe checking out one of his properties if you want to come. Bring your sister," he says.

"Is it that guy?" Lauren asks.

"It's Ben," I say. "He wants us to get sushi with him and James later tonight. We have to go."

"No" isn't an option.

"Okay, fine," she says, yawning. "But I'm not hooking up with his friend. He's too much of a pussy."

"Lauren, promise me you'll at least be nice to him, please. I really like this guy. He's fun."

"You know, you say that about any guy who gives you attention," Lauren says, reapplying sunscreen.

But Ben feels different.

"Just have fun. See where it goes," Lauren says.

The idea of spending another night with Ben gives me so much to look forward to. What should I wear? I let fifteen minutes pass before I respond: "Hey, me too. Sounds good. What time?"

"How's 7:00. Went back to James's house. We'll come pick you guys up."

I'm debating whether I should wear a black, tight-fitting bodysuit that enhances my nonexistent chest or a long, flowy skirt.

"Oh my god. That's hideous," Lauren gawks, deciding my outfit for me. "Where did you get that? Grandma's closet? Enough with the old lady, flowery, peace and love. Show your figure, please!"

She tosses me her jean skirt to try on. We're almost the same size, except I have wider hips.

Ben wants me to drive with him. James is letting him drive one of the Ferraris his mom's company was lent for the weekend. It feels off-puttingly flashy, but why not?

Ben opens the door and walks me through its manual transmission, revving the engine. It sounds like a race car. Ben's personality incarnate. He seems excited about it, so I pretend to be impressed as he describes every feature. James and Lauren have already sped off.

We pull out of Hotel Sole. James is far ahead, but Ben makes up for it quickly. His foot presses on the gas, and we go faster and faster. "I've done this before," Ben says, looking at me while switching gears.

I'm soaking up the thrill of this moment. Ben acts like he owns this town, and I feel exhilarated for the first time in a while. Like I don't have a care in the world. Ben's presence puts me at ease.

"What did you and James do all day?" I ask.

Ben takes a hand off the steering wheel to unbutton a button on his linen shirt. "Not much. I hung out by his pool while he was on a bunch of work calls for a new home he's showing. I was supposed to leave today, but I ended up booking a ferry ticket for tomorrow instead. I haven't really used my vacation days this summer, so I can miss a day at work. I told my boss I'd be on email."

"Oh, what made you stay?" I ask, raising my eyebrows.

"Nothing in particular." He gives me side-eye. "Maybe a cute writer who taught me a few things about restaurants."

I can't tell if he's trying to charm me, but it's working. Ben puts his sunglasses on his head. The sun starts to set when we get to the restaurant. James and Lauren are sitting next to each other at a table in the crowded dining room. A waiter immediately brings us four shots of sake.

"My man," James says, holding the shot glass up to the waiter, giving him a high five with the other.

Lauren pretends to take a sip. She hates sake.

"Glad you two could join us," James says, fixing the collar of his navy polo.

"Of course, how could we miss you taking us for sushi?" Ben turns to him and says sarcastically.

James ignores him. "So, what do you both like? Any dietary restrictions I should know about?" he rattles off like a waiter.

"Nope, none here," I say. "I eat pretty much anything. Lauren is the picky one."

Lauren glances up from her menu. "I mean, that's not true. I'll dabble in a little something different. I like tuna."

"Well, that's a start," James says. "There will be lots of tuna, then."

Ben tells us he's deathly allergic to peanuts, so James ushers over the waiter again to make sure they know, repeating himself like it's the most important thing in the world. "What do you say we get the omakase, then?" James says, speaking my language.

Ben turns his head toward me and asks: "Oma what?"

His trust in my expertise makes me feel valued, shedding layers of my imposter syndrome.

"The chef picks different pieces of sushi for us," I tell him.

"Oh, right. Of course," Ben says, pretending he already knew.

"Everybody on board?" James surveys the table. We nod. The waiter comes back to collect our menus, and James orders us each the tasting menu with sake pairings. I'm thrilled that this dinner could go on for hours. I hope Lauren can at least fake enjoyment. "*Arigato,*" James says, bowing his head to our waiter. Jesus Christ—Can you be any whiter?

We each have a glass of wine that the bartender gifted. James must come here a lot and leave good tips.

"So, what else did you two get up to in your college days?" I ask, lacing my fingers around the stem of my wineglass.

"This guy was a prankster. Got us into a bit of trouble," James says, putting his arm around Ben.

"Sure was. Remember when I put that mannequin in your bed with the blonde wig when you were sleeping? And you woke up texting me that you didn't remember who she was."

"Dude, you were such an asshole. That was the funniest, stupidest thing. She looked so real, okay?" James turns to us for validation.

Ben is laughing, and I'm immediately distracted. I love his laugh. It's staccato with long bouts of silence before he comes up for air, his head nodding back and forth in pure, boyish joy. He finds his composure when his eyes catch my gaze.

"I literally left her there for a good hour or so thinking she was dead asleep. I got the RA in on it too. She came in to pretend to wake her up."

James is laughing too.

"You boys sounded wild, let me tell you," Lauren says sarcastically, faking a yawn, flipping her perfectly blown-out hair.

Ben leans back in his chair, uncrossing his arms to take a sip of sake. I notice him eyeing a woman in a blue slip dress waiting for a seat at the sushi counter.

He does a double-take. "Is that?" he asks, looking at James and back up at the sushi counter. I realize it's one of the blonde women he was talking to the night we met.

"Yeah, I think so," James nods.

She struts over to our table in platform wedges, mouthing "Hi!" as she waves at James and Ben.

"Hello, beautiful strangers," she says, staring directly at Ben, overexaggerating every word in Drew Barrymore hyperbole. "Mercury must be in retrograde because I did not get a text back from either of you," she continues.

James stands up to give her a hug, his watch catching on the hem of her dress.

"These are our friends," James cuts in, introducing Lauren and me. Lauren looks irritated by the disruption. I flash a smile, tucking my hair behind my ears. I wonder if she's hooked up with Ben.

"Hey, Julia. I missed your text, my bad," Ben says, reaching for a sip of sake.

"No worries, dude. All good. All good," she says brushing a hand through her beach waves. "I know you said you'd be here the rest of the weekend, so just seeing if you both wanted to stop by a party I'm hosting at Moby's."

"Open invite, girls, of course!" She turns to us, overanimated. "It's a collab for my friend's no-waste sandal line, Salvage. I'm doing her social." She reaches into a white, woven, croissant-shaped purse. "It's buy one, give one." She hands us a 15-percent-off card. "Her dad is getting Bon Jovi to come out. Iconic, right? Miranda used to date his son," she says, pointing over to her friend in wide-leg jeans and a crop top at the counter. "And Christie Brinkley's Prosecco is another sponsor. Anyway, it'll be really fun."

Lauren smiles without saying a word.

"Thank you so much," I say. I notice Ben is suddenly so quiet, looking at his phone.

"Benjamin, we could use your drumming skills—if you're up for a nightcap," Julia says, her Juvederm lips perfectly stained in pale pink.

"I didn't know you played the drums. You didn't share that detail last night!" Lauren chimes in. I'm selfishly grateful she's steering the conversation back to us.

"I mean, it's something I do sometimes when I'm drunk, just a hidden-talent hobby," Ben says, tapping the table with his chopsticks.

Julia is still staring at him. "Text me if you want to hang," she says, giving us a double wave as she dissolves into the crowded dining room.

I'm fake smiling, wondering how much history they have. Ben's not even from here. I wonder how many hookups he's had. Am I just the latest?

"Sorry, that was awkward. We sort of met a few summers ago and keep in touch when I'm back in town," Ben says.

James turns the conversation back to himself.

"Too bad I hardly ever see this guy. He's always busy wheeling and dealing, right, buddy?" James says.

"Me? I'm always busy? He's the one who's always on conference calls. You haven't come up to Boston once since college," Ben says. I admire his ability to say exactly what's on his mind, but I can tell he might rub some people the wrong way because of it.

"I'm trying to get this guy to move out here and sell real estate with me. Dude, you could make a fortune. Let's see what my mom says about that opening. Ben is a fantastic salesman. This guy can convince me to do anything. Somehow, he persuaded me to lend him my car for half of our freshman year. Remember that, man? You took the car to sell those football jerseys? Yeah, he promised me 10 percent of all his sales if he could use my car. We made bank that semester."

"Yeah, until the dean of students caught on that we were taking profits away from their official merch."

"Anyway, the guy can literally sell anything. Remember you stole all those fireworks from that frat party, and we resold them freshman year?"

Ben seems to be the brains behind their friendship. James clearly doesn't need money. I think he just got a thrill out of semi-illegal stunts, feeling like he had his own business ventures, away from his family's shadow.

"So, have you given it any more thought?" James asks Ben, one leg crossed over the other, exposing his bare ankles and Ferragamo loafers.

"Thinking about it. But not sure what I want next," Ben says, fidgeting with his fork. "I do love my apartment."

"You'll be making so much money you can save for a baller one," James says. "I put in a good word at the brokerage."

I would second that, but it's too soon for me to voice my opinion.

"I'd need to get my real estate license first. We'll see, man. I need to make enough to really make it worth my while to leave. I'm ten minutes from the beach. I don't have it bad in Boston. The lottery startup is really starting to grow."

James sighs. "We need another agent on the team. My mom said you were the front-runner out of all our crazy friends. You have real sales potential."

Ben's expression shifts, and I can tell the compliment makes him feel good.

Our conversation pauses when a chef brings over an assortment of sashimi, slabs of three variations of tuna. I can tell the pinkest piece is toro, my favorite. I can already taste the buttery, rich bite in my mouth. One is a crispy rice variation. My mouth is watering. We all reach for our chopsticks, even though the chef said the fresh fish can be enjoyed with our hands, the more authentic omakase way. But 50 percent of our table leans mainstream in the culinary department, so I don't push authenticity. Lauren doesn't eat raw fish, but she's able to stomach a few bites of the tuna. She puts a piece on my plate, just like she'd give me half of her Strawberry Nutri-Grain Bars when we were younger. She knew I'd want it without even asking.

"So, are you girls down here a lot?" James asks, holding his hand over his mouth so he can chew. Ben is devouring his plate without care.

"Not really. Actually, this is my first time here," Lauren says. "I'm not sure I love the vibe, to be honest. Don't get me wrong. It's a beautiful place. But I mean, everyone just seems a little too stuck up, you know? Like I'm not someone who would exactly wait in a line to get into a bar, or pay one hundred dollars just to get in. Or spend twenty dollars for a green juice."

"To be fair, it is gorgeous out here," I say. I want to be invited back, no matter how shallow James may seem. "The seafood is so good. I mean, come on. The lobster roll at Lunch is epic. And also, it kind of feels like time stops here. Don't you think?" I say, steering the subject back to food.

"I couldn't agree more, Mia," James says, clinking my wineglass. "Dude, it's also way different during the off-season. Much more chill." James catches himself sounding like a bro. He takes a sip of sake and reverts to his country club script. "It's a special place, but you have to really see its roots, past the busy seasons," he says, looking right at my sister.

I can tell James has never met a girl like Lauren. She's used to calling out bullshit. I flash back to her yelling at my mom's old landlord, who gave her shit about not getting the rent in on time. James has probably never been challenged, and I can see him practically drooling over Lauren. She commands attention and respect.

"Okay, that's fair," James says, pandering to her point of view. "People can be a little pretentious. I'll give you that. Though I mean, when you live here all year, you can see how, you know, hard-working people are here.

The locals. They never stop working even when the season ends," he says, making a blue-collar pitch neither of us is really buying. It must be hard to get into his Mercedes and sell people multimillion-dollar homes. People like him are pricing the locals out by the minute.

"A little?" says Lauren, raising her eyebrows. "I can't even get a drink in this place without getting elbowed by some bitch."

"Lauren!" I say, in a big sister "be nice" voice.

"Tell me how you really feel," James says. "This girl is funny," he says, turning to Ben. I wonder if he and Lauren did anything more than kiss last night.

Ben is devouring the rest of the tuna. I always feel like I'm the only one eating when I go out to dinner with my friends, or on the rare date. He dips the last bit of tuna into soy sauce and feeds it to me. I'm eating up the attention.

Ben tells me about his summer plans. He loves being out on his mom's boat, he tells us, and I'm already picturing him taking us out to the Cape. He says he wants to visit his brother, who lives in the city, and I'm already hopeful that I'll get to see him again.

The check comes, and without missing a beat, James gives his Black card to the waiter without looking at the bill. We try to act normal as he pays. Ben rummages through his cognac-colored wallet. "You sure you got this, man?" he says.

"Yeah, yeah, yeah—of course. You came all this way. It's all good."

Ben shrugs and puts his wallet back in his pocket.

"What an incredible meal. Thank you for bringing us here," I say, refolding my napkin over my lap, my tone straying corporate, like I'm thanking a client for hosting me at a Jean-Georges lunch.

"Yeah, this was really great. I loved it." Lauren is less convincing.

"My pleasure. I'm glad you two enjoyed it," James says. You can tell he takes pride in entertaining and knowing the Hamptons hot spots. I wonder if this is typical for him and Ben, courting pretty girls together. I wouldn't be surprised. James is a smooth talker, and Ben is charming in his own quirky way. Who wouldn't fall for them?

"So, do you guys want to come check out my new listing?" James asks. "It's only a few miles away."

Lauren and I have a buzz from all the sake and wine. We'd usually discuss our game plan, but we both say "sure," in unison.

James leads the way, thanking the staff and saying a few other words in Japanese I can't understand. Ben pulls me back before we leave the restaurant and gives me a kiss, his dark-wash jeans hugging his perfect butt. I'm usually so shy about PDA, but I'm kind of drunk, and I love that he's into it. Plus, we're one of the last tables, so there's hardly anyone in sight. He tastes like sake and soy sauce, and I bite his bottom lip. He must like it because he pulls me in closer.

"I wanted to do that all night," he says.

"Oh, you did?"

"Want me to call an Uber?" I suggest, as he kisses down my neck.

"Why? No, no, it's fine. I'm cool to drive." He pulls the keys out of his back pocket. I'm hesitant about getting in the car with him after we've been drinking.

"It's, like, a ten-minute drive. We'll be fine." He notices I'm fidgeting with the clasp on my purse.

"James knows every cop in town anyway. His mom basically owns this town."

I shrug. "Okay."

We make our way down a winding street, and minutes later, hewing close to James's car, we end up in East Hampton to see what James described as his "most highly anticipated listing of the summer." It's a $7 million glass house in Springs—"the pinnacle of modern architecture," he'd prefaced.

James puts on a beam that illuminates the driveway as two slate black gates open. The glass house with black trim looks like it's glowing. It's stunning in all its modern luxury. James carries a magnum of Whispering Angel rosé that must cost $300, another drop in the bucket for him.

"It's a livable work of art," James says, and I picture him saying the exact same line to prospective buyers. I marvel at the floor-to-ceiling windows. I would kill to see this place in the daylight. I hate living in my dark, split one-bedroom that faces another building. There's sunlight for maybe ten minutes a day. Luckily, I'm not home much, but weekends get grim. The open concept house is staged to perfection. James gives us a tour, starting in the kitchen, which I know is already my favorite room in the house. I spy Sub-Zero appliances, a Wolf stainless steel stove the size of a restaurant kitchen, and two waterfall islands made of Carrara marble.

"This place is insane. I mean, seriously, I would die to live somewhere like this," I say.

"You and I both," Ben echoes, marveling at the Bang & Olufsen speakers.

"Are these all synced up to Google Home?" Ben asks. James nods. Ben finds a remote to the floating fireplace and turns on the flames with the touch of a button.

"Why don't you have a seat on the couch and relax a little?" Ben says, acting like we're playing a married couple. "Let me fetch you a glass of wine. You've had a long day," he says. I picture us coming home from a long day of work and fucking on the marble countertop, the floor-to-ceiling windows putting us on full display.

"So, who wants dibs on upstairs?" James walks into the living room with his sweater tied over his shoulders.

"What, really? We can stay here tonight?" Lauren is right behind him. We both couldn't care less at the thought of leaving the hotel if it means staying here.

"Yeah, it won't hit the market for another few weeks. It's all ours for the night. Make yourself at home. The beds are already made. Just try not to break anything, okay?"

James is looking right at Ben, still flicking the fireplace on and off, his eyes widening as the flames flicker.

Light illuminates the backyard. A pergola towers above the stone with a wooden table that looks like a backdrop from an episode of *Barefoot Contessa*. There is an infinity pool and a giant statue of a Buddha with prayer hands. Lauren carries wineglasses outside as James places cushions on the Adirondack chairs around the fire pit.

Ben is still fixated on the indoor fireplaces, playing with the remote like a kid on Christmas as the flames change colors. He ignores James when he tells Ben to put it down.

The summer air is much cooler now. James brings two sage crewneck sweatshirts embossed with "HL" for "Hamptons Luxury" from his car. It's getting easier to buy into this lifestyle. Ben carries out a portable speaker blasting "Starlight" by Muse.

"Did you take that from the hotel?" James asks.

"Yeah, they won't miss it. I promise," Ben says.

He wraps his arms around me from behind, and I jump a little, my body tense like always. I wonder when he stole the speaker. If he'll bring it back. He says he got it for me.

"Oh, I didn't see you there," I try to downplay my spastic reaction. He starts massaging my shoulders. It smells like firewood and his cologne. "What perfume are you wearing?" he leans in to ask me. "It smells amazing."

We sit around the electric fire pit. James smokes a cigar, listening to Lauren talk emphatically about the hair salon and bar concept she's saving up to open. He gives her advice about investors, but she says she won't need any. She's doing it all on her own. Hearing her talk about money reminds me of when we lived in our tiny apartment and she'd keep a stash of dollar bills, fives, and tens in a baby blue Mudd shoulder bag, tips she made while working for dog groomers. We worked at Dad's restaurant, babysat, and anywhere that would pay us off the books. She'd always loan me a few bucks without asking for it back.

Ben leans in and whispers to meet him in the bedroom suite upstairs. I help Lauren take in the wineglasses, carefully placing them in the farmhouse sink. This kitchen is a dream.

"Do you want to stay here?" Lauren asks me. She's sober, and I can tell she's fine staying or leaving.

"Yeah," I say. "Let's stay—is that okay? It's so late anyway. Seems fine to stay, right?" I ask, waiting for her final sign-off. She just nods and tells me to have fun.

"Fine, I guess I will let James try and woo me," she says.

"Really?" I ask, surprised. I know he's not her type, but I'm grateful that she's showing some interest.

"Why not? I'll see if he can keep me entertained," she says, raising her eyebrows.

I'm relieved knowing she is fine to handle herself. And I know she'll have no problem putting James in his place if needed.

My feet slide along the perfectly sleek wooden floors up the staircase to a hallway with many doors. I can see a dim light coming from one of the bedrooms. I find Ben lying on the bed, staring into his phone. He must see my shadow, because he looks up. "Hey," he smiles. "I was just checking on Terry. Want to see her?" he shows me a black and white terrier rustling with a chew toy on his phone.

He gets up, saying something about how he forgot his mouth guard.

Ben and I gaze at our reflections in the giant standing mirror. We look like a couple. Perfect. Our brunette hair, my brown eyes and his green, glowing in the reflection. Ben puts his arm around my waist. I wonder what he's thinking, and if he'll text me when I'm back in New York. I picture this house as our own. This perfect house. I gaze around the room at the warm neutral hues—a bouclé swivel chair, the mahogany dresser, dreaming that one day my shabby furniture would morph into this—all of this.

I climb in next to him. His skin is soft. It smells like the sea salt body wash from the hotel. I graze his arm with my nails. I love being so close to him. He leans in and kisses me. His lips warm against mine. He tastes like wine and cologne.

"Why don't you ever use tongue when we kiss?" he asks.

I give him a confused look. "We haven't exactly been kissing for long, have we?"

"It's been long enough," he says, moving a piece of hair from my face. I guess I didn't realize I was holding back so much.

"Open your mouth," he says, pressing his lips against mine, his tongue gently massaging mine. A full-on make-out session like I've never had before. It's so sensual. Ben isn't holding back, and I start laughing. I'm focusing so much on whether I'm doing it right. "What?" he asks. "You're killing the moment."

"You're tickling me," I say, laughing harder now. He keeps kissing me, and we both smile and laugh with our lips pressed together.

We stay up all night. Ben tells me about his parents' divorce. About how his mom had to start a career from scratch because his dad moved back to Florida and got remarried. I tell him about mine. We have more in common than I thought. Ben's grandparents helped raise him, too. He tells me how his brother in New York has been distant and that they don't really talk all that often. His sister is like that, too, and I wonder why they aren't close like Lauren and I. I've never bonded with a guy like this before or even had a deeply personal conversation about my parents' divorce. Ben tells me that the breakup with his last girlfriend was hard because he just didn't see a long-term relationship in their future. She had been dying to get engaged after dating for a few years, but Ben wasn't ready. She let him have Terry. They still keep in touch every now and again as friends.

"Do you still have feelings for her?" I can't help but ask.

"No. I don't. It was tough, but we are so different. She's immature. She drank a lot. We fought a lot. We're better off as friends," Ben says. I think about how mature that sounds and feel reassured. I want Ben all to myself.

"What about that girl from the sushi place?" I ask.

"Oh, that is nothing. We had a little fun last summer and sporadically kept in touch, but we have nothing in common. I don't know, she's not really my type," he says.

He sounds genuine, and I feel relieved.

Ben tells me about how he lived in Maine for one summer, working for his uncle's construction business, and how he gets second thoughts about his career. I'm surprised because he seems so confident, so sure of himself. He loves working for the lottery startup, but he doesn't know if it's really his calling. He says he wants to work for himself. I love the feeling of his hand on my face. We look into each other's eyes with the reflection of the outside lights beaming in. I trace a scar over Ben's right hand and show him the one on my left.

"I cut myself in college. We were playing that game—Russian Roulette," he says, and I cringe at the thought of someone jabbing a knife between my fingers. It wasn't the knife—it was shards of glass from a broken bottle that shattered on the table.

"How did you get yours?" he asks of the horizontal sliver of raised skin on my hand. "Lauren did it," I say. "I must have been seven or eight. She was trying to tell me that dinner was ready. We were at my grandparents' house, and I was playing with a Rugrats doll. I wasn't ready yet. She got so angry she took a razor blade from my grandpa's sewing machine and slit my skin so quickly I didn't have time to process it."

"Wow—ouch. She is a feisty one, that Lauren," Ben says.

"I was bleeding for hours, but I never got stitches," I say, thinking about how it wasn't unusual for Lauren to act out in rage when we were younger. She was always angry, and I was always the peacemaker, hiding so much of my sadness.

Ben feels the scar on my hand. He kisses me again and again and intertwines his body with mine, my legs wrapping around his. I don't want this moment to end. For the first time, maybe ever, I feel truly connected to someone. This person. His warm body envelops mine, and I feel lighter than I have in a really, really long time.

"I wish you didn't live in Boston," I say. "Come to New York," I demand, convincing myself of the crazy notion that maybe one day, he will. For me. Why couldn't he? He can work remote at his job. Nothing is really holding him back.

"Maybe one day," he says. "Maybe one day, we'll come back here—to this house—and we'll have the Roca brothers fly in and make us that meal you were talking about. Maybe if James hires me, and I sell enough houses.... This will be my billion-dollar listing."

"I love this idea," I say, thinking about what the future would be like with Ben.

"You'll have to convert," he says. "I'm Jewish, you know."

"Will I?" I say, being playful, but seriously contemplating. I've always pictured myself marrying a Jewish boy.

"I'm more Jewish than you are. You didn't even know that nova was lox," I say, smiling at him, thinking of an earlier conversation about bagels.

"You're right," he says, still holding my hand. I can hear my heart beating in my head and feel my mind ease as he traces his fingers up and down my arm. I don't want this weekend to end. I want Ben to come back to my tiny apartment in New York. I can already see myself loving him.

Ben presses his lips against mine. He promises he will visit soon, and we both fall asleep, our hands clasped and bodies wrapped around each other.

The next morning, I wake up to the steady sound of Ben's heartbeat, my ear resting on his chest. I'm awake, but I don't want to move and unsettle this moment.

We head back to Hotel Sole and pack our suitcases. Ben has to catch his ferry in an hour. But before we go, he asks Lauren to take a picture of us. He wants to show his mom "the nice Italian girl he met." I love that he wants to show me off to his mother already.

I'm overcome with excitement and sadness. The weekend is over. Tomorrow I'll be sitting at my desk, trolling for story ideas and stressed with deadlines. I don't want all this to end. I don't want Ben to be like all the others. I dread the familiar feeling of intoxication turning into a spiral of regret.

"You excited to go back?" I ask, muting my intrusive thoughts.

"Me? I mean, I do miss Terry," Ben says. I picture his terrier waiting for him at the door. How they'll spend hours at the beach near his apartment. I can see him so content, but I hope he'll miss me.

We say goodbye in front of his car. He kisses me once and then comes back for another, holding me in his arms. His tongue lingers on mine, and I feel myself giving him a real, genuine kiss. He looks down at the pavement and back up, then kisses me again softly.

"Mia, maybe you are worth the drive to ratty New York City," he says. I roll my eyes, but I'm smiling.

"Maybe," I say.

"I'm glad we met," he says, climbing into his car.

"Me too, Ben," I say.

I watch him pull out of the parking lot, and I flash back to us holding each other in that glass house. His warm body on mine. His hand in mine. How safe and calm I felt alone with Ben. How much comfort I found in this stranger. I think about Ben's tiny imperfections. The pranks. His disregard for what anyone thinks of him. His scar, his tiny patch of lighter hair, the sliver of gap he has between his two front teeth. The smell of his cologne. He's better for them. I picture us in my tiny New York apartment all the way home.

I cut a square of sea salt dark chocolate I pulled from the freezer and pour a glass of Malbec from an open bottle into my shitty thick-stemmed wineglasses, my evening ritual. I don't want to lose the buzz from this weekend. I text my best friend, Eva, the photo of Ben and me at Sole, then call her on speaker to debrief. She's one of the few people I can be fully myself with. She always listens with lighthearted candor, validating everything I have to say.

"Oh my god. Who is *that?*" she says. "You guys look like a couple."

"Can you even? Isn't he so cute? His name is Ben. I met him this weekend in the Hamptons with Lauren. He's exactly my type." I tell her about how we met. How she would love James's vibe. About his Black card and the omakase menu. Eva, too, has a love for all things luxury.

"I'm sending this pic to the group chat," I say, looping in our two other college friends, Carrie and Jade.

"How cute is he?" I say again. I need to hear that I'm not alone in this assessment. "SO cute. Wow. I was just going to say—this is literally the guy I would picture you with."

Jade and Carrie chime in on the group text with fire emojis and question marks. I quickly explain, but I don't want to distract from Eva, who is telling me about her weekend looking at houses in Hoboken. She's getting engaged soon; she can feel it.

Jade says she's manifesting good vibes. Carrie responds with prayer hands and says she already wants to meet this "mystery guy." I pause when I hear Eva say, "You guys look like a couple" again.

"I know. I know! I don't want to get my hopes up. I feel bad. Obviously, we already slept together, but we hung out the entire weekend. He has my number. Uh, I hope he texts me."

"Whatever, it was your birthday! It's okay to have fun. You work so hard. It sounds harmless, and the fact that you guys hung out all weekend is a good sign. You'll definitely hear from him," Eva assures.

I take another sip of my wine. Eva always makes me feel better. "I know. I know, it's just, he lives in Boston. Uh, which sucks, but I mean, it's not that far."

"Boston! No. I mean, yeah, it's really not *that* far. And Boston is so cute and chic. You guys can see each other on weekends. Okay, I love a Nantucket moment for you and so close to Boston." Her optimism gives me hope, and she reassures me about sleeping with Ben too soon. She says she would have done the same thing if she weren't in a relationship.

My body is still reeling. From being under Ben, on top of him, again and again. Our chemistry was absolutely electric. I haven't felt this alive, this charged since…maybe ever. It's only been three hours since we parted, but I desperately want him to text me. I go back into my room, all forty square feet, to watch Bravo, but I'm not paying attention. All I can think about is Ben. His nails grazing my stomach, my legs, my spine. His hands on mine, clasped through the night. I drift off to sleep dreaming of us sitting on the bench at Sole. He's holding me like he's known me my whole life. I feel like I already love him. I wake up to the chiming of my phone, and my heart starts racing.

"Hey there. I really enjoyed our time together this weekend." I can feel my smile forming, my cheeks warming as I continue reading. "The sex was nice, but I really liked getting to know you. I'll save up and plan a trip to New York soon, if you want that. Anyways, I'm home now, and I hope you got back safe." I read his text over and over, devouring his every word.

"Hey, me too. I loved meeting you, and I'm glad you made it back to Terry. I want that—the visit, I mean. Excited to see you again soon," I reply.

I fall asleep again, this time dreaming about Ben and me in the glass house. Then in New York. And I wake up to the thought of us. Together again.

Ben and I have been exchanging witty banter for the past few weeks. He sent me pictures of Terry on the beach. I rewatch the video he sends me of Terry howling a refrain that sounds like "I love you." Ben insists on taking me on a FaceTime virtual tour of his area. He's on his electric bike, the wind whistling as he jets down the sidewalk and onto the desolate beach as the sun sets. He holds the phone near the water. He tells me about plans to take the boat out to the Cape before Labor Day.

"This is why I have two roommates," he says. He's wearing a Spider-Man neck gaiter that's equally cringe-worthy and endearing. I'm learning that he's a bit of a man-child.

"Ben, that face mask is hideous. Please don't tell me you wear that out," I say, half-joking.

"This? Of course, I do. All the kids at the beach think I'm Spider-Man. They love it," he says. There's no convincing him it's not cute. "Want to see the beach?" he asks, panning the camera on a gorgeous sunset.

"Wow, I can't believe that's practically your backyard," I say. "It must be nice to have the ocean close by."

Later that night, he pours a glass of Chardonnay. I virtually "cheers" him with my glass of Cabernet in silk pajamas. We stay up nearly all night talking. We talk about the lottery app and how he could be getting a promotion. How he has equity in the company and thinks they could sell it for millions one day. Still, he says he's weighing getting his real estate license to work with James as a side hustle. He goes on about how good he would look wearing a suit rather than a sweatshirt to work every day. I roll my eyes, knowing he's right. I love the sound of that. Selfishly, I love the idea of him being closer to me.

I tell him I'll visit one day, after he comes to see me in New York first. He says he'd like that. His mom said I was "cute" when he showed her my picture. They'd had lunch at a café in his town. Ben loves French onion soup, and sends me a selfie with a bread bowl, joking, "Made by one of the Roca brothers." I smile at the message—and at the fact that he really listened to my story. I'm not used to guys flirting with me. The attention feels intoxicating.

"I favorited your author page," he tells me. I'm beaming. My mom is the only one who reads my stories religiously, and posts them on Facebook.

"You did? Really?"

"Yeah. I love your writing. I read that story you told me about—the one about the refugee chefs. And the pizza debate. Your writing sounds like you when you talk. I like the puns," he says.

That's the biggest compliment, considering how hard I've worked to need fewer edits. He tells me he's meeting a few buddies at a dive bar by his apartment. I hope he doesn't talk to any girls.

The next day, I send him a selfie of me holding up my story about Bradley Cooper's new cheesesteak shop, and a video tour of the newsroom. He's disrupting my type-A productivity at work. I think about his simple life in Boston and wish we could meet for dinner or even cook together in his apartment. It gets me excited about him visiting. Ben will marvel over the special chef treatment we'll get. I wonder if he'll like a tasting menu, or if we should stick to something simpler. Maybe I'll take him on a boat cruise around the Hudson so he can see the skyline at night.

We can order a pastrami sandwich from Katz's like tourists. The night could end with cocktails—and me not regretting bringing him home.

It's so hard to focus when all I can think about is Ben. I find myself waiting on standby for his next reply. I don't mind waiting.

CHAPTER 3

I READ THE *BOSTON GLOBE* headline, "Woman Killed in Boston Harbor Boat Crash." James texts Lauren and me: "Thought you both should know. I think Ben did this." My body freezes.

I'm scared. I lower the laptop screen at my office desk for privacy. What does this mean? I keep reading. "A woman was killed in a crash between two vessels early Saturday morning when first responders found one of the boats overturned upon arriving at the scene. A 25-year-old man believed to be driving under the influence was operating a 27-foot speedboat while making a sharp turn when it collided with another 15-foot boat, causing the smaller vessel to capsize, police confirmed. A rescue diver found 63-year-old Margaret Deerfield unresponsive and pronounced dead at the scene. Her husband, 65-year-old Frank Deerfield, was rushed into surgery at Massachusetts General Hospital." They don't identify Ben anywhere; they just refer to a "Marblehead man being treated for minor injuries."

My heart is racing. I leave my desk, hoping that no one notices. I toggle back to the text from James. "I haven't heard from Ben in days. He hasn't answered my texts," James says. Then he gets more cryptic. "Something like this happened to him in college while we were living in Tampa. He was speeding when I let him drive my car one night. He hit a guardrail and got a DUI."

My mind flashes back to the night Ben drove back from the sushi restaurant, how fast he was driving. I didn't think anything of it. I felt so safe with him. Could Ben really be a liability? I'm shattered at the thought of Ben taking an innocent life. I pray that the woman's husband is okay. This was a tragic accident. It had to be. I feel a pit of sadness in my stomach. I'm angry that the first person I've ever felt a real connection with is being ripped away from me. It feels unfair. I already feel so attached to Ben. I don't want to let go of him.

James confirms it's Ben. He recognizes the boat in the photo. He says he was on it last summer. The thought that Ben didn't call me last night keeps creeping in.

I can't focus on anything but the crime back at my desk, despite the ping of a Slack about a deadline nearing, which I chase off with a quick "Will do!"

Is this vehicular manslaughter? I google what exactly that means and the number of years Ben could face in prison if it's true. It depends on the state. In Massachusetts, it's anywhere from five to twenty years, one source says. And on top of that, they could revoke his license for life. Ben must have been drinking. How could this have happened? My hands are sweating on the keyboard.

I know I'm overreacting. I hardly know this guy. I should just forget about him and his seemingly doomed future, but I'd be devastated if anything happens to him. I scroll through my phone for the photo of us sitting together at Hotel Sole. His soft smile, with his arm wrapped around me. How he said he would visit me.

I get another text. Lauren again. James says Ben is in the hospital. I feel my chest tightening.

"Lauren, what the fuck is going on?" I had to call her.

"Hellllllo, Mia. What is it? I'm busy at work—what's going on?" She sounds impatient. Annoyed, like always, when I call her during work.

"What's going on? Lauren, *Ben*. Hellllllo?" I'm speaking in a loud whisper. I don't want my colleagues to overhear.

I hate how unbothered Lauren can be. I need her to react.

"This…this can't be true. Are we 100 percent sure this is Ben?" I whisper-shout.

"Mia, that's what James said." Her voice is calm, aloof, like she couldn't care less. "I sent you the news story. It sounds like it's him. And I gotta say, you're scaring me now. You don't know this guy. Yes, it's a terrible thing that happened, but he's basically a stranger. You need to snap out of it, Mia. This isn't something you want to be involved in. I'm not going to keep texting James, either."

"Lauren, I know. But you don't understand. We've been talking since we met. Every day. He is not this news story. Please keep asking James for updates. Please just do it for me. Tell him to keep us posted if he hears from him. Okay?" Silence. I can hear her mumbling something to another hairdresser about an appointment being late. "Lauren!"

"Okay! I will. I'll let you know what he says. But you have to stop thinking about him."

I hang up, in slight fury. How could she be so insensitive? I pace around the office kitchen, pretending to be on a call. I can't help thinking about how scared he must be. I want to know that he's okay. Something comes over me—I need to know for myself if this is true.

"Hey, heard about what happened. Hope you're okay. Thinking of you," I text him, then turn my phone face down on my desk and try to forget about it. When I pick it up an hour later, the message says delivered, but there's no response. I wonder if I'll ever hear from him again.

James group texts Lauren and me.

"Hey, Ben hasn't answered my calls. I'll keep trying. This isn't looking good. I spoke with my dad's attorney, and he says Ben will likely face jail time. We probably shouldn't get involved."

I'm gutted. "Jail time? You think it's really his fault?" I ask seconds later.

"I mean, this wouldn't be his first DUI, and the article said he had been drinking. I don't know. This is definitely not good."

"Ugh, this is so scary. I hope he's okay. Let us know if you hear from him, please."

"Will do."

I still don't want to believe it's Ben, but James's insistence is convincing. I have to snap out of this—at least, for now. I'm going to a food tasting event at the James Beard House. Chefs are flying in from all over the country, and I've been looking forward to this for months, but now I'm distracted.

Still no response. I tell my friend Leah what happens. She's the food editor at work who has taken me under her wing. She used to cover hard news and crime, and tells me Ben could be facing ten years, at least, if he's convicted. I rub my hands together. I show her the photo of us.

"You both look really happy here," she says, lowering her gaze. "I'm sorry."

I can feel my eyes welling up with tears. My jaw clenches as I try to force a smile.

"I know. I feel so terrible," I tell her, crossing my arms and changing the subject to tonight's menu. When Leah asks if I'm still up for it, I nod.

"Of course. Yeah, I wouldn't want to miss this," I lie.

I indulge in passed sushi rolls, prepared by Morimoto himself. If this day hadn't sucked so much, it would have been my ideal evening. I accidentally spill my drink on a woman in white next to me, and she gives me the dirtiest look. "It was an accident! You don't have to be rude about it," I snap, too loudly, as she brushes past.

"Are you okay?" Leah asks. Even though she's a bit older than me, I've always thought of her as a peer. We're inseparable at work, but she feels more like a mom in this moment. "Yeah, I'm fine. I'm just so shocked by Ben's accident. I just wish this wasn't true."

"I get it. I was really excited for you. He seemed really sweet. But I mean, he's probably going to prison for a long time. Better to quit while you're ahead."

I agree with Leah's practical advice, but it makes me feel worse. I keep sneaking glances at my phone. I drink to calm my nerves. Leah sees me checking my text messages.

"Mia, it's going to be okay. You will move on from this guy. We'll meet new guys. I know it's hard, but you'll be better off."

"But I don't want to meet new guys," I tell her, like a child throwing a tantrum after getting a new toy taken away. "I like Ben. We could have been perfect together."

I'm drunk at this point. I'm distraught at the thought of Ben making such a selfish and destructive choice that took a life. But this is a sober thought that scares me. My overwhelming feeling is, *Why me? Why does the one guy I finally feel chemistry with have to end up a killer?* I'm angry at the thought of losing Ben. I know it's only been a month, but I feel invested, emotionally and physically. Maybe this was all a misunderstanding? I need to know for sure. Maybe it really wasn't Ben's fault. The uncertainty spikes my anxiety. A waitress brings out mini plates of José Andrés's chimichurri wagyu. I'm eating so fast I can't even taste the flavor, just the tangy aftertaste I drown out with Chardonnay. I order another glass at the bar and take three smoked salmon canapés off a waiter's tray. Leah is telling me about a story she's chasing on squatters in a rich part of Brooklyn.

"That's interesting," I smile politely, wishing I could ride the ferry from the Upper East Side to Brooklyn all day instead of writing in a dark office tomorrow.

When I get home that night, I do something I know I shouldn't. I call Ben. But I'm not thinking straight. There could be an open investigation going on at this very moment. The call goes straight to voicemail. I know his phone didn't get lost in the accident somehow, because my text goes through. Do the police have his phone? They're probably going through all his texts. Every fiber in me desperately needs to hear from him. I exhaust myself with "what if" scenarios and read every local news story about the accident until I finally surrender my phone to my nightstand and try to sleep.

I wake with a splitting headache and knock over the water glass reaching for my phone. There's a text from Ben. Adrenaline rushes through my veins.

"I'm okay. I can't believe you're still talking to me. It means a lot," he texts. "I'll call you later if you want."

I find so much comfort in those three short sentences. I feel my body unclench. Then, I reread: "I can't believe you're still talking to me." He knows I know. It's real. I grip my phone and start sobbing. My breath gets shorter as I try to conceal my crying from my roommate. I realize Ben and I can never be together. I need to end this now.

I get to work, and all I can think about is Ben. I keep refreshing the same news stories with different variations of the same headline, while trying to write a trend story on Labor Day escapes.

I type the keywords "Boat crash Boston Harbor one dead" into Google. There's an update to yesterday's *Boston Globe* story. "Winchester natives Margaret and Frank Deerfield were high school sweethearts," their son, Ian, told *The Globe*. The two were celebrating their anniversary the night that Margaret died. Frank is in critical condition but expected to recover. "They are everything to us. The most loving parents," Ian is quoted as saying. The story is developing. They still don't name Ben as the perpetrator.

I tell myself I need to stop being a voyeur into this tragedy. But I can't help but think about how Ben must have felt when they told him what he'd done. When he woke up in that hospital bed. I don't think I could face it if I were in his shoes.

The article says that the man from Marblehead could be charged with operating under the influence and vehicular manslaughter.

Fuck. I discreetly get up from my desk to call my sister from our office kitchen.

"Lauren, I can't believe this is true.... What do you think will happen now? Like, should I have not called him? I'm worried that..."

"Mia, wake up," she cuts me off, mid-angst. "He killed someone. He's going to jail. I wouldn't talk to him anymore. This is the last thing you need." She's yelling at this point. "Listen to me. Stop thinking about him. Stop texting him. Don't call him. Get over it. It's over. He is nothing to you," she says. I know she's right, but hearing her say this—scream at me—hurts even more.

"I know. I just feel terrible about all this. We were just with him. He's so normal. Like, that...that could have been any of us. Yes, he should absolutely pay for what he did. But..." I think about the possibility of Ben going to prison.

"Mia, you're really worrying me now. You need to seriously get it together. This isn't your problem. This isn't your fault. Mind your own business and go back to work."

I hate how heartless Lauren can be, but I sometimes envy her ability to turn off her feelings and not bear the responsibility for everyone else's emotions. She always envied me for having more friends growing up, but she's always been more real. "I just feel bad. He isn't a criminal, Lauren."

"Yeah, well, you really don't know him," she says. I'm pacing around the kitchen. I know she's right. "You don't know who this guy is. Leave it alone and go back to work, okay?"

"Okay," I agree, grabbing a bag of Doritos from the free snack basket on the counter.

"Promise me you will?" she says.

"Yes. Okay, okay, I will."

I want to believe the words coming out of my mouth. But I know that I'm lying.

Ben has texted me almost every night since the accident, and I feel a strange closeness. He says I shouldn't be talking to him, but I know deep down he feels comforted by our conversations. I honestly like his company.

"I've been reading the stories you sent me. The one about the garlic knot pretzel. The...what's it called? Oh, the lede you wrote, 'Don't get it twisted,' made me smile," he tells me.

Ben says he hasn't been able to sleep. He keeps replaying the accident in his head. What would have happened if he had stayed home to help his mom install the new TV, like she had asked him? How could he lose control of the wheel? He would never be so reckless. How could he take someone's life? How he wished it were his instead. "I should be dead right now. It should have been me," he says. I don't know how to console him. If I were him, I'd probably feel the same.

When he refused to leave his room for three days, his mother called the rabbi to come pray with Ben. He wrapped his hands in leather straps, a box with verses of the Torah, the Jewish ritual of *tefillin*, he told me. They prayed for hours. And he's gone back to the Chabad near his house every morning since. He says he prays for the family. He asks God to give them strength. His rabbi says to pray for forgiveness, but Ben says he doesn't deserve it.

I think about the victims—the pain and grief that family is going through. And I can't fathom the kind of emptiness Ben caused them, how he changed their lives forever. I think about how Ben will live with this. He says he's ready for prison, that he will do whatever it takes to repent. His eyes are bloodshot from crying. "All I want to do is tell them," he tells me, his voice unsteady. "How sorry I am. I'm so sorry."

We decide to FaceTime for the first time since the accident. I'm scared. I don't know if I'm ready to see Ben's scars, but he assures me that he wasn't hurt badly, so I agree. His right eyebrow has a gash that's hardened with blood. It looks like there's a piece of glass still lodged in his forehead. There are red scratches and a line of stitches over his right eye. It's bad, but not as gruesome as I thought it would be.

"Do you see this? Look closer," he says, pointing at the top right of his forehead. I can see something shiny and clear. "It's glass. There's glass still stuck in my head from when I hit the windshield. Somehow, I was still on the boat. They didn't remove the glass at the hospital. I have to see a surgeon."

"Oh my god. That must be killing you. Are you in pain?"

"I'm okay," he says. "I'm lucky to be alive."

I don't want to ask too many questions. I'm also paranoid that his phone conversations might be tapped by the police. They must be building the investigation. He must have hired a lawyer. All this runs through my head as we gaze at each other through the camera.

"They took my license. I'll probably never be able to drive again," he says. I can see the devastation in his eyes. I know how much he finds the act of driving freeing, how much he talked about being out on the water in the Cape.

"I figured. Do you...do you have any updates?" I hesitate to ask.

"I can't really talk about anything. I have a lawyer, though. A really good lawyer."

I'm relieved to hear that, at least.

"Okay," I say. I don't want to pry, but I'm also anxious about what's going to happen to him. "Well, I'm glad you're okay," I try to reassure him. "So, what happens next?"

"I don't know," Ben says in a monotone. "For now, I've been advised to go to AA meetings every day. I'm going to my first one tonight. It's at a church near my house. I'll do whatever I have to," he says. There's a melancholy in his voice. I miss childlike Ben, carefree Ben.

"That's good, yeah," I say. "Just take things one day at a time. That's all you can do right now." More silence. He's not in his room. The background looks unfamiliar; there's a random whale poster over his bed.

"Where are you?" I ask.

"I moved back into my mom's house for a little. I don't want to be alone. Terry is here too," he says, smiling for the first time and calling the dog over to pet her.

"Well, I feel like you're handling this the best that you can right now. You know, under the circumstances."

"What else can I do?" he says. He winces, touching the scar with the glass poking out. I can tell how much pain he's in. But he never says he's scared. He seems ready to accept whatever punishment is coming. I can read the flood of emotions—guilt, remorse, fear of the unknown—flash across his face.

"I'm picking you up at 7 tonight for your meeting," I hear a woman call out. "There's steak in the fridge for dinner. Don't forget to take the dog out," she says, sounding like business as usual. It's strange to hear her rattling off menial tasks. How can she function so normally at a time like this?

"Mom, what did I tell you about coming into my room when the door is closed?" he whines like a teenager, like a switch had flipped. I hear a door shut. I think we're alone again.

"So, AA? How do you feel about it?" I ask.

Ben scratches his head. "My lawyer says it would be a good idea."

"Oh, right. I guess that makes sense," I say. Ben didn't seem like an alcoholic. He seemed to drink casually, like the rest of us. I could think of plenty of times I'd been way more drunk than I saw him be during our time together. Then I thought about the time I drove home from the mall where I worked in high school after having a few rounds of drinks. I thought I was fine, blasting music on the parkway. I felt invincible. Somehow, I got home okay.

I knew Ben liked smoking weed and having a glass of wine every now and then, but I didn't see him as reckless. I flash to Ben getting kicked out of Tampa. To all the pranks he pulled in college. Learning about the DUI in James's car. I guess his lawyer wants him to do everything he can to repent.

"It just doesn't seem like you're an alcoholic," I say. He tells me he saw a therapist a few days after the accident, someone named Gary he'd seen in the past. "Not all alcoholics have drinking problems. It's more about addictive tendencies, my therapist said."

I nod. I can see this in Ben: his fast driving, his thrill-seeking, the thrill in acting on risky behavior. I'm trying to process it. "Are you nervous about going to AA?"

"I've been, actually, once before, after I got a DUI in Tampa. I didn't think I needed it, but I wanted to straighten out my record. I went for like six months." This is news to me. "It's exactly how it is in the movies. Everyone goes around and tells their story. There's coffee," he explains.

"Well, it's good that you're going," I say, trying to be positive.

"Why are you still talking to me?" Ben says abruptly. He sounds almost angry, like he's bothered by it. "I don't get it. If I were you, I would be sprinting away from this dumpster fire. You don't owe me anything. I'm not your problem, Mia," he says, an unfamiliar edge turning on that I didn't see the night we'd met. "I'm not your problem," he says again. "I don't need you to sit here being nice to me. You know what I did was wrong."

I can feel my face turning red. I feel pathetic for sticking around. Even Ben is calling me out for it. *Does he think I'm desperate? Am I?* I question my own loyalty to this stranger. Now I feel ashamed for caring. His question confuses me, too, and I don't know what to say other than I want to be here, with him. Instead, I freeze. There's an uncomfortable silence.

"I just..." I say, trying to formulate a sentence without getting emotional. "I just know that you're a good person. You seem like—you seem like you're not as bad as what you did."

I can see him looking directly into my eyes. I can't tell whether he wants to scream or cry.

"I know I don't know you well, Ben. I know that. And I know this is crazy. I know I should be running away. But something is telling me that I can't. And as much as I should, I don't want to. When we met, I felt this instant attraction to you, but it went beyond that—beyond chemistry. I feel like I've known you for years. And I'm genuinely sad about this. You were supposed to come to New York," I say.

He's starting to get emotional. I sense—feel—that he wanted the same thing.

"I know," he says, holding back tears. "I...I wanted that too, Mia. I wasn't sure where any of this was going. To be honest, I just thought after the Hamptons, we'd go our separate ways, but I couldn't stop thinking about you. And now everything is ruined. I wrecked everything. You deserve more than me. You shouldn't be talking to me. I know I keep saying that. But honestly, Mia, I'm so grateful for you in this moment." I can feel his grief. It makes me want to be close to him even more. I want to hold him and tell him everything will be okay. I want him to feel safe, the way he made me feel that night in the glass house.

"Ben. I don't expect you to trust me. I know we barely know each other, but I want you to know that I'm here for you."

He's crying uncontrollably now. I don't know how to respond with anything other than silence.

"Mia," he says, "I'm…I'm probably going to prison for a very long time. You shouldn't be talking to me. You should be dating other guys. You know that, right?"

I do. I know we can never be together; none of this is remotely realistic. I'm just living in the moment, and Ben needs the comfort. I'm finding comfort in being there for him too.

"Thank you for being here with me. I do like talking to you too," he says. "Even though we shouldn't be."

Ben tells me his ex-girlfriend, Claire, brought him bagels yesterday morning and dropped off dog food for Terry. He says she heard about the accident and wanted to make sure he was okay. I hate that I feel jealous about it. I found a tagged photo of Claire on Ben's Instagram, taken at the physical therapy practice where she works. She has an old photo of herself walking Terry on the beach near Ben's apartment; her light brown hair is swept up in a bun, and she's wearing a pink Lululemon set. She seems simple but naturally beautiful. There's another photo of her holding a pint glass up with her friends on one of those pedal tavern bikes in Nashville.

Ben tells me they met a few summers ago on the beach. I wonder if they kissed or hooked up while she was at his place. He says it was a short encounter. She just came to say she was sorry to hear about what happened. I feel threatened by their history, but I give a "thumbs-up" to his text message and tell him I'm glad he has support.

The jealousy gives me more motivation to keep swiping on dating apps. I know I need to move forward. There's a guy named Jeff who's thirty and lives in Midtown who says we'll get along "if you like pizza." Kevin from the West Village works in sales and seems to be in a band. I swipe a few times and lose interest. When I match with someone, I send through a "Hey there" opening line, all the effort I can muster after a day of writing for my paycheck.

I stare at my phone and just give up. Maybe I'll meet someone who actually lives here and isn't a killer. Fingers crossed. I sigh at my self-pity. There's a press event tonight sponsored by a champagne label—a perfect excuse to get out of the house and eat well.

It's starting to rain, but the peppy PR woman assures me via email that the event's not getting canceled and to use the hashtag #VeuveSummer. I don't have anything else to do, so I commit. Eva is coming too, thank god. The event is at Pier 60 downtown, not far from One World Trade. I schlep down on the 4 train, which feels weird on a weekend since I'm on it every day at 7 a.m. for work. It's a different crowd—more kids and families.

I'm happy I get to the dock before Eva so I can scope out the scene. The rain has turned into a heavy mist, and the sky is so overcast I can barely see the Freedom Tower in the distance. The PR woman hands me a poncho. We're taking a Yamaha speedboat to the docked deck of a fishing boat, where the party is happening. I'm a little nervous. And like whiplash, my mind flashes back to Ben's accident.

Eva arrives looking chic as always, even in the rain. She's clutching her black Chanel bag under one of those raincoats you can buy for your purse. "Oh, I'm so glad they make Chanel-sized raincoats!" I tease.

"Of course, I found one. And how perfect is this?" She twirls around her most prized possession. It costs more than my monthly rent. But that's Eva, and I love her for it. She's obsessive about her bags. And she's the only person I know who can pull off white pants.

We're the last group to board the speedboat. The heavy mist has turned into a downpour, and I wonder if it's safe to be taking a boat in this weather. The idea of anything remotely dangerous feels triggering. "It's totally fine. Don't worry. We're going to be there in literally five minutes," the PR woman assures, but I know her fake smile is concealing what a shit show this is about to turn into. The guy driving the boat—whom I won't call a captain because this situation is far from legit—advises us to strap on life vests. "Oh, here we fucking go." I turn to Eva.

Eva is hysterically laughing, clutching her bag for dear life. We feel like we're on an episode of *The Real Housewives*. We're like the ladies in

Cabo when a storm rocks their yacht and everyone starts panicking. The waves are choppy and rocky, tossing our bodies up and down. We find solidarity in panic with two other writers on the boat.

"All this for champagne. I will not go down with this *Titanic!*" I laugh at my own joke.

"We're all going to need that drink now," Eva agrees.

Our hair is soaking wet when we finally arrive. "That boat ride was definitely a liability," I bitch to Eva. "Could you imagine if someone from *Page Six* were here? This would be an item in a heartbeat." I dab my running mascara. At this point, we're both thankful to have made it. And having Eva by my side feels like an absolute life raft—for many reasons.

When we finally regain composure, a French model lends us his seersucker-clad arm, another lookalike hands us glasses of bright yellow champagne, and all is well again. We spy a table of grapes and assorted cheeses; there's more champagne than food. I check my phone, hoping Ben texted. I take a long sip of champagne, thinking of how I haven't heard from Ben in hours. I should pace myself, but I'm desperate for a good buzz. It's been too long, and I want a break from the heaviness of life, of what might happen with Ben. He hasn't texted me since he told me about his ex coming over.

"Eva, wait, I need to tell you something. It's about Ben," I say, finishing my last sip of champagne.

"Yeah, how's he doing? Are you seeing him soon?" I can feel my smile dissolve.

"What's wrong?" she asks.

"I've been meaning to tell you, but it's so hard to explain."

"What? What—did he kill someone? Go missing?" she says nonchalantly, reaching for a wedge of brie off a cocktail tray. She's concerned when I don't laugh.

"Wait, what's going on?"

"He got into a boating accident, and someone died." I can see the shock in her eyes. Her jaw practically drops.

"Oh my god. Is he okay? That is horrifying. I didn't know he even had a boat."

"It's his mom's. He was driving it. He got a little hurt, but he's okay," I say, before revealing the dreaded detail.

"He was drinking. He's probably going to prison."

Eva's eyes widen. "What! Are you sure? How do you know? That's so scary. My mind is blown. How could this happen? How long have you known this?"

Eva is shocked and keeps apologizing and asking legal questions I don't have answers to.

"I just know he has a really good lawyer, so maybe there's a chance that he won't have to, but I don't know. I feel terrible for the victim's family. For her husband. Please don't tell anyone. Ben and I are still in touch, but obviously this isn't going anywhere. I'm just trying to be supportive. It's so up in the air. I shouldn't even be talking to him, but you know how I feel about him. It's hard to turn off my feelings."

"Of course not!" she promises. "I won't tell anyone. I'm so sorry. I've never experienced anything like this. I'm glad he's okay. I know how upset you must be. It seems like you two really hit it off. Maybe you're right. Maybe he won't have to go to prison, or maybe not for a long time, at least?"

Eva's optimism is a boon, but we both know it's not looking good. She tries to cheer me up with a cocktail, and says that in the meantime I should still peruse dating apps. I can't put all my eggs in one basket.

"Oh, of course I will be," I say, feeling the punch kicking in. "I mean, everything is so uncertain. I'm definitely going to be putting myself out there."

But Ben is the only thing I can think about. It feels so good to have him to talk to every night. The shame I feel for my dependence on him during this uncertain time, and the stigma I know his crime carries, is unsettling. I keep drinking to feel more at ease.

I shift my focus back to the event. I recognize a woman my age who works at *The Cut*. We met at a media event for a pinot grigio launch. We both cover similar beats in arts and lifestyle, and she's easy to talk to. We joke about how we're both still single and exchange tips on dating apps. Hinge was the "it" app now and was crawling with guys on Sunday nights. Tinder was for creepy assholes. Raya was for rich ones.

I can feel the waves crashing against our boat. It feels like we're moving, even though I know we're docked. Maybe I'm drunker than I think. I should stop drinking, but I'm finally fun. That's where I start to go downhill. The crowd is applauding as one of the delicious Frenchmen sabers a magnum bottle of champagne. I sip my drink quietly, thinking about which ex I haven't texted in a while. This is what I need to distract me: a night out, and endless champagne.

One of the PR reps offers to give us a tour of the boat. Eva and I take a selfie at the bow. "My heart will go on for champagne!" I tell her. We are both hysterically laughing, my bad joke funnier as we keep drinking. I take a hit of Eva's weed pen, and we both forget about the rain and how we almost ended up in the Hudson. I stumble and lose my balance and spill my drink. "I'm so sorry," I say.

I ask one of the boat workers if they have a cigarette. I am pining for one and haven't had one since the night I met Ben. The crew member comes back with one, and I grasp for it like it's a winning Powerball ticket. I wonder if Ben can still work at the lottery app. I didn't even think to ask. Eva is drunk too, and she matches my manic energy.

We are in the last group to head back on the Yamaha, only this time it doesn't feel scary. It's exhilarating having the wind in my hair, the Hudson lit up by the city skyline as we whisk through the current. The water isn't as choppy as I remembered it earlier. I close my eyes and pretend I'm flying, relishing the ease of my mind. I feel so free and think about how lucky I am to have built the life I have in New York.

I check my phone, hoping one of my exes has texted back. No luck, so I suggest a nightcap with Eva and *The Cut* editor. We decide on Locanda Verde because it's close, and it's Bradley Cooper's favorite spot. He loves the chicken. His publicist probably fed him that line, but who cares? It doesn't take much convincing. Moments later, I'm eating one of Andrew

Carmellini's meatball sliders off some banker's plate. He's probably old enough to be my father. At some point, he orders me a glass of pinot noir. It's so silky in my mouth, I know it must be expensive.

"You have to try the octopus. It's what they're known for," he says. I wait for him to feed me.

He has salt-and-pepper hair, and I try to guess his age, but he won't tell me. I'm so much more confident when I'm drunk. Drunk me thinks I'm a fucking supermodel, and I love every minute of it. I wish I could love myself this much sober.

Eva tells me she has to go. Her boyfriend is waiting up. They've been dating since college. She tells me not to think so much about Ben, that it's good that I'm out and having fun, and to text her when I get home. But I resent her for not being able to hang. I'm still talking to the hot banker, trying to understand what exactly it is that he does. Will I sleep with him? Maybe. My mind flashes back to a fling with a chef—how he cooked for me in my tiny walk-up, hiking all the way up the five floors. He was newly divorced, and I was a fun, short-lived rebound.

Back to banker guy. Maybe he lives in a penthouse? I just hope he isn't married. I notice that he's not wearing a wedding band when he loosely grips the stem of his wineglass. I hope the bartender will use his name because I don't remember it, and I don't want to seem more drunk than I already am by asking. The bartender refills both of our wineglasses.

We keep talking about his job and his kids. He says I seem mature for my age. I tell him I hate dating guys my age because they're awful and lazy and noncommittal. I don't remember what I said to make him want to kiss me, but he does, and I don't pull away. He starts blushing. I keep drinking. Turns out he's divorced, and I hope he really is.

Banker starts talking about his kids again. When did he say he had kids? He says he just told me about them. Things are getting weird, and I'm confused about where this is all going. "What? You have kids? Are you married?" I ask, getting mad at him for misleading me like every rich, powerful, stupid man in New York.

He laughs and tells me that he has a daughter around my age. She's twenty-two. He's apparently already told me all this. I tell him I'm tired. He pays the bill, and we say goodbye. The bartender offers to help me get an Uber. I tell him I'm okay and can do it myself. I hate when people try to help me. I don't need anyone's help. I go outside, hunting for another cigarette. Someone from the kitchen staff is smoking, and he's nice enough to give me one. The street is desolate when my Uber pulls up. Somehow, it's almost 2 a.m. I get in the car and close my eyes for a few minutes, and when I open them, we're crossing the Brooklyn Bridge.

"Fuck!" I yell. "We're going to *Brooklyn?*" I blurt out.

"Yes, ma'am. That's the address you gave me," the driver says.

This isn't the first time this has happened. There's a matching street address in Brooklyn, and when I don't pay attention, it defaults to that zip code on my phone. I'm so tired at this point, but the Uber man is nice enough to reroute me to the Upper East Side. I get home twenty minutes later and chug a glass of water in the dark so I don't wake my roommate. I wish I had gotten pizza. I'm suddenly so sad.

Ben and I speak every few nights.

"Hey," I say.

He calls me an hour later. "Hey. I just found out I'm getting arraigned the day after Thanksgiving."

Silence. *Fuck. Is this it?* A jolt of reality hits me for the first time in three months. The sick, psychotic honeymoon phase of whatever you call this is over. I don't know how to answer, but I want to comfort him.

"I'm sorry, Ben. I'm so sorry," I say.

"Thanks."

"I wish I was there."

"Me too."

I tell him that everything will be all right. But we both know it won't.

CHAPTER 4

TODAY IS BEN'S ARRAIGNMENT, AND I feel helpless. He'll go to court for the first time. There will be press. Camera bulbs flashing in his face. Relentless asks for comments. He can't say anything. He says he'll try and call me after.

I feverishly refresh the *Boston Globe* website, and every local paper in Boston covering the case, to see if I can find out any new details: he's pleaded not guilty to manslaughter for operating under the influence and another count of manslaughter for operating under the influence of drugs. I'm taken aback by the drug charge. I know Ben smoked weed, but I wonder what else he was on that night.

I find a video from a local Boston newscast. Ben is in a suit, walking into the courthouse. For someone so broken, he carries himself well. He has his head down, trying to ignore the reporters swarming him and his lawyer, a gray-haired, older Irishman. He doesn't look up once. I watch the two-minute news clip on my work laptop over and over. I'm proud of him for being so brave. His statement is loud and clear in his body language. He never meant to hurt anyone. He is overcome with grief and remorse.

"Authorities say Ben Cohen's blood-alcohol level was nearly twice the legal limit of 0.08 and under the influence of marijuana and prescription drugs the night he was driving a twenty-seven-foot speedboat around midnight when he crashed into a fifteen-foot powerboat."

I tune out the rest of the broadcast. I feel numb.

Ben posted the $6,000 bail—his mother must have. I try calling him after rereading the news stories a good ten times. I wonder if he has any new information. Then I race to meet my deadlines and jet out for my dinner reservation. There's a new Argentinian steakhouse in Brooklyn Heights I'm writing about for the "Eats" section of the paper. I invited my food editor, Leah, along to try it.

"I ordered us a round," she says, scribbling a list of deadlines in her reporter's notepad. "It looks like we can sample any of these meats from the barbecue. Should we just try one of each?"

"Yeah, sounds good," I say, reaching for the wineglass. A waiter brings over warm cheese bread. I devour a piece without thinking about the carbs. It's buttery and delicious—exactly the comfort food I need right now. Before I know it, there's a spread of blood sausage and beef empanadas, which are a little greasier than they should be, but I still finish an entire one.

We talk about deadlines, and somehow the conversation turns to Leah's relationship with a new guy she met last summer in the Rockaways. She's considering whether she should introduce him to her parents. I advise waiting until things get more serious. The grass-fed flank steak comes out, sizzling hot on a grill platter. We switch to a glass of 2010 Malbec. I leave Ben and his dismal situation out of the conversation, but Leah brings it up anyway.

"I'm sure Ben is a great guy, but you don't want to get tangled up in this. You have your life, your career," she says. "I just don't want to see you get dragged down by some guy who doesn't deserve you."

It makes me want to hide the truth from her even more. Of course, I don't deserve this, but I feel myself falling in love with Ben. I crave his text messages. His voice memos. I'm becoming addicted to being wanted, needed by Ben. I lie and tell her I'll be fine.

When I get home, I look through my text messages. My mom checked in to see if I was okay. I haven't spoken to her in a few days. There's another from Lauren, asking where I've been. I check to see if there's anything from Ben. Still nothing. I convince myself it's for the best. I keep swiping on Hinge. I match with an architect for Shake Shack. He seems perfectly normal. "What's your Shake Shack order?" I flirt.

The next morning, I wake up to a text message from Ben.

"Hey, I'm coming to New York."

Comfort

CHAPTER 5

MY FIRE ESCAPE IS COVERED in snow. The last time I saw Ben, we were saying goodbye in the parking lot of Hotel Sole, holding hands under the sun. Our carefree ride through Sag Harbor with the windows down, the intoxicating summer air.

I fantasize about what life would be like if none of this had happened, if Ben and I were a couple. I'm trying to take things one day at a time, but this whole thing feels like a tragic romance novel. Part of me is so desperate to know what happens next.

I didn't think Ben would be able to leave the state, let alone come to New York. But I guess it's a waiting game now, since his mom posted bail. He's coming to see his brother in the city—and me. I realize the continued contact will make it harder to let go, but I'm still excited to see him again.

I wonder if the chemistry between us will still be there. I wished him a happy Thanksgiving, and he didn't answer for days. I know it's normal for him to withdraw. He's seeing two psychologists weekly and meditating to calm his anxiety instead of drinking and smoking pot. He's still praying with the rabbi most mornings.

He texts me on a group chat with his brother. I feel awkward about being introduced to his family.

"Hi Adam, meet Mia. Mia is the writer I met in the Hamptons I was telling you about. I would love for you to meet her. Do we have anything planned? Can we add her to a reservation?" he writes. I have no idea how to respond. I don't really want to meet his family. I feel awkward imagining our small talk. I feel like they'll judge me for even being there, and the idea of putting myself through that public shame feels daunting.

"Just that comedy show at 10 p.m. I booked for us. Mia can take Mom's spot if she wants," Adam responds. An hour passes, and I still don't answer. I don't know if I want to meet his family. Ben texts me separately with three question marks, so I start typing.

"Wow, thanks so much for that intro, Ben," I write back. "That all sounds good. I don't want to intrude on your family time, so let me know when works best for a dinner or brunch."

"No intrusion at all," Adam replies. "See you both soon."

Tonight's the night. I idle in front of my closet, thinking about what to wear. Last time I saw Ben, we were mostly in bathing suits—or no clothes at all. Now he'll see me in my element. I'll probably just wear my all-black uniform, a security blanket of sorts that consists of a turtleneck and a pair of over-the-knee suede boots to look a little feminine. There's a camel-colored peacoat I've been dying to wear. I want Ben to see me as a confident, successful New York woman. I put on bold red lipstick and call an Uber. My nerves cartwheel as we weave in and out of traffic down the FDR and along the East River. I send a selfie to Eva, who approves of the red lip.

"I'm a little nervous meeting Ben's family," I tell her.

"Don't be! Just be yourself. He'll be so happy to see you," she says. "It's so nice that you're meeting them. I'm sure it means a lot." I cling to her reassurance.

Adam lives in a luxury building in the West Village. I feel like I'm walking into a first date, only with Ben and his closest family members. I'm used to being a chameleon, adapting to whatever situation I'm in to make my sources feel comfortable as a journalist. But this isn't work, it's personal, and I feel unprepared to meet the family of someone who is going to prison, someone I have feelings for.

Before I get out of the car, my Uber driver tells me I smell good, a welcome ego boost. I'm wearing the Miu Miu perfume I wore on my birthday, the same scent Ben complimented. I hope it'll take him back. I walk through the revolving door of Adam's building.

"Hi there, I'm here for Adam Cohen," I tell the doorman. He calls up as I simultaneously text Ben, letting him know I'm here, hoping he comes down so I don't have to walk in alone.

Before I even ask, he says he's on his way down, and I feel instant relief. I sit on a white leather couch, taking in the vanilla-scented fragrance in the lobby that's probably more expensive than my rent. This is the kind of building I've always wanted to live in.

I imagine all of the couples that must walk through those big revolving doors with their dogs trailing across the marble white floors, and I picture carrying a Prada bag under my arm, pushing a baby stroller with my husband. Then I see him. Ben. Our eyes meet as he's walking out of the elevator. His perfect green eyes gazing directly at me. His brown hair and eyebrows. His scars still visible but faded with the time that's passed. We both pause for a moment, just looking at each other. He walks closer, and I briefly scan his body. He's wearing a blue button-down and dark-washed jeans. I can now see the scar on his right eyebrow more closely and feel his pain. He embraces me, and we stay like that for a long moment. I feel everything for him. Sadness, remorse, the survivor's guilt he's carrying. I want him to know I'm here. I can feel in his grasp that he's relieved to see me. We may have only seen each other one other time, but we're bonded by something.

"How are you?" I say, breaking the silence. "I can't believe you're here," I gaze up and down as if I'm unsure he's really standing in front of me. Is this the same man who held me so closely that night in the glass house? After everything that he's been through. "It's been so long," I say. "But it also feels like we just saw each other."

"I know. I'm good," he says. I sense that he's nervous. "We just got here a few hours ago." He's looking directly at me, analyzing my hair, my makeup, my red lips. He's happy to see me. And in this moment, the broader situation isn't real. It's just us again.

He takes my hand, and I follow him into the elevator, hoping we'll have another moment alone. I wish it were just us tonight. He presses "PH" for the penthouse level, and I find myself leaning in close. "You're wearing the perfume you wore in the Hamptons," he says. "The Miu Miu, right?"

I can't believe he remembers.

I nod and lean back into his arms. We kiss for the first time since the Sole parking lot, and my heart ignites. His face is scruffy and unshaven, like the first time we met. He looks exactly the way I remember him, but he's even more attractive. Maybe because I know him better. Maybe because I've seen new parts of him. The elevator opens abruptly, and I regain my composure, prepping myself as if I'm about to do a work interview, only this time I'm the subject. Ben leads me into his brother's apartment.

"Hi!" Margot, his mother, greets me. Her hair is slightly shorter than shoulder length, dyed dirty blonde, and she's wearing reading glasses and a burgundy turtleneck sweater with jeans.

"How are you? Ben has told me so much about you," she says warmly, reaching for a hug.

"Aw, I'm glad. It's so nice to finally meet you," I say, taking off my peacoat and eyeing Ben, who instinctively reaches to hang it for me.

Adam and his girlfriend are asleep in the bedroom, she tells me, after a long day playing tour guide. I spot their French bulldog, Maverick, roaming around. I pet her to calm my nerves. I can feel Margot looking at me. She's smiling.

"Mom, stop being weird," Ben says, walking me to the couch.

"What? I'm just admiring this beautiful girl," Margot says, still smiling. She looks pretty put together for someone whose son could face up to ten years in prison, maybe more. People hide pain well. On a second look, her eyes look tired behind her reading glasses.

Ben motions for me to sit next to him on the couch. I consider taking my boots off, but they're too hard to get back on. Margot compliments them, and I thank her politely, telling her they're Stuart Weitzman and that my sister bought them for me, when she asks.

"Mom, Mia is going to take your spot at the comedy club tonight, okay?" Ben cuts her off mid-sentence. She's talking about a scarf she bought at one of the winter markets.

"Yeah, that's perfectly fine, honey, I know. You guys have fun. This weekend is all about you hanging out with your brother and spending time with your friends. Whatever you want to do," Margot says.

I can see her mom shield turning on. She must believe that this could be one of Ben's last normal weekends. She's trying to soften the impending doom. I can see it in Ben's face, half of him is thinking about what's next. Margot continues talking about their day and their plans, when Adam comes out of the bedroom.

"Shh, Tracy is still asleep," he says to Margot, bending down to pick up Maverick. "We can hear you from in there." He seems annoyed at Margot like a teenage boy.

Ben disregards his noise complaint and introduces me. "Meet Mia!" He bolts up. "She's a journalist," he says, like I'm a Pulitzer Prize. I'm probably blushing. I feel uncomfortable with the spotlight on me.

"Hi," I say in a tone three octaves higher than my real voice. "It's nice to meet you. Thank you for having me."

Adam returns the pleasantry, not matching my forced enthusiasm. He's handsome, and it's apparent that he's Ben's brother from his profile. They both have a pronounced jawbone that juts out slightly. Adam's is more visible because his face is thinner. He's much skinnier than Ben. He's also unshaven. He works for a cloud-based software company as an executive vice president of sales, and Ben says he works constantly, that his job is so stressful, that he barely makes time to eat. But apparently, he has great taste in restaurants—he must be making good money, with a Breville coffee machine and Le Creuset lining his stove.

Ben pinches Adam's arm and makes a muscle with his. He told me he always wanted to be like his brother. When he was younger, he'd try to hang out with Adam and his friends and buy the same clothes. They don't see each other much anymore. Adam only comes up to Boston for the holidays, and Ben never goes out of his way to come to New York either.

He doesn't like cities. "But I'll make an exception because you live here," he told me over the phone.

I can sense tension between the brothers. Adam comes off a little high-strung and type A, the opposite of Ben's lax demeanor. He's running through the weekend itinerary with Margot as jazz music plays on his fancy smart speakers. Ben is tinkering with them. He loves figuring out how gadgets work, and I can see Adam getting annoyed. Ben turns up the volume so loud we can't hear them talking anymore, and Adam yells at him to turn it down or he'll wake up Tracy.

There's a wine decanter resting on the marble countertop that makes me feel ashamed for refusing to spend more than ten dollars on my own bottles. I think about my mismatched plates and chipped cereal bowls. I know Ben won't judge my chipped bowls. Ben sits back down next to me. I can smell the ginger beer on his lips. His eyelashes are longer than I remember, his skin still a few shades darker than mine even in the dead of winter.

A blonde woman in her early thirties, curvy in all the right places, joins the living room. Tracy introduces herself, offering everyone a glass of wine. Thank god. I so desperately need a crutch to take the edge off. But isn't it a bit tone deaf for us to be drinking in front of Ben after everything? I feel bad for saying yes to a glass of pinot noir. But everyone else seems to be cool with it.

Ben even encourages me to have one. He must see that I'm hesitant. "It's fine. Don't be weird," he says, putting his arm around me. "Have some wine. You're going to need it, getting to know my mom tonight." I'm grateful that Ben can still make sarcastic jokes, like when we met. He has a way of putting me at ease.

"Do you have any more of that ginger beer in there?" Ben asks.

Tracy pours me a glass of pinot noir, and she, Adam, and I toast. Margot isn't a drinker. She sips on a seltzer. I relish the sweet, bitter taste.

COMFORT

There's already a line wrapped around the block when we get to the Comedy Cellar. I'm shocked no one has brought up the accident yet. I wonder if Ben has even spoken to his brother about it. From their dynamic, I bet not.

Tracy does most of the talking. She's a vet, and describes how a woman brought in a baby bird with a fractured wing that she rescued off the street earlier in the week. Ben cuts in, changing the subject before the story ends to ask if a type of dog food that he saw on Reddit was safe for Terry. Tracy's eyebrows arch up. She makes intense eye contact with Adam and tells Ben she'll take a look at the ingredients.

There's a lull, and when I can't think of anything to talk about besides work, I ask if they tried a Canadian bagel shop that I just wrote about. They hadn't, but Adam adds it to his Notes app. The conversation strays to hobbies, and, other than eating out at expensive restaurants, I have none. Tracy does CrossFit, God bless her. Adam puts his arm around her in the first display of affection I witness between them. I feel Ben reach for my hand, and a wave of comfort comes over me. It feels strange how normal everyone is acting, like there's an undercurrent of denial about Ben's accident.

When we finally get inside, every seat in the house is full of bachelorette parties, couples, and a few tourists. The MC is about to take the mic. I feel relieved that we don't have to keep talking. The first comedian, a chubby guy probably in his mid-twenties, with a beard and Southern accent, comes out.

"Anyone in a long-distance relationship?" he asks the audience. "It's a lot of work. A lot of hard work. Calling, texting, driving. Anyone else a sexter in the audience? I see a few of you are. Don't be shy. We've all done it. Okay, good for you, wow. Give yourself a little more credit. It's like an Olympic sport. It's a lot harder than it looks. Holding up the phone, getting the right angle. Like, it made me realize I'm not exactly ambidextrous." Everyone laughs, including Ben.

I watch him go from expressionless to hysterical, and it puts me at ease knowing that he can let go of the heaviness and just live in the moment. After the show, I thank Adam, and Ben calls us an Uber back to my apartment. I notice they didn't hug when Ben said bye.

"That was so good," I say, tucking my hands inside my jacket pockets. "I can't believe that famous comedian came out at the end. What are the odds?"

"I know, right? It was our lucky night. It's definitely because you were there," he says, smiling. He kisses me again as we wait for the driver to pull up.

I'm beyond relieved my roommate is gone for the weekend so we can have some privacy and not have to worry about making noise.

"Wow, so this is the penthouse suite, huh?" he says, wheeling his suitcase through the tiny hallway into the living space that connects to the kitchen. I'm self-conscious about my coiled electric stove and its dirty burners. They're impossible to clean, so I don't even bother.

"It is," I say, thankful that the apartment is somewhat clean, though I realize the bottles on my bar cart are covered in dust. "Do you want the grand tour?" I ask, throwing up my arms. "We'll start in my favorite part, the kitchen. Right here."

We stand in front of my refrigerator, which is covered in magnets from all of the places I've traveled. I didn't want to spend any time or money decorating the apartment because I eventually want to get my own studio, when I can afford it. Until then, the fridge gets all of my personality.

"What is all this clutter!" Ben says jokingly, staring at my magnet opus.

"This is my magnet collection. I'm kind of obsessed with it," I say, straightening the crooked license plate from LA and the cow's skull from New Mexico. "Sometimes I stand here with my coffee and think back to these trips. It's my favorite thing." It's not something I would usually say out loud, but I feel so comfortable around Ben.

"Oh yeah?" Ben says, pointing at a magnet with a couple tangoing that says Buenos Aires. "Tell me about this one."

"Oh, I like this game," I say. "Okay Buenos Aires. Hmm…my favorite memory. Well, I was covering a travel story and somehow got invited to a famous chef's home. He cooks over these giant open fires. His name is Francis Mallmann. He was on *Chef's Table*." His stare is blank, and I realize he has no idea who or what I'm talking about.

"Anyway, we had cocktails in his living room, and he cooked us this amazing dinner. It was really special," I say. "Just me and three other journalists. I learned to tango that night too."

"That's awesome," Ben says, his fingers trace over Jamaica, Newport, Rhode Island, and a hula girl from Hawaii. "I've never been." He stumbles on the magnet from Santa Fe. "I love Santa Fe. My grandparents had a house out there for a while. They collect art. My grandpa's ashes are sprinkled there, actually."

"No way. I love it out there. It was one of my favorite trips actually. I randomly went skiing there last year for another travel story. I met a bunch of writers out there, and we ended up becoming such good friends. I never smoke, but they got me to smoke weed in the parking lot of our hotel. I felt like it was an in-the-moment type thing."

I immediately regret sharing that part because Ben hasn't smoked since the accident, and I'm afraid he might want to again. It must have been so hard for him to quit cold turkey. He's staring down at my laminate floors.

"Wow, you are X-rated bad," Ben jokes, and I can feel his sense of humor coming out again. Like he's remembering how to flirt with me. I roll my eyes, giving him the validation he wants.

He moves on to my food column headshot. I'm wearing a gold statement necklace. "So modest," he says, pointing at the placement of my headshot under my Little Italy magnet that reads, "Not only am I perfect, but I'm also Italian too."

"Shut up! It's a great photo," I say, sure of it. I do look great there.

"It is. And you should be proud, having a column in a major newspaper. That's pretty unbelievable."

I like hearing the praise from Ben. My mom tells me all the time, but it's different.

Ben questions my roommate's crystals along the mirrored console in the living room, and I tell him they aren't my style. I point him towards the fake Andy Warhol portrait, a still life of a dinner table called *After the Party,* his pop art from 1979. Ben says it feels more like my vibe.

We make our way to my bedroom, which is filled to the brim with books. Ben jumps on my bed and grabs a book that's sticking out. It's John Irving's *A Prayer for Owen Meany.* I ask if he's read it, and he says he hasn't.

"We read it in AP English in high school. My senior quote is from that book."

"What is it?" he asks.

"It was something like, 'If you're lucky enough to find a way of life you love, you have to find the courage to live it.'" I haven't thought about that quote in years.

"I think you're pretty courageous," Ben says. "It takes a lot of guts to live in New York by yourself. And to put your writing out there on such a public platform, especially today, with social media and all the trolls. Oh, and you're definitely brave to put up with the rats in this city. They're everywhere." He gives me a coy smile.

I'm charmed by his compliment.

"Thank you," I say. "The rats aren't so bad."

He puts the book back and admires how comfortable my bed is. It's surreal to have him in my apartment. He hasn't tried to kiss me since we were outside.

"You're being shy," I call him out and pull him closer to kiss him. I get a rush of excitement, like when we first met. The chemistry hasn't gone away. If anything, it's just intensified with the anticipation of finally reconnecting.

"I have to be honest with you," he says, looking down. "I really didn't think I'd get here. I'm so happy we met. But I wonder every day why you're still here...."

"I don't know. I feel terrible about everything, Ben. And I can't make sense of it either. All I know is that I really, genuinely like talking to you."

I feel like, for the first time, I can be myself around someone. Like I'm not performing or having to be on. I feel a sense of freedom with Ben because I know he can't judge me. That he's isolated from my world and it's only us.

He doesn't say anything for a while, and I need to fill the silence.

"I know all of this is crazy, and I probably shouldn't be involved in your life, but I'm glad you're here with me now. I feel a connection with you I've never felt with anyone."

I know I shouldn't get attached. It's only going to get worse. But I can take care of myself, and I know I'll always be okay. I've never really cared about someone enough to know what that might feel like anyway. I've never been in love.

"I know," he says. "Me too. I'm happy I'm here." He kisses me again and again. Ben says he can't talk about the accident; all of the legal stuff is still being processed, and I tell him I understand.

"Life is so uncertain for me now, Mia. You know that. I can't keep any of my promises because I don't know where I'll be or how long I have left with you. But I promise—I mean—I'll do my best. I'll do everything possible not to hurt you," he says.

I want to believe it. I want to believe him. How is it possible that I care so much about someone who is tangled in a lifetime of pain? But I knew from the night I met Ben that I could love him. Now that there is an inevitable deadline, I see the two sides of a potential life with him. Loving him and losing him.

He presses his lips against mine, his tongue migrating to the inside of my neck, my collarbone. He takes his shirt off, then mine, carefully unbuttoning my jeans. We're both kneeling on my bed, his warm body up against me as he unhooks my bra, kissing my bare chest down my stomach. His tongue travels between my unsteady legs, like the night we met, staring up at me with his green eyes. He takes off his boxers. I wrap my legs around him, tracing my hands on his faded tan lines as he plunges inside me.

"You feel so good," he tells me, our bodies interlocked. He holds my hands overhead. I feel his muscles tighten, my body reeling with him inside me.

Ben props me onto my knees, cupping my breasts from behind as he presses against me from behind. Again and again, until we both start to come at the same time.

"Fuck, Mia," he says, collapsing on top of me.

I'm filled with a sense of relief when I wake up with Ben next to me. I inch closer into his arms, feeling his warm body against mine. He's still sleeping. He doesn't snore; I remember that from the Hamptons. He's shirtless, and I trace my fingers over his back. He twitches for a minute out of deep sleep. "Wake up," I whisper. "Let's get breakfast."

Ben yawns and sprawls his legs over me in a deep morning stretch. "What time is it?" he asks.

"It's almost 11," I say, surprised at how late it is.

Ben tickles me from behind on our way to the kitchen. He's remembered how ticklish I get. I make us both espressos as Ben blasts music on Spotify from the bathroom. I'm afraid it'll wake up my neighbors, but I don't want to kill the vibe. He's acting more like himself.

I take Ben to my favorite diner on Eighty-Ninth and Second. The one where I relished gossiping with Eva, before she moved to Hoboken. Ben orders pancakes and poached eggs.

"I've been indulging a lot lately," he says. "Comfort foods."

"I hear you." I look up from my menu. "It's necessary sometimes. Treat yourself." I order an omelet. And we both get a coffee.

"I feel like a regular," he says, scanning the packed booths. "This place reminds me of a diner near my house. I hope one day we can go." I love the sound of that.

"Maybe," I say, turning my phone facedown so my Hinge app doesn't ping at the table. I know this won't last, but I feel weird about Ben knowing I'm actively pursuing other guys.

"So, tell me a secret, something I don't know about you," I say.

"Well, you know the worst thing that's happened to me. Um, let's see. There was this semi-traumatizing thing that happened when I was younger, that Adam did."

I brace for whatever it is he's going to tell me.

"I got lost once when I was a kid. I was in second grade. We were visiting my grandparents in Miami, back when we lived in Boca. I remember we were on that busy street, Lincoln Road, the one with all the restaurants and shops. Adam was with his friends. He was maybe ten. I must have been six or seven. We were watching this steel drum band play in a crowd. I loved the drums. I begged him to let me stay and watch, and then, all of a sudden, I turned and I saw him running out of the crowd with his friends.

"They were gone. I felt a weird panic come over me. Like I was completely alone in this foreign place. I couldn't find him anywhere. I looked in a clothing store, a Cuban coffee shop. I remember a woman tried to help me, but I couldn't understand her. She was speaking broken English. She said 'police,' and that made me nervous, so I ran out and found a bench a few blocks down. It started getting dark. Adam finally showed up like nothing happened. He was at a GameStop the whole time and pretended like it was my fault. He told our mom I ran away. When I told her Adam left me, she grounded him for a month. He wouldn't let me live it down. He's pretty much bullied me ever since."

"Okay, that sounds traumatizing," I say, watching him fold the corners of his paper placemat. "What a shitty thing for him to do."

"Yeah, I mean, we all were kind of out of sorts during our parents' divorce. It was a tough time."

"I hear you. It wasn't easy for Lauren and me either. Thankfully, we had each other. You mentioned having a sister?"

"Yeah. Alana. She's three years younger."

CHAPTER 6

I TEXT LAUREN THE PHOTO of Ben and me at the office. And another group shot we took with his family.

"Wait, you already met his mom?" Lauren texts back, and I already regret giving her too much detail about our weekend.

"They're pretty normal," I say, trying to convince her that Ben does not come from a bad family.

"Why would you want to meet them when he's going to prison?" she asks. She has a point, but Lauren's judgment makes me want to tell her less. But she's my sister. How can I hide this from her? I wish she could be more understanding.

"I know, I know. And honestly, I felt super weird meeting his family," I say, pandering. "But they're so normal. We ended up having a nice time. And his brother seems really successful. He's a big sales executive. We all had a nice time at the comedy club." It's a final attempt to humanize Ben.

"I mean, listen I'm still on dating apps. There are a few other guys in the mix. I just—he was in New York. How could I not meet up with him?"

"I know you like this guy, Mia, but you will find someone else who is not involved in a crime."

Her harsh delivery makes me feel worse. Like I have to keep this a secret. I call Eva after we hang up. I know she'll be more understanding.

"You did nothing wrong. He was in New York. Why wouldn't you see him?" she tells me on the phone, complimenting my outfit in the photo of Ben and me in Central Park that I sent her.

She reassures me that Ben's family doesn't think I'm crazy for sticking around, that they probably appreciate my presence. I feel a lot better.

"Thanks, and just, please keep this between us. Like I said, I don't know where anything is going, and I'd rather not make it seem like I'm all in with him. Jade and Carrie don't need to know just yet," I say.

"You know I won't," Eva assures me. "It sounds like you guys had a nice weekend."

She's right. The visit was better than I could have imagined. I'm already thinking about when I'll see Ben next. His texts feel like a dopamine IV. I'm smiling more. I'm happier at work when he texts me. I fantasize about him being my boyfriend, but I'm also ashamed of his crime and how people would see me if they knew I was standing by him through all of this.

I'm already too emotionally invested. I open the Hinge app and make plans with Jeff, the guy who had the profile about loving pizza. He's originally from Michigan and insists we try a Detroit-style pizza place in Chelsea. "Can't wait!" I text him.

Then I bury myself in work to distract from the lingering uncertainty of Ben's case. I get an assignment about a story on dangerous toys for the holidays, and I have to test out a new electric bike outside the newsroom. I nearly fall off, but it makes for a great first-person piece. I send Ben photos, and he can't stop talking about how badly he wants one. He begs me to "work my magic" and get him one.

Ben has more time on his hands since he and his boss mutually agreed it would be best for him to take a leave until his trial. I can sense that the lack of a schedule is driving Ben crazy. He sweetly texts me Reddit threads with story ideas. He says his ex, Claire, came over again to check on him and take Terry for a walk earlier. Reiterating that their relationship is completely platonic. I pretend I don't care.

The trial keeps getting pushed back, and Ben asks if I want to see him for New Year's. I usually hate staying in the city, but maybe that's because

I never have anyone to spend the holiday with. I remember a publicist friend emailed about a party downtown with views of the fireworks. It would be the perfect night. My daydream is abruptly interrupted when I get a call from my dad, who is frantic about a chef and a waiter not showing up for work. He'll be alone in the kitchen and carrying out food if I don't come help.

"Mia, please come up. I'm begging you. I need the help. It's only for a few hours. Haven't I always been there whenever you needed me?" he insists, his voice panicked.

"Dad, I can't. I just. There's an event at the Central Park Conservancy tonight. I've already RSVP'd." I think about the vintage silk Dior gown I rented hanging in my closet.

"Mia, you think I want to beg you to help me? I'm desperate. Your sister can't do it because she has the business, she's running around. I need your help."

I hate how guilty he makes me feel. It kills me to see him running around, making the food, waiting on tables. I see how overwhelmed he is in the kitchen. He works so hard, and I wish he could just find good help and keep it together. I can't drop everything to play waitress. I know I'll never hear the end of it if I don't.

I leave the office and toss my hair in a messy bun on the 6 Train to Harlem, then the Metro North. I don't even bother to ask my dad to pick me up from the train; he'll guilt me about that too. He's prepping the dough for tonight. The restaurant is a ten-minute walk.

"Mia, come on, answer the phones—it's starting to get busy!" he says, overwhelmed. "Put your phone down! It's just for a couple of hours."

I think about Ben and our New Year's weekend. The phone ringing jolts me back to the present. "Thank you for calling De Luce's. How can I help you?" The refrain sounds weirdly nostalgic, like I'm a teenager again, working through summers in college. I punch in the penne alla vodka, the calamari, and the large Sicilian into the POS system, easy, like riding a bike.

December always flies by. Maybe it's because deadlines are rapid before everyone goes home for the holidays.

I met Jeff, the graphic designer living on the Lower East Side, at the Detroit pizza place in Chelsea. I ordered an IPA and delivered a monologue about the best Neapolitan restaurants in New York. We agreed on Paulie Gee's, but there was no spark beyond that. He told me about his obsession with Nintendo Switch, and something about a comic book he was writing. He asked me on a second date, but I haven't responded.

Ben shows up at my apartment on New Year's Eve with roses. I kiss him, inhaling his cologne, as he wheels his suitcase to my room.

"Are you sure you don't feel weird about going on this river cruise tonight? We can still cancel," I ask him, unsure if he said yes just to appease me. I got an invite to a New Year's party on a yacht charter that anchors in the Hudson for the fireworks before midnight. Ben assured me that he would be okay. "I'm just thankful we'll get to spend the night together," he said.

"Mia, I'll be fine. This is a once-in-a-lifetime experience for you. I wouldn't want you to miss it," he says, convincing.

"Okay, just making sure," I say, taking out two champagne glasses as Ben joins me in the kitchen. "Now that you're finally here, it's time for a toast," I say, swaying the mood more celebratory, even though I still feel awkward about drinking in front of Ben. We "cheers" with kombucha and Veuve Clicquot, a gift from the press event with Eva. I'd been waiting for a special person to share it with. Even if Ben can't drink, tonight feels appropriate.

"I'm so happy to be here," he says. I can tell he means it. He combs his hand through his hair, gripping the back of his ear. "I've been in my head a lot lately. You know? A lot more than usual. And I just keep thinking about the trial."

He's staring at my dusty bar cart. I regret the "Smile, There's Vodka" frame hanging above it. "You ask me why I'm up so late watching TV. I can't sleep. I can't turn off these thoughts. And then when I finally do, I don't want to wake up. I don't want to be awake. Because I feel like after everything I did, I shouldn't be here."

I reach for his shaky hand. "Ben, it was an accident. You didn't mean for this to happen." I know deep down this could have been prevented. I know if Ben hadn't been drinking and high, things would be different, but my mind keeps flashing back to instances in college and high school when friends drove when they shouldn't have, and in much worse circumstances.

"I know." He's getting choked up, fidgeting with the Barcelona shot glass.

"Well, I'm just happy to be here. But I feel like I shouldn't be allowed this happiness. I feel guilty for being here, even though there's nowhere else I feel like I can be calm."

I selfishly feel delighted that my presence calms Ben. I wonder if he knows he does the same for me. For my restless mind. I admire his ability to be completely vulnerable with me. He's not sugar-coating any of his emotions, unlike my own impulse to lighten the mood or change the subject when things get serious.

I know he's dealing with a lot, but he gives me something to look forward to every day, even if this is a dead end for both of us. I lean in to kiss him. He presses his lips on mine, grazing the back of my head with his hand.

"We have a lot to look forward to tonight!" I pull away, trying to lighten the mood.

He takes another sip of his drink, seemingly snapping out of his sadness. He unzips his garment bag draped over the couch to show me his navy suit. I know he'll look perfect in it. He puts on The Killers, and I get nostalgic for high school and college—a carefree feeling. I can sense Ben settling in again. Like he feels safe here.

I sing along to "When You Were Young," as we get ready, curling my hair in the bathroom.

We both know every word to this song. Ben sings the refrain. He actually has a pretty good voice.

The music relaxes us, and Ben has a way of undressing my invisible layers. I feel comfortable showing him more of me, physically and emotionally. He's seen me without makeup plenty of times now. While we're apart, I ask him to FaceTime until we both fall asleep on the phone together.

Ben downs an energy drink while I steam his suit. I put on a lacy black slip dress and try to keep my hand steady as I trace a cat eye with eyeliner.

Ben pauses to get a closer look at me. "Wow," he says. "You look stunning. You're so beautiful."

"Thank you," I say, smiling and reaching for my champagne glass. Ben makes me blush. Being the center of attention is uncomfortable for me. I wonder if he can tell. "You look great too. Handsome," I say, telling him he wears a suit well. It's perfectly tailored in all the right spots. He has a tie with fireworks, which sounds tacky, but it actually works with his look.

We zip down the West Side Highway toward Chelsea Piers in an Uber. Wind blows through my hair by the water, and Ben holds on to my arm. "Wait," he says, letting go to fix my hair. "Let's take a picture." He pulls me in toward him. I love being so close to him. I can feel his smile on mine.

"Wait, one more." Ben's eyes look like he's really smiling in the photo. He wants to send it to his mom. "I want to remember tonight," he says.

People wait in fur and puffer jackets on the dock, swaying as we descend to the boat around 9 p.m. It must seat fewer than twenty people at tables lined around the enclosed windows. A four-person orchestra plays in the background. It's an intimate setting. We make our way to Bill, the publicist's, table. I didn't realize we'd be in such close quarters and dread having to be "on" all night. I pull Ben aside. "Hey, I feel like we shouldn't bring up the accident," I say.

"Of course not. Mia." His eyes lower. "I'm not even supposed to talk about it. You really think that's what I would lead with? Here?" He sounds angry.

"No, I know, I know. I'm just making sure." I feel stupid for even saying it, but I know how unfiltered Ben can be. I just worry he might say something uncomfortable in front of my colleagues. A waiter greets us with a tray of champagne. Just as he's about to hand Ben a glass, I interject. "Oh, no, that's okay. Just one, for me. He doesn't drink."

"Do you make mocktails?" Ben asks. Thankfully, he doesn't seem annoyed that I spoke for him. The waiter says he can order at the bar. I'm dreading the thought of someone asking him why he doesn't drink. I wonder what he'll say. I hope he doesn't say he's in AA. I'm praying for surface-level conversation, but I know how honest Ben can be. I feel like I have to be on guard tonight. My reputation means everything to me, and I don't want Ben to say the wrong thing. I can feel my body tense up.

Ben reaches for a top hat decorated with "Happy New Year" in glitter and hands me a matching crown. The fur coat crew has morphed into a sea of mingling silver, gold, and black sequined blazers and dresses as the boat gently rocks. A few of the older men are dressed in suits and ties, and Bill walks over to greet them. Ben and I are the first at the table, and I savor our moment alone.

"This feels like an Old Hollywood party, like *The Great Gatsby* or something, doesn't it?" Ben says, looking around the boat. He seems less outspoken than usual, but not out of place. "I've never spent New Year's like this. It's usually those overpriced, all-inclusive drink packages at some club with a million people crowded around a dance floor."

"Yeah, that sounds about right," I say, watching Ben as he looks for a server.

"I'm going to get you a real drink," he says, glancing at my almost empty champagne glass.

It feels nice to have Ben by my side, even if I do feel nervous that he might say the wrong thing. By the time he comes back, our table is half full. There's a journalist, Veronica, who is twice my age and reports for a local New York TV station. She has a camera hanging from her neck, and silver hair. She's with a man I assume is her husband. He's got jet-black hair graying at the roots and a goatee.

Ben and I introduce ourselves, and I prod Veronica about how she pivoted into broadcast. I'd always wanted to do TV, but my path naturally veered into print. Ben and her partner are laughing about something; they seem to be doing fine on their own. I'm relieved that I don't have to handhold Ben. He's so charismatic and friendly; I start to relax about his situation. That's not what tonight is about. Bill makes his way toward Veronica and me. He's one of those old-school New York PR guys, the sweetest and ever-hanging on to youth. His teeth are whiter than mine, perfectly straight, and too big for his mouth. His lips are bursting with filler.

"Hey ladies," he says. "So glad you two met. Mia is a writer and does a lot of event coverage."

"Yes, I know she was telling me," Veronica says approvingly.

"Mia, who is this new arm candy? He's so handsome," Bill says. I can feel myself blushing.

"Isn't he?" I gush. Ben makes eye contact and walks over. "We were just talking about you." I reach for his arm.

"Oh yeah, I could tell. I could see you staring at me from across the room. I didn't realize I was already the life of the party," Ben says with a wink. There's that confidence again. I'm impressed at how easily he can turn it on.

Bill looks him up and down, Veronica too. Her partner, Pat, is taking a cell phone video of the boat, oblivious that she's checking out Ben. Our host for the evening, clad in a black tuxedo and black sequin tie, has a mustache like the Monopoly man. He clinks his glass. We all sit down as the chatter winds down. Ben brushes my knee under the table, a flirty reminder that he's here—with me. The band starts playing a jazzy rendition of "Gimme! Gimme! Gimme! (A Man After Midnight)," as the dance floor pulses with single women.

"So, how did you two meet?" Bill asks.

I haven't rehearsed our story. I hope my version lines up with Ben's. Mine certainly won't include the one-night stand part. "We met in the Hamptons," I lead. "I was there with my sister, a birthday trip, and he was visiting a friend."

My eyes find Ben's.

"Yes, you and your sister were all over us," he chimes in at the perfect moment. "My friend's family is in real estate, and he was throwing a party for his new magazine at Hotel Sole."

Bill looks intrigued. He smiles and leans in.

"Mia and her sister couldn't stay away," Ben quips. I give a flirty eye roll.

"No, you and your friend begged us to go out with you," I say. "Of course, out of the million guys in New York, I meet someone from Boston!"

"I'm not surprised. It's impossible to meet people in New York these days, right? With all those apps? Twinge? Hinder?" Veronica's attempt at being relatable. Her partner is still videoing the dance floor like a dad making a home movie.

"Yeah, it's terrible, so this worked out." I smile at Ben, who confidently starts talking about working at the lottery app, leaving out the part that he's on leave from work. I reach for a dinner roll, still anxious that the accident could come up.

The band is getting audibly louder. "Do you want to dance?" Ben asks, the perfect segue out of this conversation.

"Um, yes! Why not?" I say, inching my way out of the booth.

"Great exit," I say, resting my hands on his shoulders. "We would have been stuck there all night, chatting."

"Hah, what do you mean? Those guys are awesome," Ben says, poising to spin me around.

"What were you and her husband—is that her husband? I couldn't tell. What were you guys talking about the whole time?"

"Oh, he started telling me about how he used to do shrooms," Ben says in a hushed voice, laughing. "He offered me some of his mushroom chocolate under the table."

"What? You didn't take it?" I wasn't surprised that Ben got some stranger to open up within twenty minutes of meeting him. It's just his personality.

"Some ice breaker, huh?"

"You did not have that chocolate, did you?" I ask again, my tone stern now.

"I couldn't resist." Ben raises both hands like it wasn't his fault. "He was insistent. It was just a small square. I saved you a piece so you can loosen up," he says, patting his pants pocket.

My eyes widen. How could he be so stupid. Taking an edible on this boat while the investigation is still ongoing. "Stop. You are kidding me right now."

His silence gives way to a full-body laugh. Thank god. Another one of Ben's pranks. "You should have seen your face," he says.

"Oh my god. I literally thought you did mushrooms with that random old guy. You're so annoying. What were you guys really talking about?"

I have an underlying need to control the narrative tonight.

"Come on. Tell me," I say.

"We were just hanging at the bar, and I ordered another mocktail. I told Pat not to judge me for being sober. I told him I couldn't hang, trying to be funny, but then he says, 'Make it two!' Apparently, he's sober also."

"What? Huh, that's interesting. So, what about the shrooms?"

Ben's stupid prank was so convincing that now I'm confused about what did or didn't happen.

"No, Mia, there was no chocolate. Come on. He was telling me about his crazy college days. He worked as a photographer before he got into IT and just did all of these psychedelics for inspiration. I don't know, he really opened up. Anyway, he nonchalantly mentioned he was in the program."

"And you told him you were too?"

"I mean, yeah. Why not? He brought it up."

"You didn't say anything about the accident, did you?"

"Yeah," Ben says, his face looking more serious. "I told him."

My stomach starts to turn.

"What?" I ask, recovering from the whiplash of his last prank.

"Mia, relax. I told him I don't drink for health reasons."

I feel a sigh of relief. I don't want people knowing my date is an alcoholic, and the accident is no one's business. I feel guilty for having these thoughts, for being ashamed of Ben's situation. I'm already trying to hide parts of Ben to protect myself, but I can't let people in. Leah thinks I've already moved on. I've barely updated Lauren. I take a sip of my champagne.

"Relax," Ben says.

The skyline illuminates the sail, and I pause to take in the incredible scene. We're on a private boat in the middle of the Hudson, in this amazing city. How exciting it feels to finally have someone to share it with. Someone I could love. The realization is at once romantic and devastating. I feel a sadness creep in, a reminder of how lonely I am. Ben is a great distraction.

I want to freeze this moment while he's still holding my hand. So I don't have to be alone. Ben is taking it in too. He's quiet, sipping on his mocktail and looking out at the glowing city. We sail past the Freedom Tower as we approach the Statue of Liberty. It's 11:30, and we have the perfect spot for the fireworks.

Ben wants a photo of me by the Statue of Liberty. It's windy, and he tucks my hair behind my ear. I hold up my half-full champagne glass, smiling and hoping my red lipstick isn't smeared.

He leans in to kiss me. I sense he's getting emotional. "Are you okay?" I ask.

"Yeah, I'm fine. I'm just really happy to be here with you," he says. His eyes look glossy.

"I'm happy you came. I really am," I say, breaking my PDA rule to give him another kiss.

The fireworks start, and we both stare at the sky like marveling kids. The reflection of the fireworks over the Hudson River. The light from the city skyline. We're part of it all, just two onlookers watching the spectacle.

Ben starts to cry. "What's wrong? Ben?"

"I just…" He's choked up. I realize the last time he was on a boat was the accident. "It's just hard to allow myself to feel happy. I feel so grateful to be here. To be here right now with you, in this amazing moment. But it's just…I don't deserve this. I shouldn't be happy after everything I've done. I shouldn't be here. I feel so bad for feeling anything right now," he says, echoing his feelings from earlier.

"Ben, you made a mistake. But it doesn't mean you're a bad person," I say, trying to comfort him.

"It's just every time I feel happy, I think about the woman. Her family. How I ruined moments like these for them. They will never have this. They will never…" He's now sobbing. "It's all my fault. I did this. I did this to them. I will never forgive myself, Mia. I can't. I can't."

It's the first time I see Ben get this emotional about the accident, and my heart sinks. Breaks for him. For them. For these strangers I've never felt so heartbroken for. I don't know what to say. How do you tell someone it's going to be okay when you know so deeply that it's only going to get worse? That this will never heal. That he can't fix it. That I can't fix it.

"Ben. You are not the man that made that choice that night. You are not a killer. You are not. You are not. You are not," I say, in tears. Ben can see how distressed his pain makes me. He looks up at me; my mascara must be running. He looks into my eyes, and I've never felt more seen.

He hugs me for a long time. The explosion of fireworks sounds in the distance. We regain our composure as the lights beam on the boat. On our faces. The crowd is chanting, "Ten, nine, eight, seven…" But Ben isn't here. He's with them. And I feel selfish for even wanting to kiss him. I look away, but he wipes the tears from my eyes and kisses me.

"…Five, four, three, two…" His lips on mine. Fire over the river. The chaotic sound of the fireworks. The relentless finale popping, crackling in the sky. The cheers, the horns blowing. The sirens sounding off the West Side Highway. Ben's body leaning into mine. His lips. His wet face. His hand on the small of my back. Our bodies, just two bodies under a mosaic of fire.

"I don't want to lose you too," he says.

"One."

I wake up early for work the next day and tell Ben he can sleep in until his bus. I'm hit with another wave of sadness. Why am I doing this? Why am I voluntarily putting myself through all of this pain? As I lean in to kiss him, he stops me and thanks me again. We hug for a long time. I can't help but cry. I'm embarrassed, but I can't stop. "Do you think I'm crazy?" I ask him.

"No, I don't think you're crazy," he says, pulling back my hair to wipe my tears.

I can tell he's thinking something that he's not saying. He's quiet for a while.

"What?" I ask self-consciously.

"You just…"

"What?" I repeat.

"How do I phrase this," he says, gathering his thoughts. "You just want to be loved."

Bliss

CHAPTER 7

I WATCH CLUMPS OF MY lifeless hair fall to the floor.

"You've got to cut it off," Lauren says, holding a handful in her hands. "At least three inches. The longer you wait, the worse it gets." She's looking down at me in her salon chair. I haven't gotten a cut since before the spring. She's finally opened her own place, and I'm one of her first customers. She did it, just like she said she would.

"But I like it long. I want to leave it. Just trim the dead ends. I want fun and sexy, long layers," I say, trying to convince her that my thin hair can withstand a voluminous curtain bang. I watch more fall to the floor.

"I can't believe you're seeing him again this weekend. What's the update? Is he going to jail or what?" Lauren has no problem cutting right to the chase.

"I'm not sure, honestly. He has to hear back from his lawyer about a trial date, but that could take months. He's basically free to just live his life until further notice."

I realize how ominous that sounds. I'm happy I can at least talk openly to Lauren. I can tell she doesn't fully support it, but at least she's accepted the idea of us being together, for now.

"As long as you're okay with all this. I mean, you seem happy. You look happy," she says, meticulously measuring pieces of my hair against each other, trimming the uneven ends.

"You know, it's weird. I really am. I don't mind the long distance. I'm busy with work. We've seen each other a few times. It's something to look forward to. I know realistically this can't go anywhere, but for now, it's good," I say.

I'm meeting Ben at a casino in Connecticut this weekend for a food festival, our halfway point. Lauren tells me to have a good time, and I can tell she means it.

I stare at my reflection in the mirror. My hair is shorter and darker than I anticipated, but I wanted something beyond my simple trim. I run my fingers through my silky hair, feeling as bold as I look.

I was hesitant about bringing a sober Ben to the casino, but he assures me that nothing will tempt him, of his unwavering commitment to sobriety. We'll see how this goes. We're going to a food festival. There'll be plenty to do.

I get off the Amtrak and into a cab, but I wait to text Ben. I want to touch up my makeup before I see him. I get the hotel room key and sneak up to our room. But Ben is already there, waiting with his shirt off.

"I told you to call me when you were ten minutes away," he says, pulling me in for a kiss. "Is this your sexy new hair cut? I love it. You look amazing." His body instantly warms me.

"I wanted to surprise you," I say. "But it looks like you beat me to it."

"No, I wanted to surprise you! And you ruined it," he says, biting my lower lip.

He walks me into the bathroom of our suite. The tub is bubbling, and there's a tray of chocolate-covered strawberries and champagne in front of a bath. He'd strategically arranged it all himself—I can tell.

"Aw, Ben. This is so sweet. You did this all?" He nods, smiles. "You did surprise me! I love it. You're so cute."

Moments later, Ben helps me undress. I can tell we're going to be late for dinner. "We have that comedy show. Don't forget," I say. He hushes me to be quiet.

Ben strips off his boxers. He loves being naked, and I can't blame him. He's got a great body. He motions for me to come to the window.

"People will see!" I say, shyly. He glances back at me, fully naked. "Close the curtains!"

"Make me. Come on. No one can see us. We're all the way up."

I take a long sip of champagne. There's something about Ben that makes it so easy for me to just give in. He presses me against the glass, pulling my hair back as he gently kisses down my neck, easing my tense body. By the time he makes it down to my legs, I stop caring about someone seeing us. He picks me up, and we fall onto the bed, my legs clenched around his waist.

"We may miss the dinner," he says, thrusting deeper. "Should I keep going?"

"Don't stop."

The casino banquet room smells like smoked meat. Hundreds of chefs from the Northeast have gathered for the food festival. I spot a woman around forty dressed in a "Stressed Is Desserts Spelled Backwards" T-shirt. Retweet. There's a giant poster of food celebrities, like *Chopped* star Alex Guarnaschelli, Wolfgang Puck, and José Andrés. A group of middle-aged women clamors to take a selfie with Bobby Flay. I spy the strawberry-haired, blue-eyed chef signing cookbooks while three sous chefs plate lobster over squid ink fettuccine fra diavolo. I interviewed Bobby at a charity food festival in Sagaponack years ago. Since, he's recognized me and always remembers my name, once complimenting my "passionate" interview style.

"I want to introduce you to Bobby," I tell Ben, reaching for his arm. "Come on. Let's say hi."

"You know him? My mom has all of his cookbooks. She watches him on that Food Network show."

"I know, so does my dad. I'm gonna call my dad and see if Bobby will say hi to him. He'd be so happy," I say, not ashamed about the annoying ask.

We inch closer to the fan-girling moms. Bobby waves me over. Ben plays it cool, following behind.

"Hey, Mia. I didn't know you were going to be up this weekend," he says, dropping a half-signed cookbook to make eye contact.

"Yeah, you know I couldn't miss a food festival with you headlining," I say.

"Is this the squid ink fettuccine from Amalfi?" I'm sure it is.

"Yes, you remember it from the opening?" he says.

"Of course, it was the best item on the menu," I say. He's smiling at me and Ben, who I forgot is standing beside me. "Oh, sorry, this is Ben," I introduce them, feeling awkward for not using a title, but I'm not sure what to call him in this moment.

"Nice to meet you, Bobby. Big fan," Ben praises. He plays it cool, but I can tell he's feeling shy. I chime back in.

"So, I don't think I told you this last time we spoke, but my dad is a chef and a big fan. Would you say hi if I called him right now?"

"You know I hate doing this, right?" he says, still smiling like he'll make the exception.

I call my dad and put him on speaker. Ben is cracking up, getting a kick out of the whole exchange. "Hey pal, I'm going to be your next challenger on *Beat Bobby Flay*! My food is out of this world. I got the best meatballs in town," my dad quips, his confident charisma coming out as he talks about food to one of his TV idols.

"We'll see about that, buddy," Bobby says, as I mouth, "thank you so much."

He smiles and winks, then instructs his sous chefs to hand us each a plate of the squid ink pasta dripping in fra diavolo sauce, just as the crowd of middle-aged women swoops back in. We savor the heaping portions, still reeling from the encounter.

Ben swipes through candid photos he took of Bobby and me. "I'm sending these to my mom. She won't believe it."

"It's not me. It's my business card," I downplay.

The chef's tables are lined up side by side; it's barely noon, and there are already streams of people holding up plates for baby back ribs and Bloody Marys. I lose Ben in the sea of eaters, then spot him on his way to the meat carving station. I'm tempted by the craft cocktail section. A mixologist is shaking up mini espresso martinis, and I grab a glass. I find Ben, who is dissecting a plate of ribs and a burger topped with brisket and bacon, oozing with egg yolk. He has a bottomless stomach.

"How is it?" I ask. "Lots of red meat going on here, I see." I point to his bleeding plate.

"Incredible. These guys have a barbecue shop in Back Bay I never even knew about." He's holding their business card, his fingers glazed in barbecue.

Watching Ben get excited about food makes me happy. I always have fun at these events on my own, but I realize how nice it is to share with someone.

"What did you get?" Ben asks.

"Espresso martini."

"Looks good," he says, eying the foam on top. "Let me try the espresso." He takes my straw like a dropper and siphons a tiny bit out.

"Hey! I don't think that's a good idea."

"It wasn't even a sip. I just wanted to taste," he says, brushing it off.

I'm distracted when I hear my name. It's AJ, a chef I interviewed at his Jamaican restaurant in Midtown.

"What's up, Mia! I didn't know you would be at the festival. Let me make you a plate," he says, motioning for us to follow. At his stand, chicken is charring on a makeshift grill lathered in Jamaican jerk spice, a perfect medley of tangy onion and garlic with brown sugar and warm allspice. He playfully refuses to tell me what else is in the secret Jamaican jerk recipe. I wave at his sous-chef plating pickled red onions over basmati rice.

"Great article, by the way," he tells me. "We had a line out the door after that story dropped. I'm not even kidding. It means a lot." I can't help my shy smile.

I'm so happy to hear the story is bringing customers to Chef AJ's small business. I think about waitressing at my dad's restaurant through college, and even still today. I wish he could find better help. "Oh, this is Ben," I say, overthinking what to call him again.

"He's in from Boston." I bring Ben into the conversation.

"Hey, nice to meet you," Ben says, reaching for a handshake.

"You too, man. You're in good hands with Mia. She obviously has great taste."

I can feel myself starting to blush despite my confident demeanor. Ben isn't used to seeing this side of me at work—so in my element and sure of myself.

"She does, doesn't she," Ben says, putting his arm around me.

More customers flock to AJ's stand, so we say bye and move on through the next food maze until I can't physically stomach another bite. Ben somehow gets his hands on a skewer of quail eggs. I politely decline. I'm enamored by a ramen burger from a Brooklyn chef. "I think I just found the next big hybrid viral food," I text Leah, already thinking about the headline.

"We should spotlight this new ramen burger I just tried, and the chef behind it. He's so cool. He started making these out of his tiny apartment in Bushwick." She gives the picture I sent her a thumbs-up emoji.

"Who are you there with?" she asks, likely wondering why I didn't invite her. We go to practically every food event together.

"It's my friend Eva's birthday," I lie. "I surprised her with an extra ticket. You know you obviously would have been my first choice, but she is obsessed with Bobby Flay."

"That's sweet," she texts back. "There will be more! Smorgasburg starts in a few weeks. Have fun and take pics. Maybe we can run that photo you took of the Ramen burger."

I feel bad for lying, but the less she knows about Ben, the better. I spy him weaving in and out of dessert tables. He comes back with an assortment of cookies and brownies, and I wonder how the hell he's not two hundred pounds. I'll have to work out for the next month to burn this off. But he looks so happy.

A cocktail waitress on the casino floor comes around asking what we'd like to order to drink. I still feel guilty about ordering cocktails around Ben. "Maybe you can get a nonalcoholic beer," I suggest.

"Hmm, yeah, I could probably do that. Do you have any?" he asks the waitress, who says they serve O'Doul's. I'm drinking a martini and definitely have a nice buzz going when Ben suggests we play blackjack. "I don't know how," I say.

"That's okay. I'll teach you," he says, eyeing two open seats at a table.

It smells like old man cologne and cigarettes near the slot machines. If there weren't a food festival, this place would so not be my vibe. Ben vows just to play for a few minutes. He shouldn't be gambling his money away right now, especially with all the legal fees. I order another drink. "The goal is not to go over twenty-one," he tells me. That's all I really get, because numbers go over my head, and I'm not really paying attention.

He puts down fifty dollars, and I stand behind to watch. I lose track of what's going on when I see the ramen burger chef. Now is my chance to lock in an exclusive interview if I want to feature this epic new Frankenfood before someone else discovers it. It's obviously made for social media, and I can help take this story viral.

"Hey, chef! I'm Mia. I cover food, and I loved your ramen burger. I'm hoping we can set up a time for an interview. Would love to hear more about you and how you came up with this," I say, digging through my purse for a card. The chef is so excited to meet me, and I email him on the spot, asking him not to speak to any other reporters. I want to be the first to write about it. He agrees, and I'm thrilled at the thought of breaking an exclusive food story. Leah will be proud. I walk back to the blackjack table to find Ben. He's cupping his head in his hands.

"Where did you go?" he asks, looking up at me. "I was looking for you."

"Hey, I'm sorry. I didn't want to interrupt. I was just—I saw that ramen burger chef. I just had to get his contact info for work. What happened? Did you win?" As soon as the question comes out, I regret asking.

"No, I lost. I lost big time. I should have known when to stop. I shouldn't have even played," he says, his tone laced with remorse.

"How much did you lose?"

"Five hundred bucks," Ben says, shaking his head. "I guess it could have been worse. It's my fault. I told myself I wasn't going to."

"Honey, don't beat yourself up. It's a casino. That's what people do," I say, trying to lift his spirits, but I'm still tipsy and not quite comprehending the gravity of Ben's loss. He doesn't respond, and we go back to our room. The next morning, I try to comfort Ben. I know he's beating himself up for letting his impulses get the best of him.

My editors eat up the idea of the ramen burger. They want to make it the cover of our next Eats section, my first big food spread.

"Mia, this is a great get," Leah praises. I'm beaming and can't wait to tell Ben about how we discovered it. But when I call, he just says, "that's great," in an aloof monotone—not the celebratory cheerleader I was hoping for. He tells me about the AA meeting he went to back in Boston. I still don't think he has a problem, but I try to support him.

"How was it?" I ask.

"It was fine. I feel like I needed it," he says. He sounds a little tired.

"Oh yeah? Why? I thought you were fine?" Apparently, he told his sponsor about the taste of my cocktail and about ordering the nonalcoholic beer, which apparently did more harm than good. His grim tone makes it feel like it's my fault. I feel guilty again for putting him in that situation, but I hadn't realized how taxing it was for him. But I realize he's the one who said yes to the drinks.

"I mean, they said my first big mistake was tasting your drink, and getting the O'Doul's," he says. I wonder if he had more when I wasn't watching.

"But why the O'Doul's? There's no alcohol in it. Why is it bad?" I don't really get it. He's being so hard on himself.

"Because it mimics drinking, and makes me feel like I need it. I knew it was a bad idea, too."

"I'm sorry, sweetie. It's my fault. I didn't mean to make you feel pressured."

I can't help but feel guilty for exposing Ben to that kind of environment. But so much of my work revolves around this type of scene. It's how I got my cover story. He says that he understands but that next time he should probably avoid those kinds of trips, at least for now. I just wanted someone to share the experience with. I wanted us to have fun, but I understand. He's right.

My mom picks me up from the White Plains train station in the Chrysler Sebring I learned to drive in when I was sixteen. She worked overtime to pay for private lessons when I failed my road test, encouraging me to retake it until I passed. When I did, I remember the freedom I felt driving on my own.

I stare at the American flag air freshener and a wooden rosary wrapped around the mirror. The prayer card from my grandpa's funeral is resting in the cup holder filled with coins.

"Hi, Mia. How was your trip?" she asks with her full smile. Her dyed jet-black hair smells like my sister's salon. She's wearing a knit sweater I got in high school. I envelop her in a hug, noticing the back seat is filled with my newspaper stories.

"It was good! So fun. So many chefs, so much food," I say, knowing I need to tell her about Ben. I'm relieved to see her. Just being in her presence makes me feel like everything will be okay. We head to the diner. I figure we can spend some time together before I head back to the city. It's still early afternoon on a Sunday.

"Do you have an ad in the paper today?" she asks, innocently calling my stories ads. I know what she means.

"Yes, I have an article in the paper today—it's my first food cover story!" I say, feeling free to share my excitement. "Did you buy today's paper?"

"Of course, I did. I want to see it. Where are my glasses?" She fumbles through the glove compartment.

"They're on your head," I say, giggling.

"Oh," she says with a smile.

I flip through the paper inside. We both order coffees at the diner, mirroring each other's mannerisms. She reads over my story, taking a picture with her cracked iPhone, which has a photo of my sister and me from high school on her home screen.

"Mia, who is Ben?" she asks. I tense up immediately. She already knows his name. "Lauren told me you met someone. Who is he?" she asks again, looking up from the paper.

I reach for my coffee. "You would love him, actually. He's a nice Jewish boy. But he lives in Boston. Still, it's really not too far. He's really sweet. We'll see where it goes. I want you to meet him at some point." My mom doesn't pressure me to settle down. She raised us to be independent and to take care of ourselves. Her standards for us are high, but she's never really seen me get serious with a guy, so I can tell she's at least hopeful, more for my happiness than anything.

"Yeah, I want to meet him! When will you see him next?" She cuts me a piece of her waffle.

"I'm not sure. I think maybe in a few weeks. He invited me up to Boston for President's Day weekend. It's only a few hours away."

My mom has never been to Boston. I try to explain what it's like, and she gets excited seeing how happy I am about Ben. "So, what's new with you?" I ask, changing the subject before the accident comes up. I told Lauren not to say anything. My mom has spent her whole life worrying about us. Taking care of us. The last thing she needs to hear about is Ben's wreck.

"What's new with me? Oh, nothing really. I'm taking care of grandma. You know, she's doing okay. It's hard. And I'm looking for another job, but no one will hire me," she says.

It breaks my heart that my mom should be retiring but can't afford to, despite having worked her whole life. She lost her job at the school. She's driven buses. She's delivered mail. She's worked in a bank. Her last job was making food at the community college in our town, but the men in the kitchen talked down to her. It was no place for a woman to work, especially at her age. She quit and started working part-time in another kitchen, making minimum wage. I can tell she's feeling defeated, but hearing me talk about my work makes her smile.

I'm sitting in the front row at a Michael Kors fashion show. I wish I could tell him how much his fashion meant to college Mia. The gold statement watch. Feeling brave enough to wear his zebra print handbags. And now being here, at his iconic ready-to-wear show. No one appreciates this more than Eva, so when I got an extra ticket in the front row, I immediately sent her an invite.

"We've certainly come a long way from our matching oversized men's watches, haven't we?" she jokes, clutching her red Chanel bag.

"Honestly, give me back the confidence I had pairing that watch with a statement necklace," I joke, remembering a few of my fashion flubs. I did feel great wearing them.

I'm happy to see there are models with curves strutting the runway. I marvel at a woman wearing a gorgeous black overcoat studded with black roses. She's toting a perfectly chic, black leather bag. It's so New York. And it takes me back to when I proudly carried around my MK bag to lunch in high school like I was the queen of the cafeteria. I spent all the tip money I made at my dad's restaurant to buy it at Macy's. There was a confidence

I found in his monogram. I'm mesmerized by a red gown with a plunging neckline. It looks like the couture version of the dancing girl emoji. I picture myself wearing it to a gala.

"What's going on with Ben?" Eva asks. I tell her about our casino weekend and how he surprised me with champagne. How he was the perfect date. I leave out the part about me sort of blowing up his sobriety. I still feel bad about it. I change the subject back to fashion.

"I need to start wearing more color. All I wear is black because it's basic and cheap and still looks presentable," I announce. I'd love to pull off something bold, like fuchsia, and feel as confident as the Mia who once wore that statement watch.

"One day, I will buy myself one of these dresses, just because I can," I vow to Eva. She fully supports this decision, having just put a $400 Journelle silk nightgown on her Amex.

Later that night, I walk along Fifth Avenue, passing the Plaza Hotel, then turning onto Park. I gawk at the homes, the estates, imagining what kind of money I'd need to have to own one. Life is different for these people. I relish this long walk alone. No one is on the streets. I see a chef smoking a cigarette outside. For some reason, the realness of this moment and my complicated gratitude for my working-class roots make me cry. I think about how hard my parents worked so I can be here. How they'll never be able to retire comfortably. I identify more with this stressed-out chef than any of the women living in a bubble in the front row. But I made it there. I built this life for myself. Then my thoughts turn to Ben, and the pain of losing him grips my chest.

Crumbs litter my keyboard as I stress eat a bacon, egg, and cheese croissant, trying to get a story in about a viral, thirty-dollar single chicken nugget that comes topped with caviar at an upscale Korean fried chicken restaurant downtown. I'm calling it the most elevated adult Happy Meal in New York. I tease the story with a photo of the nugget paired next to a glass of champagne with the caption, "How fabulous is that?"

I wish I could say the same about my love life. Eva and Lauren are the only ones who know about Ben's accident and my continued relationship with him. Leah thinks I've long cut ties with him because I've rattled on about the surface-level dates I've had since.

There was the hookup with Jade's former co-worker, who works at a competitive law firm. Our texts fizzled out because he had too many work trips. A tennis player I met on the Roosevelt Island tram when I missed the transfer to the Q train. He suggested drinks at a bar near the Queensboro Bridge after I clung to him in panic, swearing I felt the tram sway midair for longer than usual. Then there was the cop from Jersey City, a mistake I made one night after an Amy Schumer comedy show in Newark when Eva and I kept doing tequila shots. The morning after, I chased the Plan B pill with an iced coffee on the way to the Path train.

I make my way through packed tables decked in checkered tablecloths, when I see Jade and Carrie sitting down with two cocktails. I'm nervous about having to disclose more about Ben's situation. We planned a night to cheer up Jade, who just got out of a four-year relationship with a guy she'd been dating since we were in college.

"Therapy is saving my life," Jade says, tucking a piece of her strawberry-blonde hair behind her ear.

Carrie nods, gripping the stem of her martini glass with her ballet slipper–pink manicure, her blue eyes glowing from behind her oversized, clear-framed glasses.

"I promise, being single isn't so bad," I lie, holding my martini up to meet hers.

"I've been single! We're all in it together now," Carrie says in solidarity. She's worked as an analyst for a global bank, and I'm constantly impressed by how calm she stays under the pressures of having to dissect data from international markets and translate it to global business stakeholders.

We're all two martinis deep, and I'm feeling my emotions heighten.

"And now I finally have you both as wing-women again. Seriously, this is a blessing in disguise. You are so much better off," I lie again. I couldn't be more fucking lonely without my dead-end relationship with Ben.

"You're so much smarter and so much more successful than he is. I'm telling you, it'll be fine," Carrie assures her. I wish I could convince myself of the same thing. The vodka and our optimism get Jade smiling again. Mission accomplished.

"I know, I just couldn't take it. And that shit he pulled the night before the bar exam? How selfish is he?"

"He was threatened by you," I tell her. "You made all the money and did everything for him."

Our burgers are bleeding rare. I adore the no-frills, cash-only nature of this place, even if the waiters act like they're doing you a favor.

"Wait, Mia, who have you been dating? What ever happened with that guy, Ben? You haven't mentioned him in a while," Carrie chimes in, mid-bite.

"Wait, I didn't tell you?" I say, bathing a cottage fry in blue cheese sauce to buy time, hoping they can't tell I strategically left out the bombshell in my personal life. Does that mean they're bad friends for not asking sooner, or am I just a good liar?

"Oh, you're not going to believe this. It's a lot to unpack. Buckle up," I preface.

Jade leans in, chewing in anticipation. "Mia, tell us!" she says.

"So, everything was going great," I say, chomping on a cottage fry. "We texted almost every day after we met. And he had plans to come down to see his brother in December, and then, like literally a month after we met, he was out on his mom's boat one night and got into an accident," I swallow. "And a woman died."

"Oh my god," Carrie says, her eyes widening as she fixes her glasses.

Jade's face sobers. "What? Was he drinking?" she asks like a good lawyer.

The vodka on my tongue burns. I swallow and take another sip. "Yeah. He was," I say, feeling a knee-jerk response to defend Ben. "It's so sad. He was in shock. I was in shock. It could have happened to anyone."

Carrie looks shocked. "She really died?" she asks in disbelief.

"Yes," I say.

"That's so scary. We had a kid in our high school class that happened to. He was driving drunk and killed another senior in our town. He was all over the news. I think he's still in jail for it," Carrie says, abandoning half of her burger when the waiter comes to collect our plates.

"Where is Ben now? Is he okay?" Jade asks, steering the conversation back to Ben. "Wait, is he going to jail?"

"I'm not sure. I mean, I think so. It's all really complicated. I just feel terrible."

"I mean, yeah, you're right. That's insane. Mia, I'm so, so sorry. I know you guys really hit it off. This sucks."

I'm uneasy thinking about Carrie and Jade gossiping over Ben's accident to our broader friend group, but how could I not give an update? I try to make light of the situation. I leave out that we're still talking nonstop. The food festival. His visits to the city. "I know. We had so much chemistry."

"Are you still talking to him?" Carrie asks. I'd rather lie to avoid judgment. I wish I felt more comfortable being open, but the less they know the easier this will be.

"I mean, it's tough because they're doing an investigation. I told him how sorry I am, but that I need to take a step back. There's really no way this will work if he's going to prison." I wish it were that simple. It's only been an hour since we last texted.

"I just really, really liked him. He was the first guy I felt like I had a genuine connection with." I take another sip of my drink.

"Excuse me, can we get another round?" Jade asks the grumpy waiter. I'm relieved that she can sense we all need another.

I try to make it clear again that it was an accident, that Ben isn't some reckless, insensitive person. "But I mean, he wasn't wasted. It really could have happened to anyone. That's why it's so scary. And so sad."

"I understand. Trust me I do," Jade says. "Mia, this is awful. I'm really sorry. You don't deserve this. We'll meet new guys this summer."

"Yes, cheers to that," I say, faking positivity, relieved by their support.

My third martini arrives cloudy, the olive juice barely cutting the acidity. Then I get a text from Ben.

"I can't wait for you to leave the big city and come spend time with me in this little town."

Ben stayed with his mom a week or two after the accident for comfort but retreated back to his place. His mom's been helping him pay rent since he stopped working. I've only seen glimpses of Ben's apartment on screen. Mostly the gray and white patterned curtains in his bedroom, the backdrop for most of our FaceTime calls. The back of a brown couch he sits on playing video games while I write. We sit in silence, taking comfort in the quiet of each other's company. There's a partition of doors in his room that leads to the enclosed front porch to his makeshift office. I've seen glimpses of his roommates when he pans the camera as he microwaves frozen meals in their shared kitchen.

I'm excited and nervous to see Ben's world in real life. Us, in his element. I head up to Marblehead for the first time for President's Day weekend. I don't tell anyone I'm going to visit Ben, besides Lauren. Leah thinks I'm hooking up with a friend of Eva's boyfriend, but I tell her it's still early, and I don't see it getting serious.

When I get to Ben's, I'm starving and a little moody from sitting on a bus for five hours. Ben is much better at not complaining than I am. Terry is at his feet and much bigger in person. Ben's holding a bouquet of sunflowers and leans in to kiss me. I wonder where he'd managed to find them in the dead of winter without a car. It doesn't matter; I'm already in a better mood. "I can't believe I'm in your house," I say as he hugs me.

"You are. And I can't wait to give you the grand tour," he says. He is smiling so big. He hugs me again and holds me for an extended moment.

Ben lives in an actual house, with three bedrooms and two other roommates, Eddie, who I haven't met on FaceTime yet, and Victor, a Brazilian who works at a discount jewelry store and sometimes shares his home cooking with Ben. Ben showed me his seafood paella a few weeks ago on FaceTime.

Ben hangs my jacket in the communal closet. The kitchen is open and outdated, with dark brown wooden cabinets and plastic flooring. Red curtains hang above the wooden dining room table. Everything is clean, but the fixtures are so old it makes it feel worn. But there's something endearing about the lack of frills.

He carries my bag into his room. Terry follows behind, and I already feel a sense of familiarity with the space. Ben has very eclectic taste. His room is a postcard of all the places he's traveled to for work and relics from his childhood visiting his grandparents in Santa Fe. Most men I'd been with in the city had places void of any personality—the same basic Ikea bed, dresser, and nightstand. Everything in Ben's room is either a souvenir from his travels or pieces from his grandparents' art collection.

There's a turquoise ladder from his grandmother's old house resting near his window. A pair of green wooden cacti on a dresser. A picture frame in the shape of a dog bone with a photo of Ben and Terry with the Blue Ridge Mountains in the background next to his bed, along with a row of self-help and history books.

"Well, I can assure you there are no Roca brothers in this town. And nothing nearby is exactly Michelin-star status, but I did make us reservations at the best Italian spot in town," he says. "You do like Italian, don't you?" There's that sarcasm again.

"That sounds perfect," I say. He holds my hand as we climb down his icy stairs. It snowed last night, and the sidewalk is covered in black ice.

Walking feels like an Olympic sport. Being outside in Ben's town feels surreal. It's dark, and it seems like we're the only ones awake.

"I can't believe I finally made it to this one-horse town," I joke. Ben feels so much pride in his beach town. It's his sliver of calm, especially now with the trial looming.

We get to a place called La Vita. It's homey in a suburban way. I order the safest thing on the menu, chicken parm, and Ben keeps asking if I'm sure I want something so basic. Yes, I'm sure. I need comfort food. He orders a veal pasta dish. I raise my wine glass to his can of root beer.

Ben recites our agenda for the weekend. He has a Duck Tour planned in Boston, a dinner, and a show. I'm so excited to see the city again. It's been years, and I don't mind doing the touristy things. He pays the check, and when we get back to his place, I'm so tired I fall asleep in his arms.

He grabs me by the waist under the covers and pulls me in closer to him the next morning. "Do you remember what you asked me last night?" Ben says, yawning.

"What, no what did I say?"

"You asked me if I was okay."

"Did I? I don't remember, why?"

"I don't know. It was really weird. I was thinking about the accident, and you just woke up and said that. I couldn't go back to sleep," he says.

"Really? I don't even remember. That's so weird. Maybe I just sensed it?"

We lay in bed for a little longer, and then Ben pops up to make me coffee. It's sunny out, and the snow has melted. He remembers my love of diners, and we walk to the Shoreline Diner, a tiny luncheonette across from the beach, five minutes from his apartment. It's been around since the '80s, maybe longer, judging by the brown plush chairs.

It's buzzing with energy. I love the simplicity of the place and immediately go into people-watching mode. It's the journalist in me. I want a sense of who lives in this town. There's a table of teens eating thick-cut French toast in sweatpants; an older couple eating pancakes. They must have money. I can tell because the woman is wearing a designer jacket that I recognize. Then there's Ben and me.

Ben waves at a mother-daughter duo on their way out. The daughter has long brown hair and looks around my age, wearing a workout outfit. She gives Ben a distant smile and a wave.

"Who is that?" I whisper.

"That was awkward," he says, taking a sip of his coffee. "Her mom knows my mom, and tried to set us up on a date after I broke up with my ex. We went out a few times, but I wasn't feeling it. Haven't seen her until now. I sort of ghosted her. Anyway, nothing to worry about there."

I hate the idea of Ben with anyone else. A waitress brings over heavy ceramic mugs, and we order eggs.

We sit in comfortable silence. I'm still trying to get a read on the ambiance, but I feel a sense of calm, a refreshing change from the urgency of my life, with its deadlines and New York energy.

Ben recognizes that I'm deep in thought, thinking about the woman we just saw, and mimics the stare I must be giving. When I reach for my coffee, he grabs his, and we begin playing a childlike game where he copies my gestures. I purposely blink, and he blinks. I scratch my head, and he does too. I stick out my tongue and roll my eyes, and it's like we're two five-year-olds playing Simon Says. The waitress catches him with his tongue out when she brings our food. He snaps out of boyish mode.

"I can see the love you have for me in your eyes," he says, catching me off guard.

"What do you mean?" I ask, taking a sip of my coffee.

"I just know," he says.

⸙

Ben lives near Salem. I've never been, but I've seen all the movies about it. He says it's like a college party town during Halloween, but I'm excited to see it during downtime. The streets are desolate when we get off the train.

"I was never big on Halloween," I say.

"If you grow up here, that's the time locals avoid," Ben says, looking into The 1692 Salem Witch Museum window. It's closed, so we decide to browse a vintage shop instead.

The jewelry counter catches my eye. There's an assortment of brooches and old pins. Everything looks like junk until my eye meets a silver ring with three bands intertwined and a row of diamonds across the middle. I find Ben, wide-eyed.

"I think it's a David Yurman ring, and they're only selling it for twenty-five dollars," I whisper. "They probably don't even know what it is."

"You want it?" Ben asks. "I thought you hate buying used things."

"No, no, it's fine. I don't need it," I say. "I just think it's funny that they have such a nice piece of jewelry in this place." But before I can finish my sentence, Ben presents me with a brown paper bag with the ring inside. "Stop it. Why did you do that?" I say, so flattered that he actually bought it.

"Put it on," he says, slipping it on my ring finger. It fits perfectly. "It was meant for you," Ben says, smiling. "Maybe you're a thrifter after all."

I never thought about my wedding, or even getting engaged. It feels weird to have a ring like this on. I think about what Ben would be like as a husband. The thought shouldn't be crossing my mind. It hasn't until now. I remind myself that a future with Ben will never be a reality. But it's hard not to picture it in this moment.

We thank the sweet manager on our way out, strolling past a shop called Wicked Good Books. Ben jokes with the guy behind the register that we just got engaged. A woman comes out from behind one of the bookshelves to congratulate me, and I can feel myself blushing.

"Yes, he did, today. Isn't it sweet?" I say, holding up the ring and my gray manicured nails, laughing at our inside joke. When I examine the bottom more closely, I see that a part of it is rusted, and I feel like an idiot for thinking it was real.

"Wow!" The woman said, putting on her glasses to glance at my ring finger. "He's a lucky guy," I joke.

We take the train into Boston to meet our Duck Tour group. We get a spoonful of Boston Tea Party history at the Charles River, and midway through the tour, we stop at a famous spot for Boston cream pie, and Ben insists we try it. He has a sweet tooth. He feeds me a bite.

Ben asked three of his friends at the lottery app for a great recommendation for dinner nearby, and we wander through the Boston Theater District to a restaurant called Aria. Ben swears it's not a tourist trap. It's "seasonal Mediterranean," and the dining room has a modern yet inviting ambiance. We sit in a dimly lit table for two. I love how much effort Ben put into this whole day, and how he still relies on me to interpret the menu, trusting my choices. We decide on an escarole salad with burrata and a handmade pappardelle pasta that comes with a runny egg yolk in the middle. It's delicious. Midway through dinner, Ben gives me a sly smile and says, "I thought you told me you loved me last night. It was so cute."

I didn't. Even if that's how I feel, I wouldn't be the first to say it, but the conviction in his voice is making me second-guess myself. I know there's an expiration date on us. I can't get attached. Telling him I love him would make it that much harder. But so much of me wants him to know. I want him to tell me he does too. I feel brave enough to at least let him know the thought has crossed my mind. How could it not? We've been talking nonstop every day for the past six months.

"Maybe I was thinking it," I say. He stares at me for a long time, his eyes getting watery. I can tell he wants to say it.

"I love you," he says, taking my hand in his. Though I know the feeling is mutual, it's still a shock hearing him say it out loud. Adrenaline rushes through me like it did that first night we met. That first night he kissed me. The night we spent in that glass house, holding each other close. Before everything changed. Before I realized he would never be mine. Every odd is against us. These thoughts tread through my mind, like Ben's feet in the water that first night. I smile so hard, I'm almost crying. Because every time I think of how happy Ben makes me feel, I'm flooded with sadness because I know what his future is. We both do.

"I love you too, Ben," I say, reaching for his hand. The candle flickers as we hold onto each other.

"I love you," he says again.

On the way out of the restaurant, I reach for a pack of matches. I want something to remember tonight. Something tangible I can keep forever, like my magnet collection, to remember Ben when he's gone.

CHAPTER 8

BEN WANTS TO SEE HIS grandmother on his father's side before the trial. He says it may be his last chance. He invites me to come with him to her home in Asheville, North Carolina. I didn't really want to impose on Ben's grandmother, plus, I didn't really want to spend money on a plane ticket. I told Ben that he should spend some quality time with Grandma M, but he surprised me with a plane ticket. I felt like I couldn't say no.

Ben's grandmother moved to Asheville after her husband, Caleb, died. They met in Boca and lived there most of their lives but vacationed in the Blue Ridge mountains in the summer months, where they bought property and turned a mobile home park into summer vacation rentals. Ben's father and brother worked on the property growing up. They taught vacationing families kayaking and canoeing on Lake Lure overlooking the Blue Ridge Mountains.

Maude, or as Ben calls her, Grandma M, painted landscapes of the lush mountaintops and sheer granite cliffs. She'd sit on the porch for hours while Caleb smoked his pipe, rocking back and forth in the old wooden swing. Life was easy there, until he died.

Grief made Grandma M lean on her vices more, a wineglass stain etched on her nightstand. Ben remembers sneaking into her bed after a bad dream when he was a kid. She'd sip slowly, while watching old reruns of *Family Feud* until she drifted off. An old teddy bear Caleb gave her now replaced his indented spot in their king-sized bed.

I forgot how much brighter the sun shines in the South. No buildings to block the beaming rays. We sit on rocking chairs outside the Charlotte airport when Ben's uncle pulls up in his "don't fuck with me" Chevy Silverado pickup. He's balding and has a bit of a tummy. I climb into the back seat, dreading the small talk.

Ben hasn't seen his uncle since college, when he worked at his grandfather's property mowing lawns and doing maintenance for the cabins. I roll down the back window and feel the cool breeze. There isn't an ounce of humidity, and I relish the fresh air. Uncle Michael isn't much of a talker. We exchange a brief pleasantry, then Ben commands the conversation. I'm relieved that I can just sit and absorb.

Michael is a lawyer by trade, but he used his knowledge solely for the family business of selling and renting summer homes. He complains that Ben's dad, Daniel, still hasn't gotten his real estate license and hints at some dispute they're having over selling parts of the property.

"Have you spoken to my dad?" Ben asks.

"He was down here last month closing a deal with two of our new renters," Michael says, somewhat monotone.

"Business has been slow, but we just had three new cabins built and they can't sit empty. Your grandma has been hounding us to sell them. It hasn't been easy."

Ben's dad hasn't answered Ben's calls in weeks. We pull up to the dirt road entrance of Meadowlark Ranch, acres of log cabins and private homes overlooking Lake Lure.

You can't hear a sound for miles inside those log cabins, Ben tells me. There's no electricity in most of them. We walk up to one of the more luxurious cabins that Michael converted into a model unit and office. Inside, there's a stone fireplace next to a giant wooden statue of a black bear and Grandma M's turquoise pottery, like in Ben's room.

"Do you still keep your guns here?" Ben asks. I look at him, puzzled.

“Guns? What guns?” I ask, remembering for a moment that we weren’t in New York or Boston. We are in prime hunting country. But the idea makes me nervous. I don’t think I’ve ever seen a gun in real life. So, when Uncle Michael pulls one out of his desk, I feel uneasy. He and Ben are just nonchalantly handling this death weapon.

“Can we go outside and shoot?” Ben asks.

“In a little, sure. I’ll load it up,” Michael says.

I give Ben a “what the hell are you doing?” look. He can see I’m visibly alarmed. I’ve never held a gun before or stood close enough to hear a shot fired. I follow Ben outside. He looks like a natural. He’s done this before—all those summers coming down South and hunting with his grandfather, the two of them camouflaged in the woods, chewing tobacco as they waited for the right shot. It’s all so unfamiliar to me. Like this whole side of Ben has been a blind spot. He puts on a pair of shooting earmuffs. There’s no target. He just points the gun toward a tree in the woods. I stand behind him, inching my way back farther and farther until he fires a shot that sends my heart pounding out of my chest. He takes a shot at another tree. I can see in his face: this is clearly just fun for him. But I want him to stop. I don’t like the sound, and I don’t like guns.

“Okay, I think that’s enough,” I say finally, wondering how we’ve been here for only five minutes, and already we’re shooting guns in the woods. But that’s Ben. He needs a constant thrill—an adrenaline rush to calm his mind. It makes me anxious because I hate recklessness. Ben tells me I need to get more outside of my comfort zone. And while I admire his fearlessness, I’m sometimes afraid of where this quality takes him. His disregard for speed limits. The DUI in Miami. The boat crash. The upcoming trial. He never intended to kill anyone, but I worry his thrill-seeking was really the trigger all along. I suddenly feel so far from home. There’s an unsettling in my stomach that makes me feel unsafe for the first time with Ben.

He puts the gun down and walks toward me. “How’d I do?” he asks, like he just parallel parked in a tricky New York City spot rather than casually fire an assault weapon. “I can’t even see where the bullets went.”

He brings the gun back inside to Uncle Michael, who's finishing up with a client. It gives us just enough time to tour the ranch. A fog starts to roll in, the air still cool as we walk around back to where one of the luxury mobile homes is parked with a For Sale sign. "Let's go in. I'll give you the tour," Ben says. I can see the glimmer in his eye. He's looking for another rush. He takes my hand, and we walk up the stairs. The door is open.

"Should we go back?" I say, not really in the mood to explore. Sometimes Ben's constant chase leaves me exhausted. I feel more like his babysitter than his girlfriend.

"Mia, I want to show you my family's property. Don't you want to see how hard my uncle worked to build these? This could be the last time I get to see this place for, like, years."

The guilt trip triggers me. I don't want to disappoint Ben, so I try to act engaged. He's right. Who knows when he'll be back here? So, we start to walk toward some small campers parked in a clearing in the trees. "You can buy these?" I ask, as we climb a small staircase into the vacant mobile home.

"Yeah, they're like $20,000. People also rent them for the summer. They're actually really nice. Like a mini home. The kitchen is redone and everything. Look, these are marble countertops," he says, smoothing his hand over the countertop. He locks the door and closes the curtains.

"Let's do it in here," he says, like an excited teenager. "Like right in there. Quickly, before my uncle comes back."

I can't be more turned off in this moment. First the guns, now this? I'm still nervous about being here, let alone getting naked on this property.

"Your uncle is literally right outside," I say. "He could come in at any second."

"Come on, Mia, we are so fine," Ben says. "You know you want to. It'll be ten seconds. How fun would it be to say we did this here? No one will come in—I promise." His persistence is starting to drain me. I don't have the energy to entertain his mind's amusement park. My shoulders are raised and tense as he starts kissing me. He pulls me into him. I can smell his cologne and try to go along with it, following Ben's lead. Do I even want this, or am I just trying to appease Ben? He kisses me harder and harder.

"Let's not. Ben, come on. I don't want to embarrass myself here. It's not a good idea," I say, walking toward the door. Ben beats me to it and puts his hand in front of the door, blocking the exit.

"Mia. I promise no one will even know. We could have already been done by now," he says, with a slight attitude in his tone. He starts a chorus of "you're no fun" chants, like a child.

"Ben, shut up!" I say, fearful that I'm losing the "cool girl" persona he's attracted to. I straddle him on the chair and start kissing him. He grabs my hips and picks me up, my legs around his waist. My mind is a rush of nerves, hoping we don't get caught. He throws me onto the bed and reaches for a condom in his wallet. I didn't realize he even had one. I close the blinds in the bedroom to make sure no one can see. He thrusts his body into mine, and I pretend to enjoy it to appease Ben, but I'm too worried about getting caught, the ultimate turn-on for Ben. When he finishes, we're both breathless. I'm happy he came quickly.

"That was amazing," Ben says, pulling up his pants. "See. I told you we wouldn't get caught."

Seeing Grandma M's condo for the first time is like walking into a southwestern art exhibit. It's a cluttered tribute to Santa Fe, every inch of the living room. A blown glass sculpture by Dale Chihuly in the shape of a green flower sits inside a clear box on her coffee table. There's a giant outlaw statue with a white cowboy hat and holster hanging over the living room sofa. That's Ben's favorite. A turquoise pottery set lines the TV console like an art walk down Canyon Road, with a sky-blue landscape of New Mexico with a white ram's head next to it. A small table near the window is fully covered in a three-hundred-piece puzzle that's about a third of the way done. Grandma M clearly has time to kill.

The woman is petite, maybe about four foot nine, and is wearing a sparkly gold strand that looks like a party streamer in her hair. She's stoic, with a hint of Ben's sarcasm. Her skin is tan like Ben's, powdered with blush. She's stylish, hip even, wearing a black fringe suede jacket reminiscent of Georgia O'Keeffe. The place smells like carpet and potpourri.

"How was the flight?" she asks from the table littered in puzzle pieces. She doesn't get up.

"It was super quick," I say, taking off my shoes.

Ben takes my bag into the guest room, and I follow, feeling like an awkward intruder. We're staying in a Victorian-looking room with a floral bedspread and dusty-pink ruffled pillowcases. There's an odd, almost frightening porcelain doll collection that lines the armoire, and more staring at us from a wooden rocking chair near the bed. We go back to the kitchen, where Grandma M is cutting pieces of smoked salmon and wrapping them in Saran Wrap to freeze.

"Maude, this is just a thought," I say, handing her the box of hamantaschen cookies we carried through TSA from Breads Bakery. I wasn't sure if she celebrated Purim, but I figured she'd at least appreciate the gesture, maybe be impressed that I even knew what it was.

"Oh, I haven't had these in forever. You can't get good ones in North Carolina, and I don't bake. This is sweet, thank you," she says, not really smiling. I can't read her. Grandma M isn't outwardly warm like you'd expect a grandmother to be. She's cold, not in a rude way, more like a cat you have to warm up to. But it catches me off guard. I grew up with a warm Italian grandma asking what I wanted to eat every five minutes.

"Grandma, where is Josh?" Ben asks. That's his cousin, who lives with Grandma M.

"He's at work. His friend usually drives him home around 6."

Ben's cousin Josh is three years older than Ben, who described him to me jokingly as a "wolf." I thought he was kidding until I saw a photo of him covered in facial hair with sideburns like Wolverine from *X-Men*. But his half smile looks warm and approachable. Josh is gay. The only person in Ben's family, as far as he knew, who is out. He's been talking to a man he met online. Their plan is to move to Austin next year once he can save up enough money. But "next year" keeps getting postponed, Ben says.

When Josh comes home, he and I exchange a few pleasantries, and then silence fills the living room. Ben breaks the ice by insisting that we go out for barbecue. We pile into Uncle Michael's car; Grandma M, Ben, and I are in the back. She looks out the window and chats about how she and a friend went to a Broadway show that was on tour, "Fun Home." It had made its way down South a few years ago after hitting it big in New York.

I probably haven't said more than six sentences at this point. Ben is in the middle. He grabs my hand, trying to be cute, but I shyly pull away. I'm still turned off by his behavior earlier. Grandma M insists Luella's is the best barbecue spot in town, but Uncle Michael begs to differ. Michael, I'm observing, is reactive to even the slightest criticism.

Once the meal starts, Grandma M begins probing me. She asks in-depth questions about my family's money, which I find a bit bizarre considering I'm a guest, but makes no inquiries about my life—where I grew up, my career as a journalist in New York, what my parents do, or if I have any siblings. But honestly, I'm thrilled not to have to talk too much, though slightly uncomfortable by my own silence. I'd rather just be a fly on the wall and watch this family dynamic, observe where Ben comes from.

"Do you really have the money to go to Disney World right now with Cara and her friend?" Grandma M questions Michael gingerly, breaking apart a piece of cornbread. "You have her college deposit coming up. How will you afford it? Maybe you should talk to your brother. He always knows better about managing money, like your father. Just don't come running to me—you all have tapped me out."

I can see Michael's fists tense.

"That's it." He slams his hands on the table loud enough to make me jolt. I didn't see it coming. He gets up and storms into the parking lot.

"Grandma, not cool," Ben says, following his uncle outside. I freeze, not knowing how to react. I've never seen Ben embarrassed like this, and he's been so good at regulating his emotions lately. Maybe he's just been bottling them up.

"You need a drink," is the politest thing Grandma M says to me in the six whole hours we've been together. I gladly comply, asking for a glass of Chardonnay, and we sit in uncomfortable silence.

Josh gives me an eye roll in solidarity, throwing up his hands as if to say this happens all the time and he's unfazed. Grandma M goes back to eating her cornbread.

"He's such a baby, you know?" she says finally. She pauses to take another bite. "He kind of reminds me of Ben as a young boy." I'm taken by her directness. "Is it okay if we drink in front of him?" she asks, referring to Ben's situation. It's the first time I've heard someone else bring up his sobriety, and I don't know how to navigate it. We're all dancing around the uncertainty of his sentence.

"Oh, yeah. Yeah, of course. He's totally fine with it," I say, reassuring her. "He doesn't drink, but he won't care if we do."

It was all the validation she needed to order another glass of merlot. "How has he been?" Grandma M looks up from her plate, finally getting down to business. The meat of this visit. His goodbye, for now. She wants information about the accident. It's the first real question she's asked me.

"Good. He's, uh, been doing really well, you know, under the circumstances," I say, a little surprised she would bring this up after the blowup with her son.

"Do we know anything about the court case?" she asks. "What will happen?"

"We don't know anything yet. I mean, he was released on bail. He'll have to go back to court in a few months," I say, hearing the uncertainty in my voice.

The truth is, I'm in the dark. We both know prison time is on the table. We just don't know how long, or when he'll be sent. Either way, Ben seems ready to face the consequences. I'm still not sure if I am.

"Has he reached out to the family?" Grandma M continues.

"No, he hasn't. His lawyer advised him not to," I say, unsure if I should tell her that or if he wants me to. He wishes he could.

She takes another sip from her wineglass, and I notice her French-manicured nails. "He seems a lot better than before," she says.

"Before?" I ask, thinking out loud.

"The accident. He was impossible before the accident—the drinking, the fast driving. No one could tell him what to do or how to do it," she says, folding her lipstick-stained napkin neatly in half. "He was always a little out of line." Grandma M goes in for another sip. "He lived with me for a few months when I was still in Boca."

I feel a little uneasy. I didn't think Ben was an actual alcoholic. I thought he was going to those AA meetings out of guilt and legal advice. I didn't realize how things were before, but I guess I didn't know him. Maybe I still don't. I think back to the weekend in the Hamptons. Ben boasting about his pranks. Getting kicked out of school. Hearing this from Grandma M makes me think that Ben may have always had a problem. With limits. With knowing when enough is enough.

"That's why his father stopped seeing him. When he got that last DUI, he said he was cutting him off. He didn't know how to help him anymore; he had his own demons to deal with. Then two years later—this accident."

I already knew what she was talking about. I read about the DUI he got in Florida. He was driving too fast again. Drinking too much. It caught up with him. Thank God no one was hurt that time.

"How do you think Ben's dad is taking all this?" I ask, regretting the question as soon as I ask. Maybe I'm overstepping—though Grandma M seems to be a straight shooter.

"He doesn't talk about it," she says. "He won't bring it up."

I'd never met Ben's father, and I wasn't sure I wanted to. Ben calls him a coward and an alcoholic. Right then, Ben comes back inside with a sheepish Uncle Michael, bowing his head like he's ashamed of his tantrum.

"I apologize for that outburst," he says, still looking down at the table.

Grandma M clears her throat.

"Your food is getting cold."

CHAPTER 9

I'M GLAD TO BE BACK at work, writing about a three-Michelin-star restaurant popping up in East Hampton, where their usual $300 tasting menu is condensed into affordably priced à la carte items, some just thirty dollars. The fresh-caught oysters in grape mignonette and fluke ceviche with radishes are to die for. I also rave about the charred corn and black truffle flatbread and the perfectly buttered lobster roll. I take great care with this review but feel such a sense of relief when I finally submit it to Leah.

Now I can relax. Ben is at my apartment, getting ready for his brother's engagement party. It wasn't really a shock, he says, since they went ring shopping months ago. Ben seems envious of his brother's seemingly limitless funds, but he is genuinely happy for them. As usual, he's blasting his music—"Safe and Sound," by Capital Cities. I can hear him belting the lyrics in the shower.

He gets louder and louder, echoing the song title in the refrain.

"Ben, we need to leave in ten minutes!" I yell from my room.

I got a blowout earlier in the day. My hair is always pin-straight. Tonight, I wanted a little more volume, especially since I'll be meeting more of Ben's family. I wasn't sure what to wear, so I went with a strapless black dress. Ben throws on a suit and a shiny silver tie. He looks so handsome, and I know he didn't put in any effort.

"You look amazing," Ben says, pulling me in for a kiss.

I tell him he's the most handsome man in New York City.

"Just in New York?"

"There's that ego."

We cut through Central Park on our way to the Soho Grand Hotel. Adam and Tracy are the perfect New York couple, what I aspire to be. They're successful and can throw money at whatever they want without being flashy. Oh, and they're happy, obviously. Or at least they seem content. I gush to Ben over their New York lifestyle as we breeze down the West Side Highway.

"Adam is never home. He works twenty-four seven. He's always stressed," Ben says. "That could be us, but you would never see me. And we have more chemistry than them. We actually feel things." I guess he's right. I haven't seen much affection from either of them, but everyone expresses things differently.

We take an elevator up to the hotel's rooftop. It's a perfect sunny day. The red benches are already filled with people holding champagne glasses. There's a sea of Ben and Tracy's family members. Ben walks over to Adam, and I follow, hoping I don't look like a trainwreck in my four-inch strappy sandals. I never wear heels. Adam looks tense, but Ben hugs him and says congratulations. Adam thanks me for coming.

"I wish I could be here for the wedding," Ben says. I can tell Adam didn't expect that, and he gets choked up.

"Let's not do this now. We don't know what's going to happen yet," he says. Ben's eyes are glossy, but he brushes it off.

"Let's get a drink," he says, rubbing his eyes.

He returns from the bar with my martini spilling over with vodka and sips his ginger mocktail. Tracy emerges in a baby blue dress, perfectly accentuating her thick blonde hair. She seems happy yet composed, her emerald-cut diamond sparkling as she holds it up. Everyone claps, and Adam gives her a kiss. I wonder how many carats the ring is. It's at least three, maybe four. I keep sipping my strong drink. Maybe it was a bad idea to come on an empty stomach. Still, I say "no thank you," to the passed appetizers. Though the pigs in a blanket do look good.

I try to stay under the radar. I don't feel like mingling, but Ben leaves my side and returns with his father and stepmom. Daniel, his father, is bald and much shorter than Ben. He has round glasses like Andrew Zimmern from the Travel Channel. His eyes are smaller than Ben's.

"Mia, we've heard so much about you," he says. I try to shake his hand, but he goes in for a hug instead, and our bodies awkwardly fumble into an embrace. I wonder if he really has.

I can't help but notice the black-haired woman in six-inch heels next to Daniel. Ben's stepmom, Iris. She's so thin and looks like Eva Longoria with her big brown eyes. She's wearing a black silk dress. She has a smoky cat eye, and I wonder how she's the same age as Ben's mother, who looks much older. I'm blinded by her cushion-cut ring, another three-or four-carat production. God, these guys know how to buy their women diamonds.

I'm sipping on my second empty-stomach martini and having an amazing conversation with Iris; though, I'm not exactly sure what it's about, but she seems like a safe person to talk to. I feel like I can be myself around her without judgment for whatever reason. I suggest we take tequila shots—I'm not sure why, but here we are, downing them. I'm mixing vodka and tequila. Not the best idea, but I finally feel comfortable in this very, very awkward setting. No one has brought up Ben's accident, thankfully. I see Ben talking with his dad in a corner—maybe they are. It's all too heavy and serious for me at the moment. I'm trying to stay positive, and Iris is an amazing distraction. Then she starts in on Ben's mother. I try to play neutral, but she's very animated. I just nod and pretend like I'm listening.

"And God only knows what this wedding will bring," she says. She's bitching about her son not getting invited tonight and how he better be invited to the wedding. I keep drinking.

"Do you have a cigarette?" I ask, clearly on a drunken whim. Obviously, Iris has a cigarette. We go through the service kitchen and emerge on a terrace down a set of stairs. We're pseudo-bonding, and I'm relishing the nicotine in my lungs with every single puff. I'll feel bad about this tomorrow, but for now, it feels pretty fucking euphoric. Iris sprays her mini perfume to cover the smoke. I look down at my phone. I have three texts from Ben.

"Where are you?!" he says. "Mia, they're about to serve the cake. Where are you?"

I get a missed call in between the messages. Another missed call.

"Mia, are you okay? Please come back upstairs."

"We should head up," I say to Iris, slurring my words.

We go back upstairs, and I try not to look as drunk as I am. I must smell like vodka and nicotine. I see Ben jetting toward me, as if I'd been kidnapped. Has it really been that long?

"Mia, where the hell were you?" he says, almost reprimanding me.

"Ben, not to worry, not to worry," I say, wondering why I sound British. "I was having a fabulous. A fabulous conversation with Iris, who might just be my new favorite family member of yours!" I speak loudly, hoping Iris will hear.

"Mia, what are you doing? You smell like smoke. I'm getting you a water," Ben says.

"*No!* I'm fine. Ben, I'm perfectly fine. If I were drunk right now, would I be able to do this?" I pull him in and push my tongue down his throat. He abruptly pulls away and holds his lip. I must have bitten it. I think it's bleeding. "I'm so sorry! Come here!" I make him follow me into the women's bathroom. It's a single stall, so I lock the door. I run water over a paper towel and press it on his lip.

"Ben, I'm sorry. Relax, okay? Everything is totally fine."

"You're so drunk," he says. "We need to leave. We need to leave now."

"Stop!" I say, blocking the door. I start taking off my dress, lowering it below my hips and revealing my lacy black bra. I'm waiting for him to seize this moment.

"What are you waiting for? Come on, Ben. No one will see. No one will notice," I say, egging him on the way he did in Asheville. I'm mad that he won't listen to me. He's shaking his head, saying I'm too drunk. He helps me put my dress back on. I try to kiss him again, but he pulls away.

"Why don't you want to fuck me right now?" I ask. That's the last thing I remember.

The next morning, I wake up with an excruciating headache. I forget Ben is sleeping next to me. My heart slows down a bit, feeling a sense of relief knowing he's by my side. I think about last night and realize the end is hazy. I shouldn't have had that last martini. I remember smoking a cigarette with Iris. *Fuck. I hope no one saw that.* I remember telling Adam how happy I am for him and Tracy, and asking Tracy if I could try on her ring.

The last thing I remember is wiping the blood off Ben's lip in the bathroom. I'm mortified. There are three ways to play this—like I don't remember anything, repeat the refrain, "I never do this," over and over again, or own up and apologize.

"You're awake," Ben says, turning toward me. He must hear my deep breathing.

"Yes, barely," I say. I most likely have mascara everywhere. I chipped a nail. What was I thinking?

"Do you want to get breakfast?" I ask. Food is always a safe topic. Ben is always hungry. He sits up.

"Mia, do you remember anything from last night? You were really embarrassing. Like, really, really drunk. My whole family was there," he says.

A sense of dread fills me—this awful, anxious feeling I've had before, but worse because Ben is calling me out.

"I know. I know. I'm so sorry. I don't know how it happened. I must not have eaten enough. One minute, I was totally fine, talking to your dad and Iris—was I really that out of control? I feel like it wasn't that bad."

"You tried to fuck me in the bathroom. At my brother's engagement party."

I open my mouth to respond but hesitate. Wouldn't he like that? What about his insistence on having sex in the trailer with his uncle right outside? I still hope no one saw us go into that bathroom.

"Oh my god. Did anyone see us?" He can hear the remorse in my voice. The shame.

"I don't know. I tried to get us out of there. Everyone was in their own world, but still, it wasn't a great look—especially with everything going on. And it's more than that, Mia. I worry about you losing control. When you get like that you get really, really flirty. With everyone. Someone could have easily taken you home. Obviously not at this party, but in general. When I'm not here. I don't want you drinking like that. It's not safe. Something bad could happen," he says.

I know he's right, but the criticism seems harsh considering this is the exact behavior that got him in trouble in the past. He's the one who got into the accident, not me. He's being hypocritical, and I resent this double standard. Yes, I should know better with everything going on, but his shaming me isn't making it any easier.

"Ben, I'm really sorry. I just got so excited meeting everyone. I had too many drinks. I won't do it again," I say.

CHAPTER 10

I'VE BEEN SLOW TO RESPOND to Ben's texts. I don't like the way he shamed me for getting drunk at the engagement party, and the uncertainty of his trial is another added stress I don't need.

Lauren took a Saturday off to spend time with me. She could sense I was uneasy about Ben. I need a hobby that doesn't involve men, or work, or drinking. We decide to go to a wheel-thrown pottery class at the 92nd Street Y with an instructor named Polly Anne, who talks about pottery like a poem. I watch her hands slowly shape the clay slab into a malleable bowl, her navy clog delicately pressing against the foot wheel.

I cup my hands over the base of the clay, pulling the inside until the edges rise higher and higher. Lauren, of course, is a natural. I watch her gray slab become a vase, while my wheel spins the base of a tiny bowl.

"Mia, you're doing great, sweetie," she says in a Kris Jenner voice. "Don't be afraid to get your hands dirty," Lauren encourages, clay splattered all over her apron, her hair.

"I know, I actually love this," I tell her, feeling a meditative calm over me as I feel the clay spinning through my hands.

"I can tell you're thinking about him," she says, looking up at me, her nails caked in clay.

"I'm really not," I lie.

Polly Anne walks through the room, helping us put our masterpieces on a shelf to dry.

"So, I told you about the neighbor who keeps flirting with me, right?" Lauren says, talking with her clay-stained hands. "He finally came over. Let's just say, he is doing just fine down there." Her hands gestures the length of the pottery wheel.

"Oh my god, Lauren! Love that for you," I tell her.

"He is just beautiful, let me tell you. We had a jolly time. He brought me over sushi, and we had a little evening on my couch. But wait—it gets better. We start hooking up, and all of a sudden, I hear him almost say, 'Amanda' right when he was, you know," she says, surveying the room of mostly seniors. "Getting *very* excited. Then after he finishes, he gets up to go to the bathroom and, you know me, I obviously look at his phone, pants down and all, and see a text from, I kid you not, from someone named 'Amanda Miami Freak.'"

"Stop it!" I say, sipping on the green tea I brought to the class. "Lauren, no you didn't."

"Oh of course I did. He comes back out, and I go, 'Who is 'Amanda Miami Freak'? You are a forty-one-year-old man, why do you have someone stored in your phone as 'Amanda Miami Freak'? Aren't you embarrassed? Why is her name popping up when you're in *my house*?"

"I cannot believe you called him out. Lauren, you're fucking killing me." I'm hysterically laughing, picturing her berating a half-naked grown man in her apartment. I forget we are surrounded by parents and old people as Lauren proceeds to tell the entire class about straddling her neighbor.

"Anyway, we cleared that up. He's taking me out for dinner next week. We'll see where it goes. What is going on with Ben?" she asks. I'm grateful that she asks, even though she doesn't agree with us.

"I've been distant. I told him I needed some space. I've been on Hinge again."

"Good!" she says. "You should be. Don't let him hold you back."

"I know. Exactly," I say, rolling my eyes. "It's a lot."

I wash my hands and see a text from Ben. It's a picture of "I love Mia" carved out in the sand with a heart at the beach by his house. Terry is perched in front.

"I'm sorry I got so mad at you at the engagement party," he says. "I love you. Please don't be mad at me."

Ben and I have been talking on and off again. He kept apologizing and sent sunflowers to my apartment with the photo of us from the Hamptons the weekend we met. It's hard to stay mad at him. He'll be here any minute. James invited us out to Sag Harbor for the weekend to celebrate my birthday with my friends and Ben. He buzzes up, and I'm excited to see him with his suitcase when he gets to the door. He strips off his shirt like always. He claims it's more comfortable. I wonder if that's really the case, or if he just wants to show me his chiseled abs and defined back muscles. I love the way they flex when he grabs something from a shelf I can't reach.

Ben must read my mind because he pulls me close and starts kissing my neck. I'm caught off guard but excited he's in the mood to play. He lifts me onto the tiny countertop and kisses me, my tongue on his tongue. Then he takes off my shirt and his pants. He's holding my hair in his fist and keeps kissing down my neck. I don't want him to stop. He lifts me up, and I'm reeling just looking at the bulge of his biceps. He's so strong. He holds me up with my legs wrapped around him. Then he gently places me down on the counter again. His boxers are off, and I catch a glimpse of his perfectly toned ass, the hottest thing that's ever been in this kitchen. He's not using a condom, but I don't care because he's careful. I'm always a little worried, but I trust Ben. He lifts me up again, and I feel him inside me.

We are both breathless from heating up the kitchen. I get us mismatched glasses of water and set my alarm for 7:45 a.m. I love the feeling of our bodies intertwined.

I've memorized so many things about him in the year since we met. The smell of his skin, the way his hair feels after a haircut, the scar that we both share on our left hands, how he brushes his teeth in the shower to music, how he scans every menu to make sure there are no peanuts. We fall asleep on the Jitney to Sag Harbor, waking up in the salty air. Back at our happy place.

"Life's a beach," I caption a photo of the tide rolling into Noyack on Instagram. Our footprints are etched in the sand. I've architected my idyllic life in cropped, filtered boxes, strategically showing only parts of Ben. His back turned, walking toward the tide. His sunglasses in a selfie. Ben, to the outside world, is a mystery. Because I've made him one.

I don't want people googling him or finding out about the accident. My biggest fear is a forced coming-out party for my ugly reality, for people to learn that my life isn't what I've been letting on. I've been hiding behind this manicured facade for months. I can curate my life on Instagram, but I feel like I'm being held together by duct tape. I'm consumed by my impending loss, like an airbag about to explode in my chest. Sometimes I have to remind myself just to breathe.

My mom still doesn't know about Ben's accident. I keep telling my friends that Ben's investigation is still pending, but I know I have to start letting people in. So, I've taken a first step and invited Jade, Carrie, and Eva to meet us here for my birthday weekend.

"I can get used to this," I say, holding Ben's hand. He's smiling back at me when his phone rings. It's his AA sponsor, Randy, calling to make sure he's staying on track. Ben tells Randy that he has nothing to worry about, and they make plans to catch up over dinner next week. It makes me happy that Ben has such a support system. Randy is also letting Ben work a few days in the office of his insurance company. He understands how important it is for him to keep busy.

"I'm really lucky to have him," Ben says, hanging up the phone. Randy went to prison more than twenty years ago. I'm not sure for what, exactly. I think it might have been for selling drugs, but I don't want to be impolite and ask. He's been sober ever since, and Ben admires how much of a boss Randy is. He's almost sixty and runs a successful business.

"He's talked me off a few ledges. And he says I can work for him when I get out, so at least I have that to fall back on, in case I can't get my job back with the lottery app. That's something I guess, right? I can even study real estate while I'm away."

It's the first time I hear Ben talk about life after prison—and he hasn't even been sentenced. Sometimes I forget how heavy all this is, how much Ben is carrying, despite his ability to be present with me. Sometimes I feel like we're in our own world, but I know the situation is weighing on him. Why he snaps sometimes. And I know I can't hide it much longer from the rest of my world; I can't rewrite his future, but I'm dreading having to explain it. I wish we could keep this a secret forever.

I need some liquid courage before my friends get here. I fill my glass with prosecco. I promised Ben I wouldn't get as drunk as I did at the engagement party. I told my friends there's been no update on Ben's investigation. I want them to know Ben for Ben, not his crime. Still, I know they'll have questions.

Carrie's blonde hair is even more golden in the sun under a backwards Mets hat. She carries a cooler under her arm, her wrist decked in Cartier. "Oh my god. Is this the famous Ben?" she says, embracing him like they've known each other for years.

I give Carrie a tight hug, absorbing her warmth. I shut out all the negatives. This weekend is about fun only. Eva carries a bottle of café Patron for espresso martinis, and Jade waves in the distance, mouthing that she's on a work call.

"Mia has told me so much about you girls," Ben says, taking Eva's beach bag off her hands.

"So excited to finally meet her mystery man. And so chivalrous," says Eva, who quietly knows every detail. She raises her sunglasses to get a full look at Ben. I'm grateful for her being my unpaid therapist for all of these months. We've talked through the situation practically every day since I met him.

"Wait," Carrie says. "You really look like a couple." She's peering at us like we're this exotic Barbie and Ken.

I feel myself blush. "Who wants a drink?" I change the subject. Ben reframed his lecture about my drinking last night. Saying he's just looking out for me. I assured him I wouldn't make him babysit me, but it's my birthday and my friends are here—I'm going to enjoy myself.

"Make mine a double anything," Jade says, still flustered from work. "Oh my god, hi!" she says to Ben, mouthing "he's so cute" to me.

"Great to meet you, Jade. I hear you're a big lawyer in the city. That's awesome. I know who to call if I ever need one." Ben seems to miss the double entendre. I hope Jade does too. I laugh nervously.

"Ladies, I'm at your service for the weekend. I make a mean…anything. Drinks on me—all night," Ben says, holding up a Solo cup.

I fall back into my beach chair. Carrie jokes, "Empty your tip jar!" to Ben, impressing us all with his hospitality. James meets us with provisions for a beach barbecue, asking Ben to help start up the grill. I'm grateful for a moment alone with the girls.

"Wait, Mia, he's so hot," Jade says, putting her hair in a ponytail, already halfway finished with her glass of rosé. "He seems so sweet. What's the update?"

"Update?" I pretend like I don't know what she's talking about. I take a long sip of my spritz.

"With his trial," she whispers. "Like, is he going to prison? Obviously, I won't bring it up, but what's going on?"

"What? Oh, oh, that." I rub my hands together nervously.

"Oh, you know. Everything is okay for now. He has a really, really good lawyer. I mean, he may face charges, but the investigation is still ongoing, so for now, it's just one day at a time. We have to wait and see what happens." I take another sip to buy more time, then try to put a positive spin on it.

"We're just enjoying our time together." But Jade is a lawyer and knows how this process goes. I catch her eye, and I can tell from her look that she knows I'm lying.

"Oh, okay. Well, yeah, I hope everything works out," she says, bringing the conversation back to safety. "I can't imagine how hard it must be for him. Seriously."

I appreciate her concern for Ben. But I'm drowning in the exhaustion of having to put on a brave face. I guess I make it seem like I'm fine, because she never asks how I'm feeling. Part of me wishes she would. Eva says nothing, listening and sipping from a Solo cup of rosé. She knows how hard this has been on me, and she doesn't judge. She doesn't tell me to run from him like Lauren.

"What did I miss?" Carrie comes out, blissfully unaware. I don't feel like recapping Ben's doomed fate.

"I was just getting us more drinks!" I say, pivoting to hostess mode.

Jade is distracted again by a work email. Hopefully, this conversation is officially closed.

James walks toward us with a cooler. He's wearing the mint green bathing suit Ben wore the weekend we met. I'm getting hit with waves of nostalgia. I haven't spoken to James since those text messages. I take another drink. And another one. It's so hard to act like everything is fine.

"Mia, hey, how are you?" James hugs me, and I wonder if he means it, despite everything that's happened, or if it's just a blanket pleasantry.

"Good, good! Everything is good," I say, overly enthusiastic. Another sip of my drink. Everything is so fine.

"Yeah? Good to hear it. How's our buddy over here?" He points to Ben, his voice more serious. I realize we're having "that" conversation.

"Oh, you know. He's okay. He's hanging in here, despite the circumstances. He's not drinking."

"I figured," James says, more serious than I remember him. He seems to genuinely care.

"He'll be so happy to see you. He hasn't seen many of his friends lately," I say, my voice lowered.

"You're amazing for being so strong," James says. I don't know how to take it. I just force a smile.

"Oh, you know, it's just one day at a time," I say, like an AA bumper sticker. I need a stronger drink.

I'm thankful that James is confident enough to introduce himself to my friends. I don't feel like entertaining. I've dodged and mined enough questions from people, and it's only been an hour. Maybe this was a mistake.

"Ben, do you want a drink?" I hear Carrie call out.

"Hey, no, I'm good," Ben says.

Things go over her head sometimes, and I can tell she innocently has no idea that his not drinking is related to the accident.

"Are you sure? I made Jell-O shots," she says, holding one up to his face. "Let's all do a welcome shot!" she chants. Eva's head is down. Jade is even confused that Carrie isn't catching on.

"Ben doesn't—"

I try to steer the conversation, when Ben blurts, "I'm sober now. I don't drink anymore." He's not nervous, just blunt. I feel relieved that he can speak for himself; I just don't want my friends to think he has a problem.

"Oh." Carrie seems confused and caught off guard. I can see Jade mouthing "the accident" when Carrie's eyes widen.

"Oh my god. I'm so sorry. I totally forgot."

"It's cool. Are you kidding? Mia drinks like a fish around me. If anyone would have driven me to drink again, it's her."

I'm relieved he makes light of the situation, even if it's at my expense. "True," I chime in, grabbing a Jell-O shot and feeling exposed. "I can't get him drunk and take advantage of him anymore," I joke.

Ben goes back to manning the grill. I'm happy that he can hold his own, but I'm dreading any follow-up questions from Carrie. "Oh my god, Mia. I'm sorry. I hope I didn't offend him! I totally forgot about the accident," she says, putting her hand on my arm.

"No, it's fine. I should have briefed you guys about the drinking."

"Wait, can he still not drive?" Jade asks.

"No, not until after the investigation. He can't really talk about the accident," I say, trying to end the conversation. "Everything is still so up in the air. I'm just trying to be supportive."

"You are, totally. He is such a nice guy," Carrie says. "He seems so normal. Just like one of us."

"Yeah, I mean, it's really a terrible situation. He seems like a great guy, Mia." Jade sounds genuine, and I appreciate their concern, but I can't open up anymore today. I'm still trying to deal with my own feelings.

"You taking over, buddy?" I overhear Ben say, watching him hand a spatula to James. I'm not confident the kid has ever cooked a thing in his life, but I'm relieved for a meal interlude. Food is always a great distraction.

Jade changes the subject, polling who is pro Ben Affleck and Jennifer Lopez as their divorce unravels. "Such a toxic relationship," she says.

Jade is pop culture obsessed and can rattle off all of the latest headlines and Bravo drama. I'm grateful this conversation temporarily distracts from my own.

Ben comes behind me, massaging my shoulders and kissing me. I politely back away. I don't want this PDA in front of my friends. I'm just not in the mood to be flirty.

"Who wants burgers?" James calls out. I can see a blanket of char caked over the meat. At least we know they're cooked.

Ben takes two burgers and helps himself to a mountain of potato salad. The sun is starting to set on the beach, and our bonfire mingles with the wood chips James tosses into the flames. The tide subsides into a soundtrack of waves as we discuss the looming end of summer and how lucky we are to have reserved this serene spot on the beach.

Eva brings out a cake, and everyone starts singing "Happy Birthday" to me. Ben grabs my waist, pulling me in close, and I'm overwhelmed. This time next year, I'll be alone. I force a smile and blow out the candles, praying my wish will come true. Candles won't fix this. Not for the victim's family. Not for Ben. Not for me.

The candle smoke clouds the darkening sky. Ben and I linger by the fire. Jade and Carrie are singing the lyrics to "Jumper" by Third Eye Blind, reminiscing about when they performed at our college's Spring Fest. Eva is showing me the oval diamond ring she wants. She thinks her boyfriend will propose by the end of the summer. She hopes, at least. Everyone but Ben is buzzed as the night ages.

He tosses his T-shirt off and pressures James to come for a night swim. "Come on man. Let's go. Don't be a baby. One swim—the water is so nice. And all these ladies want to see those abs. Come on. Show us your abs."

Suddenly, Eva, Jade, and Carrie are chanting "show us" in chorus. I'm embarrassed for James. I wonder if this is Ben chasing another high. He's watched us drink ourselves into a summer haze all day. I can tell he needs something to fuel him. The ocean must be freezing. I get chills just thinking about it.

James finally rips off his shirt. It's hard to say no to Ben.

"I'm jumping in," Ben tells me.

"It's freezing, Ben. No, don't," I say, knowing I can't stop him.

"I'll be fine!" Ben says. "I'll be right back."

He sprints into the ocean, James following his lead. I hear them screaming and cursing once they're bodies hit the water. I can make out their shadows for a bit, but they eventually blend in.

"What will you do?" Eva leans in, asking in a soft whisper. We both know what she means. The other girls are far enough away. "When he leaves?"

She offers me a hit from her weed pen. I take a deep, long inhale, trying to fill Ben's absence. It's dark enough to hide my tears. I can't hold back anymore.

"I don't know."

CHAPTER 11

THERE'S NOT A STRONG ENOUGH concealer to hide the bags under my eyes. I dab at them with my ring finger; I still wear the rusted band Ben bought me. He'll be here in half an hour. We're celebrating Lauren's housewarming party. Her business is thriving, and she's saved enough for a down payment on an apartment. It'll be the first time Ben meets my family. I'm nervous, but the spotlight will be on Lauren, so that takes some of the pressure off.

"What is that?" My mom asks when she sees the ring.

"It's an engagement ring," I say, knowing she is naïve enough to believe it.

"What?" Her eyes widen in disbelief, grabbing my hand and seeing the tarnish close up. She rolls her eyes. "What did you do that for?"

I smirk. She's so easy to fool. "Ben got it for me in Boston."

"You're not going to move there, are you?" I can hear the worry in her voice. "Move there? God no. I would never leave New York. If anything, he'd move here." I pause, realizing it's impossible. "One day."

"One day? Why can't he move? What's stopping him?" my mom bridges the topic I've been avoiding.

I know I have to delicately explain to her about Ben's accident. She's someone who sees things as black-and-white, right or wrong. And I don't want her to condemn Ben. I don't want her to think he's a villain. I wish this conversation had come up after she got to know him.

"It's complicated. He got into an accident."

"What?" She looks stunned again. "What kind of an accident?"

"He took his mom's boat out one night. Like, a little over a month after we met. And he crashed...and...and someone died."

There's a long silence. I don't want to give more information than I need to.

"Well, was he drinking? Speeding? How does that just happen?" I can hear the concern in her voice.

"I don't know," I lie, knowing she'll take my word for it. "They're still investigating everything."

"If it's his fault, you know they're going to throw him in jail." Her voice is three octaves higher than normal.

"Mom, I know."

"Mia, why didn't you tell me this?" Her hand cups her forehead. I've given her another thing to worry about. "Now I'm going to be a nervous wreck thinking about this, thinking about you getting involved with someone in this situation. I don't want you to get hurt. You don't need this. You have your whole life ahead of you."

I'm regretting having this conversation just moments before Ben gets here, but I know there will never be a good time.

"Mom, I know. And, you know, right now everything is okay. I'm not looking at the long term. He's a great guy. He really is, and I just feel terrible. This could have happened to anyone."

I can tell she's still in shock. She spends the next ten minutes spitballing her worries. How she doesn't want to see me get hurt. How she doesn't want me involved in his legal issues. I assure her there will be an expiration date, if and when he has to leave. Only, I know it's just a matter of when.

"But he'll be here soon. Please, just be nice to him. I know you'll love him," I say. "And don't ask him about it. He's been through enough."

"I won't say anything," she says. "You know, I'm your mother. I won't let you get hurt."

"Mom, I know. Everything is going to be okay." I feel a subtle weight lifted after telling her. Sort of. Now, at least if Lauren slips, she won't be completely in the dark. Or if Ben happens to bring it up today.

Lauren storms in the front door with her sunglasses on. I feel so relieved. "Hello, what are we doing? Everyone will be at the clubhouse in, like, ten minutes. The food still isn't here."

"I knew we should have gotten it catered," my mom scoffs, crossing her arms. Thankfully, she has another problem to worry about now. My father.

Lauren is the only person in the world I know who would make a registry for her own housewarming. But I do get it. I can't think of a single thing more gratifying for someone her age—our age, really. And she did it all on her own.

"I raised you girls to be independent. See?" Lauren is hugging my mom.

"Yes, you did, Mommy," My sister says in a baby voice.

"Lauren, how long have you known about your sister's situation with Ben?"

My sister gives a fake look of shock. "Me? Not long at all. What did she tell you?"

"That he got into an accident. He crashed into another boat. Why didn't you tell me sooner?"

"Mom, I didn't want you to worry," I say.

Lauren thankfully steers the conversation back to her. "Mom, stop worrying. Anyway, today is about me. And how I've worked so hard to afford this apartment, and how I'm saving up to get you one, too," she says, knowing exactly how to redirect her attention. "So I can take care of my mommy. My next place will have a guest house on my property, okay?"

My mom is smiling again. I know she will be happiest living near us. I just wish she could care for herself the way she does for us. Her makeup is creasing under her eyes. She deserves to retire in peace.

"Lauren, I cannot believe you registered on Pottery Barn for this. You're ballsy," I say, lightening the mood.

We relocate to the clubhouse of her apartment complex. There are tables covered in my aunt's zesty lemon cookies caked with vanilla frosting and sprinkles. She always makes them for our birthdays and graduations.

Ben comes armed with a bottle of Grey Goose for my dad, who is late, and a bouquet of purple tulips for my mom. I smile, remembering he asked me her favorite color yesterday.

"I heard you liked flowers, Stella," he says, handing my mom the bouquet. "I know you probably have a million guys lining up to bring you them, so I hope these don't get lost in the shuffle." He plays up his charisma.

"Oh, and unlike Mia, you and I are the only ones who seem to still love Dunkin' Donuts," he says, handing her a gift card. I told him she goes there every morning, and she beams at the thoughtful gesture.

"My daughter has told me so much about you, Ben," she says, putting the tulips in a vase. "I hope you won't live in Boston forever."

"Mia hopes that too," he quips, smiling at me.

"What can I help with?" Ben says, eager to impress my mom. I like watching him be "on." It's a refreshing break for me.

Ben and my mom fold napkins together, and he tells her stories about working as a waiter. He's making her laugh, and I can tell her smile is genuine.

"You have the most beautiful daughter," I hear Ben say. I can't help but smile.

"Excuse me!" Lauren chimes in, never missing a beat. "You mean daughters."

"Of course, I do! Hey, congratulations. Wow, this is your big apartment?" Ben says, spinning around the clubhouse dining room, pointing at the dated armchairs.

"Yes, I pay for this too," Lauren jokes.

I can tell my mom already loves him. I love how he's interacting with my family. My dad is late with the food. I would be mortified if guests arrived before the food, but Lauren couldn't care less about what anyone thinks. She's just having the party for the gifts, anyway.

Finally, he walks in, carrying a tray of chicken marsala with two dish rags in his chef's jacket, mumbling about the line at Restaurant Depot. His chef's jacket is covered in flour. He says he left the cook alone in the kitchen to be here. He calls the restaurant to remind him to turn the music on the outside patio and to push the lobster bisque.

"Dad, this is Ben," I say. I can tell he's distracted.

He hands me the tray. "Put this in the kitchen," he motions, telling me to set the oven to 350.

I hope he's not going to be rude to Ben.

"Hey, pal," he says, giving Ben a firm handshake. "Hey, help me out with the food in the car." I feel embarrassed that my dad is already putting Ben to work, but Ben follows him out to his truck like a puppy.

I'm walking on eggshells, hoping that Ben and my dad will get along, but they hardly talk for the rest of the party. "Dad, please don't be rude. Can you at least try to engage with Ben?" I ask. I know he's on edge being away from the restaurant on a weekend, but I wish he could just enjoy this moment—and be happy for me.

"Okay, I will," he says, putting his phone in his pocket. He takes a drink of his Grey Goose with club soda. I notice the wrinkles on his forehead tanned from high blood pressure. The bags under his eyes. How I savored his days off, eating Chinese food on a folding table in front of the TV. How proud I was to tell my friends at school that my dad was a chef. I remember the time he brought in a seafood pizza and a six-foot sub, like a hero, to my marine biology class. The pit of sadness I felt when he wasn't around. He always did the best he could.

"So, buddy, what do you do up in, where are you from? Boston? I like it up there. We went there when they were kids." He points to Lauren and me. "We did that Duck Tour," he says, trying to find common ground.

Ben goes on a monologue about the lottery start-up and scrolls through the app on his phone. They bond, briefly, over my dad's love for vintage cars. The conversation is surface-level at best.

When my dad excuses himself, Ben and I have a beat to be alone. "He seems nice," Ben says. I can tell he's intimidated.

"He'll come around," I tell him. "Just don't say anything about the accident. It's not the time." Ben nods and returns to the kitchen to help my mom plate the cake.

When my mom encourages me to ask my dad if he'll drive us back to the city, I figure it's worth asking. I don't feel like taking the train.

"Dad, do you think you can drive Ben and me back to the city?" He stops eating his cake, as if I've said something to offend him. His raised, bushy eyebrows already make me regret asking.

"Drive you back to the city? Are you crazy?" he scoffs, with a mouthful of cake. "I just busted my ass making all these trays of food for the party. You think I'm going to drive you down to the city? Fuck's the matter with you? Ask your mother." He tosses the paper plate on the coffee table.

I can feel my face turning bright red and my blood boiling. I would be mortified if I weren't so angry. I hope Ben can't hear this.

"Dad, it's fine. I was just asking. It's getting late. We just didn't want to take the train all the way back. Mom always picks me up and drops me off. Sorry to inconvenience you," I say, throwing in one sarcastic jab. I really want to explode and tell him to fuck off. The one thing I ask him to do. But I censor myself because Ben is here.

"What's the matter with you?" I can hear my mom calling out from the other side of the room. "You know, you should be ashamed of yourself. You show up late, and you can't take your daughter home?"

Ben comes out of the kitchen like a deer in headlights. He looks afraid, like he doesn't know how to act amid this abrupt family feud.

"Okay, dad, that's enough! Leave her alone," Lauren says, throwing her hands up. "If anything, I should be the one yelling at you for being late."

I can't imagine Ben's initial meeting with my family going any worse.

"Okay, does anyone want caw-fee?" My aunt holds up a glass pot, a signal for everyone to finish and leave.

I regret even having this conversation. I should know better by now. It's exhausting having to walk on land mines with my own family. If my dad had it his way, Lauren and I would work at his restaurant. I think about how he must have driven my mom crazy. All of those manic years she spent running the business. How grateful I was for my job.

"It's not my fault you wanted to live in the city. I ask you to come up and help me with the restaurant, and you can't even do that," he says.

The guilt he hurls is so convincing. I've been up working at his restaurant at least once a month, answering the phones, frantically running plated dishes of chicken francese and penne alla vodka to tables. It's never enough. I'm proud of the living my dad makes, but I wish he could see that my path is different and not make me feel bad for building my own life. If this is how my dad is reacting to Ben without knowing his circumstances, there's no way I'm going to divulge anything more.

Lauren and I stand by what's left of the antipasto platter. The salt from the warm prosciutto pierces my chapped lips. "You can't tell dad about Ben," I tell her. "Promise me you won't."

"Obviously," she says, as if it was already understood.

"Oy," I sigh.

The breeze cools in the darkness of her deck. We're sitting in her patio chairs, just the two of us. Ben is napping in her room. We used to escape like this when our parents fought over not being able to pay the bills. We would carry our pink double sled up the hill across from our one-bedroom apartment. Our getaway. Her tiny hand in mine. The joy of flying downhill.

Lauren leans in. Her cigarette lights mine. I inhale the menthol into my lungs. I need vices like these every once in a while to let off steam. To exhale. My foot shakes restlessly against the coffee table. Why can't I be still in my own skin?

Our smoke hangs over the deck like scars in the sky. Our bare feet on the coffee table. She touches mine, a prompt to be still.

CHAPTER 12

SOMETIMES I FEEL EXHAUSTED BY it all—the travel, keeping Ben a secret, the status of his pending trial. I'm consumed with second thoughts as we arrive at a Victorian-style Marblehead mansion, a sweater draped over my black strapless dress. It's the beginning of fall, and the weather is perfectly crisp for Ben's younger sister's engagement party. There's no shortage of celebrations for this family despite Ben's shitty year.

Ben looks handsome in a light-blue pinstripe button-down. He has the sleeves rolled up, just enough to show his muscular forearms. Luckily, no one notices our late entrance. People are eating balls of mozzarella and cured meat, mingling.

Iris looks like she is yelling at Daniel for something. She's throwing her hands in the air as he backs into a corner of the living room. Adam and Tracy are sipping wine and chatting with Adam's old college friends. Alana, the bride-to-be, comes down the wooden staircase wearing a gold and black dress that puffs out a little, with Ken doll Kevin, her fiancé, standing handsomely behind her.

I sneak away from the small talk to graze near the trays of pasta. I grab a glass of pinot noir and take a big gulp when I notice Grandma M watching from the corner of my eye. She's standing alone.

"Hi Grandma M," I say, finally. She stares at me for a while before responding.

"How's everything going with the case?" she asks. She's the only one in this family who seems to acknowledge Ben's accident. The world keeps turning for everyone else, or they just want to avoid it. I'm again taken aback by how bluntly she brings it up. It's odd that she doesn't seem to know anything. This family doesn't communicate, or maybe they just avoid the real issues. I probably don't know much more than she does, anyway.

"It's going as good as it can under the circumstances," I say, taking another sip. "I mean, he's stayed out of prison for this long. I think the lawyer is working hard to get the best possible deal. It's all still unclear."

"But what are you going to do if he goes away?" she asks. The question I've been dreading. The question that's been consuming me. *What will I do? Will I wait?* I don't know. I have no idea. I'm here now. I want to be here for him.

"I don't know," I say, in what feels like the first honest answer I've given his family. We're both quiet for a while.

"You don't want to face it," Grandma M says, not in a rude way, more introspective. She doesn't have a drink in her hand. "It's too hard."

I take another sip. Drinking makes me so emotional, too emotional for this conversation. I can feel my eyes start to tear up. I'm fighting as hard as I can not to cry.

"How do you do it, knowing that he could be gone for such a long time?" She's not prying. She just wants to know why someone would willingly mourn the living when she knows what it means to really lose someone.

My eyes start to fill with tears.

"Somehow, it hasn't been all hard for me. He makes me happier than anyone I've ever been with. If he's gone, I'll just have to do my own thing for a while. Occupy myself with work," I say honestly, optimistic without intending to be. I'm still trying to rationalize it all.

Our glossy eyes grow heavy. I can see my reflection in Grandma M's glasses.

"Can you get me a glass, please?" Grandma M asks. I nod.

Later at the dinner table, I notice an empty seat next to Grandma M.

"Who's supposed to sit there?" I ask Ben.

"My dead grandfather," he says.

CHAPTER 13

MY EDITOR, LEAH, IS STILL blissfully unaware that I not only didn't take her advice about Ben but plunged myself further into this black hole of uncertainty. I'm in too deep to come clean now. Plus, I just got an exclusive interview with Jean-Georges about a new restaurant in his food hall in the Seaport District that should keep her at bay. It's running on the cover of the Eats section, and as a reward, I get the day after Thanksgiving off, a day I usually always work.

This is the first time I've brought someone home for Thanksgiving. It's usually only me, Lauren, and my mom. This year, we're gathering at Lauren's new place.

Ben carries the turkey inside and helps Mom baste it. They're bonding over their mutual love of Dunkin' Donuts, which Ben quirkily pronounces "Donkey Donuts." His corny humor makes my mom laugh hysterically. Seeing them interact so seamlessly in the kitchen puts me at ease.

"Lauren, you have any more coffee?" Ben asks. He's already on his third cup. He chugs the Nespresso shot like it's water. I can sense Lauren quietly judging, like he has a problem with overdoing it, but I don't draw any more attention to it.

When we sit down, my mom suggests we say a prayer. Ben volunteers, even though he's Jewish and they never do this at his house.

"Thank you for letting me crash your Thanksgiving and for this amazing, amazing food. This is my first Italian Thanksgiving. Who knew that my favorite side dish would be draped all over the turkey?" he says, noting our tradition of dressing the bird in cured meat.

Lauren holds up a meme on her phone of a burnt turkey with the caption: "This is what you get when you marry Megan," and another image of a perfectly golden bird captioned: "And when you marry Maria."

It makes us all laugh. Especially Ben.

My mom is driving south on the highway, her face as distraught as mine, when we drop off Ben at the Westchester airport. He waves at us with both hands, walking backwards and blowing me a kiss. I can tell she feels how much Ben's situation is weighing on me. She asks me when I'll know more about his sentencing. I can tell she loves him, because she sees how much I do.

"I don't know," I say. "He's waiting to hear back from his lawyer."

"It's terrible what happened. I read about his accident online. I know he was drinking," she tells me. I can hear her voice cracking, her eyes welling up with tears as she fixes her mascara in the rearview mirror.

"What he did was wrong. Absolutely. There's no question." I can feel her voice growing more conflicted. "I wish you told me about the accident sooner. I wouldn't have let you get so involved. You should have never been involved. It breaks my heart."

"Of course, what he did was wrong, Mom, I know that. It was a terrible mistake, but Ben is not a monster. He is not. I wanted you to get to know him like I did. Before he made this horrifying mistake."

"This will destroy you," she says, more seriously now. "It already has, I can see how much it's hurting you. You have to put an end to it. I don't want this to bring you down."

I tell her it won't. I tell her she can't possibly think I would ruin everything I've worked so hard for. For a man. "You don't have to worry about me. He'll be gone soon," I say.

I draft a hypothetical text I'd send to Ben. That we need to end this. It's too much for me. That I'm grateful for our time together and will always have love for him. But I'm gutted at the thought of losing Ben forever. What's the point, when I'd be miserable no matter what?

I can't let go.

CHAPTER 14

I HAVEN'T DRIVEN IN FIVE years. I have crippling anxiety behind the wheel, especially on highways. My palms sweat on the steering wheel. I start humming to distract myself as we merge onto 287 toward the Taconic parkway, my cat-eye glasses glued to my face—I'm so nearsighted.

Ben insisted we take my sister's car for an escape in the Catskills to an old bed and breakfast we'd been to once before. I'm excited, but I can't relax with the two-hour drive ahead. I put my blinker on to signal left onto the highway.

"Ben, I can't do this. I'm freaking out." He's sitting in the passenger seat—calm—trying to navigate us.

"Baby, relax. You're doing great. You can do this. I'm not worried," he says, so sure. How does he trust me to drive us? I don't even trust me. "It's just like riding a bike, okay? I'm going to get us there. You're doing fine. Now get ready to merge."

I can barely keep up with traffic. I'm going under the fifty-five-mile speed limit. My chest tightens and my body goes numb as I watch the cars speeding past. I'm taking deep breaths. "Ben, this isn't a good idea. I'm literally having a panic attack! I can feel my face turning red and the sweat sticking to my turtleneck."

"Mia, do you think I'd insist you do this if I didn't think you could? I wouldn't push you out of your comfort zone," Ben says. I realize he's putting himself at risk in this situation too.

"You always thank me when things like this are over. You're always happy you just did it, right? Less thinking, more doing."

I wish I hadn't agreed. This is a bad idea. I hate that he can be so demanding sometimes. Maybe he enjoys this kind of adrenaline, but it's not for me.

"You're doing great! Seriously, sweetie, you don't have to worry about anything on the road. I'm your eyes. Just keep going," he says. I repeat that line in my head, just keep going, over and over.

"I hate this shit!" I scream. "Turn on the radio. I need a distraction."

I need something to calm my nerves. It's not normal to feel this high-strung. Why do I always get like this? I love Ben, but sometimes I feel even more stressed around him, like he fuels my anxiety.

I hear a familiar song by The Hues Corporation and turn up the radio. It reminds me of the oldies my dad used to play at the restaurant. My sister and I would belt them out with flour in our hair from making pizza, our black shirts stained in red sauce, not caring about the customers watching.

My mind starts to drift away from fear and lets the music take over. My shoulders start to lower as we approach the Tappan Zee Bridge.

Somehow, I got us to New Paltz in just under two hours. There's an electric fireplace turned on in our room as we unpack our suitcases. "I can't believe it's been a year since the fireworks on the Hudson." I turn to Ben.

"Yeah, this year really flew. I hope the years we're apart go by just as fast," Ben says. We both get quiet. It's hitting us. Ben's court date is coming up. We have one month left together.

"I don't want you to go," I say, holding him close. "I wish you didn't have to leave."

"I know, Mia. Me too. This has been the best year of my life."

"Me too," I say, realizing this could be our last New Year's Eve for a long time. It's already dark, and I watch Ben unfold some of the items

I packed for him. He wants to go in the hot tub. It's freezing cold, but I appease him and put on my bathing suit.

He read a National Geographic book with a profile of the Ice Man recently, some guy who had weathered the coldest places on earth naked. And by defying the body's standards, he'd created his own perceived tolerances. Ben is now obsessed with this guy's ability to master mind over matter. He runs outside in his swimsuit as I watch from behind the glass sliding door.

"Ben, what the hell are you doing? It's freezing out," I call, watching him run around like a puppy.

"It's so warm!" he yells back. "What are you talking about?" He comes running back and jumps into the hot tub.

I'm shivering. "There's no way I'm coming out there," I call out to him.

"Come on, baby. You can do it. Fill your body up with a deep, deep, breath, then breathe heavily in and out to warm up."

Ben's constant pushing makes me feel exhausted. As much as I try to relax and be cool like Ben, I'm just not a daredevil. These highs he chases are wearing me out. I sometimes wonder how things would be without the accident over our heads. Would I be able to tolerate Ben's rollercoaster mind forever?

Suddenly, he rushes inside, grabs my towel, and carries me out to the hot tub.

"I'm going to kill you!" I say, shivering.

The hot water feels good on my freezing skin, and Ben laughs. "Come here, baby. You did so good driving today!" he says, handing me the glass of pinot noir I was gripping before he dragged me out.

"I'm sick of you putting me through all these challenges!" I say, only half joking.

I always feel a little better after facing a fear, but Ben seems to prey on my fight-or-flight tendencies. I've barely come down from the stressful drive. Give me a fucking break.

"See, that wasn't so bad now, was it?" he says.

"It was awful," I say, taking a long sip of wine.

We press our heads back against the hot tub, the jets massaging our backs. I stare up at the stars shining like Christmas ornaments in the sky. I forgot how amazing stars are.

The next morning, we decide to take a drive into town. I set off through the winding back roads, getting distracted every now and then by the snow-covered trees lining the road. The roads are less daunting off the highway, so my mind is a bit more at ease. I can see why people live up here.

I can't parallel park, so Ben insists on doing it for me. It's risky, but we don't have a choice. Main Street is pretty empty, aside from a few cars parked outside a local bar. There are Christmas decorations on the street lanterns and a big string of lights set around the giant ball that will drop tonight.

We walk into a vintage thrift shop cluttered with old furniture and sections of Pyrex. I still hate buying used things, but Ben is in his element rifling through old records and tangled-up plugs from electronics. I go to the bookstore while he rustles around.

I pick up *The Year of Magical Thinking*, and I'm contemplating whether to buy it or borrow it from the library when I see Ben. He's holding up two tiny gold heart charms.

"I'm buying these for us," he says, reaching into his wallet.

"They're so cute. What are they for?" I ask.

"I'll take one, and you'll take one. It'll be something for you to remember me by when I have to leave," he says.

I get a sudden feeling of emotional whiplash, my mind jerking from the present to the future. The thought of losing Ben. It's more than I can comprehend. Still, I love that in his mind we'll be together forever, because part of me wants that too.

He places the tiny heart in my hand, and I put it in the zipper part of my wallet. When we walk out of the bookstore, we both notice a mosaic of navy blue and white tiles that say, "You are loved."

Ben places his brown snow boots over the edges and motions for me to do the same. He takes a photo of our feet on the tiles and promises he'll always love me.

"You have my heart forever," he says, his eyes watering.

"You are the best thing that has ever happened to me."

I can't find any words in this moment. I'm overwhelmed by my love for him—and the grief that I've carried, even though he's still here.

CHAPTER 15

I'M ON DEADLINE AT WORK, filing a story about a pickled pizza trend when Ben calls.

"Hey, I'm at work. Is everything okay?" I'm worried. He usually texts me first.

"I just left a meeting with my lawyer."

"How'd it go? What'd he say?"

"I'm going away for seven years."

Silence. I feel a tightening in my chest. I'm in shock. Seven years feels like an eternity. I knew this was coming, but it didn't feel real until now.

"What? Are you sure?"

"Yes, at best. We're going to sign a plea deal next week. If I go to trial, it'll be worse. It could be ten, fifteen years, maybe more." It sounds like the decision has been made. I can tell he's crying. I can hear it in his voice.

I am frozen.

"My lawyer says if we take the seven years, I may be able to do five with good time."

"Okay, I'm at work right now. I'll call you in a little," I say, looking over at Leah, who has her headphones in at the desk next to me.

I reach for my glasses to hide my watering eyes.

Where was I five years ago? Ten years ago? College, interning, maybe? My grandpa died. I wore the same all-black H&M jumpsuit I wore on the first day of my internship. I didn't even have an apartment then. I think about all the things that have changed since then, how different my life was. And I can't imagine how much things will change in another five years. I try to stay strong because I know I have to be. For Ben. But I can't fight back the tears fast enough. I can't stop feeling.

My boyfriend is going to prison. I let the reality of that statement sink in, swallowing the red wine I've been holding on my tongue until I feel the bitterness make it blister. I knew this was exactly where I'd end up, halted at the intersection of anger, self-pity, grief, and loneliness. This is my own fault. I let this happen. I allowed myself to fall in love with Ben, knowing he had killed someone. But I was too selfish to let him go. The saddest part is Ben thinks we can make this work. I wish we could. I tell him what he wants to hear, but I know I can't wait for him. I've always known that. It's just real now, and the comfort his presence brought me is being ripped away.

I'm drunk. I've had a lot of wine. Maybe three glasses. Maybe four.

I swipe on Tinder for a hookup. I need an escape. I need something to get me out of my head.

I go to the bar around the corner from me, and I meet a dirty blonde with blue eyes. Not my type. I can't remember his name. Why can't I remember his name? It doesn't matter. He's funny. But why am I crying? He tucks my hair behind my ear.

"Is it something I said?"

"No, no it's not you. It's okay. I just had a hard day. A very hard—but you're so, so nice. You're so cute. Promise me you won't hurt me?"

He looks at me strangely.

"Um, I won't. No, of course not. Why would I hurt you?"

"Let's have another drink?" I suggest.

A drink turns into a shot. And we're smiling and laughing again.

The bar turns into the wood floor of my apartment. His hands are holding down my arms. How did we get here? Do I have work tomorrow? What is his name?

I feel his soft skin on mine, and for a minute, I can't breathe.

"Is this okay?" I hear him ask.

"Is what okay? Of course, it's okay!" I hear myself slurring my words. I would rather give in to this than be alone tonight.

My head is on fire. My spine paralyzes in panic when I feel him massaging my back. *Not again. How could I let this happen again?*

"Hey, I'm so sorry. I have to get up for work. You have to leave."

"But it's Sunday," he says. "You work on Sunday?"

"Yes, unfortunately," I lie.

"Are you sure?"

I nod and watch him layer on his clothes while I survey the floor for a condom.

I feel a nervous relief when he leaves. There is a road map of bite marks on my waist, my neck.

"Breathe in problems, exhale solutions..." That is a direct quote from Tina, a yoga instructor and self-proclaimed healer at Canyon Ranch. Tina, sweetie, if you only knew.

I take a long inhale, holding my breath for five. Four. Three. Two. One. Deeply exhaling for five. Four. Three. Two. One. Again and again.

I break my focus, disdainfully staring at my chipped black pedicure on my yoga mat. The sunlight beams through the floor-to-ceiling windows at this five-star health resort at a mansion in the Berkshires.

Ben is sitting with crossed legs and eyes closed. He's deep in a meditative state.

My editor sent me here to cover a story on spa getaways. This place is solitary confinement for rich people. Limited dairy. Limited gluten. No alcohol. No phones. White walls.

I think about the bites on my body as we flow through our last Vinyasa, praying Ben doesn't notice.

We lay like starfish in *shavasana,* Ben reaching for my hand across the mat.

Ben sees a missed call from his dad when we get back to the room. He hasn't called since the sentencing news. Ben calls him back on speaker. I hear Daniel ask if his lawyer found any loopholes in the case and insist that this can't be the final verdict. Maybe there's something he missed. He keeps pressing.

"How do you know?" he asks again. Ben snaps, diminishing the calm he'd cultivated in the meditation.

"Because when I came out of the fucking hospital after realizing what had happened, it was the most devastating, awful feeling. And you know, it wasn't even about prison. It was about what happened. The way that I felt, and the actions that I took, and the consequences of those actions on other people, and making other people feel that pain."

He's fighting back tears.

"It fucking eats me up inside. You have no idea. It's the worst feeling ever, okay? And I felt all of that from the moment I found out what happened."

Now he's crying.

"You weren't there. I got taken away on a stretcher. I was looking up at the EMTs, and I said to them, 'Is anyone else hurt? Is anyone else as hurt as bad as I am?' That was the first thing that came out of my mouth. Is anyone hurt as bad as I am?' And they told me no. They lied to me. It wasn't until I got to the hospital that I found out what had happened."

"What did they say to you?" Daniel asks.

"They lied the entire time. It wasn't until I called a friend, and she said she'd gotten a news update that a woman was killed on that boat. I found out over the phone, in the hospital. Before I even got the MRI."

This is the first time I've heard him recount that night. He's told me he couldn't talk about the accident. His lawyer told him not to, so I didn't press him. I can't imagine the horror he felt when his friend told him that someone had died. To learn that it was his fault.

"But you knew at the time?" Daniel presses.

"And they continued to lie to me. The doctors and the nurses, everyone that checked on me kept saying everyone else is okay," he said, his voice trembling. "But my friend told me someone had died. That's when my heart dropped. That's when I realized what was happening. That's when I realized it was because of me. Because of what I did."

He cries harder. His dad is silent.

Ben's mom retained a prison coach for $500 to meet us not far from Canyon Ranch for an hour. I had no idea this was even an industry.

We're in a coffee shop when this buff, Irish-looking man named Jim walks in. He doesn't tell us what he did, just that he served twenty years at a state prison near Boston, and he shows us the tattoos he got while doing time. This feels like a movie.

"First thing you need to know is—nobody is your friend. You got me?" he starts.

Ben nods. He's already scaring the shit out of me.

"This is what's going to happen. You're going to get to Walpole. You're going to be in a cell for twenty-two hours of the day. So, get comfortable. Maybe you'll get a book, but don't bet on it. It's only temporary though. Keep telling yourself that. They'll take weeks to place you. Judging by your record, you could be going to the farm."

"Farm?" I ask.

"It's one of the less dangerous facilities," he says. Ben's face seems calm, somehow. He's not asking questions, just listening.

"I can see you've been working out. That's good. You'll be able to do more of that once you get settled in. Try to stay strong. You want to keep a low profile but still have people be intimidated by you. Once you get there, the first thing you gotta do is make sure you get money on your calling card. You'll have someone out here set it up so you can make calls." He then proceeds to rattle off rules of "etiquette" he says can have dangerous consequences if not followed, like cutting the lunch or phone lines.

"I know it seems like a lot, but once you're settled in, it won't be so bad," Jim says.

"I'm not worried," Ben says. He has a brave face on. "I'll just be worried about passing the time. Just doing everything I can not to think about it."

"It'll fly by. It may seem like an eternity. But let me tell you—I know people doing life in there. My twenty years flew. The days are long, but the years are short."

This relationship feels more like a sentence for me too.

CHAPTER 16

I'M BACK IN BOSTON THE weekend before Ben goes to prison. I pulled a few strings to get us into one of the top new restaurants in the city. It's a modern French place, and the owner was on *Top Chef*. I know this will be our last dinner alone before we're inundated with goodbyes from Ben's family and friends. Before we're overwhelmed by the packing and boxes and last-minute errands. But I can't think about all that. I just want us to enjoy this last dinner, just us.

I order my first glass of wine, a Bordeaux that's silky on my palate. I've been so stressed. Ben's mother has been bombarding us with questions. Does he want to keep the TV? Is his roommate going to pay for the couch he's leaving behind? Did he send in the last rent check?

I take a big gulp of wine, feeling at ease for the first time all weekend. Ben orders a Coke. He seems so calm. Ready to accept the sentence. It puts me in a better place too.

He's been going over his apology letter; he'll recite it in court after accepting the plea bargain. He was up for hours and hours writing it. He isn't expecting forgiveness, but he needs to express how deeply sorry he is.

Ben punctures a hole in the middle of the bubbling Gruyere in his French onion soup, and it hits me that this is his last restaurant meal for a long time. I no longer have an appetite. He scoops up a spoon of broth and wraps the stringy cheese.

"Oh my god. This is amazing," he says, savoring it.

It's almost 9 p.m., and the restaurant is dying down, a reminder that we aren't in New York. Soon, Ben and I are the only ones in the dining room. The waiters delicately slip by every so often to refill our water or take away empty side plates, but they leave us alone, like they know we need every last moment of this meal.

"I feel like this is the last supper," I say, abandoning the last of my lobster gnocchi.

"Yeah, well, it kind of is," he says, savoring the last of his duck confit.

"At least you got your duck."

"I'm going to miss sushi the most," Ben says.

"Of course, the one thing not on this menu." I shake my head.

"This is perfect. I'm going to miss these productions of yours," he says, asking me to smile for a photo.

We had yet to make headway on the foie gras plated with yuzu sauce and grilled scallions which, shockingly, work better than I anticipated.

I don't have the heart to tell Ben he's eating liver when he devours a forkful—though I don't think he would really care. He wants to experience everything he can before leaving.

"What are you doing with the espresso machine?" I ask, realizing the Nespresso I got him would just collect dust for the next few years.

"I think Alana wants it. Unless you want it?"

"No, I bought that for you. It's yours," I say.

"There will probably be a new model by the time I get out."

It makes me sad thinking about it.

"Then we'll just get another one," I try to reassure him.

As we order dessert, I'm consumed with flashbacks. The dinners we shared. The trips. The first time Ben ordered a cappuccino in Salem. Our waiter brings us two hot ones with cinnamon. We sip them in silence, staring at each other.

"I'm really going to miss this."

"Me too," Ben says, reaching for my hand across the table. We are disrupted by a text from his mom saying she's in the car outside.

The next few days are going to be hell, and all I want is a few more minutes of alone time.

"Will you please do one last thing for me?" Ben asks with his mischievous smile.

"What is it?"

"Can you come see Gary with me?"

Ben wants me to see his long-time therapist. He knows I don't like therapy. I hate being vulnerable and opening up to strangers, but he insists because our future is so uncertain. He thinks that I'm going to leave him, that I can't possibly stay committed. But his trying to control our situation isn't making it any easier. It's like he wants an answer that I can't give him right now. We've been going back and forth about it for weeks.

"I already made an appointment," he says.

"Ben, come on. I just want to enjoy these last few hours together. This whole thing is sad enough. I don't want to talk to some stranger about us right now. This weekend is already a lot," I say, knowing that he won't back down.

"Please? Please! Come on. It'll be good for both of us. Just do it for me? Gary really wants to meet you."

A black cat greets us at the door, and there's a giant Buddha in the hallway. It smells like incense. Candles are burning, and there's a Zen garden in the waiting area. This is the last place on earth I want to be, but then the thought of going to see Ben in prison dawns on me. I can't imagine it. It makes me uncomfortable just to think about. What people will think of me. Why I would be dating someone in prison. I can't picture myself there, and I don't want to.

"Hello, Ben. Hello, Mia," Gary says, extending his hand. He looks a little bit like Gilbert Gottfried.

When we sit down, Ben explains that he's worried about our future when he goes away. He's worried that I won't be able to handle it. But I think he's more afraid that I won't stay fully committed to him. He needs the reassurance that I won't leave him. But how can I possibly say that for sure? I love him, but how can I give him five to seven years of my life just waiting?

"I just think that you don't know what's going on in my head all the time," I say. "You need to trust that I'm capable of making my own decisions. Obviously, I wouldn't be here if I couldn't. You know?"

"But you've been dreading coming here," Ben remarks.

"Yeah, because it's a tough weekend, and it's been a long few weeks. I'm not ready to have a full-on therapy session."

Gary chimes in.

"If I were in Mia's situation, I'd kind of dread it too. Your court hearing next week is going to be here before you know it. So, there's a big question mark out there. Aren't you dreading it a little bit yourself?"

Ben shakes his head.

"Nope?" Gary seems surprised.

"I go to bed every night. The only thing I think about is how many pillows I'm going to get when I go in there. If I get one pillow, can I buy another? I just, I can't. I don't have the mental real estate. If I think about what I will go through, I'll fucking—"

"I understand what you're saying, and I think that's very smart, but don't make her do it too. Take the love that she is projecting onto you and make it precious rather than repulsive. You're kind of pushing it away," Gary says. "The fear of her leaving you is ruining the love that you have right now. You have to stay in the present."

"So, don't tell her that I think she's overdramatic?"

I roll my eyes at Ben. Yes, I'm dramatic because this situation is pretty fucking daunting.

"Right, let her have her feelings because they are valid."

I'm grateful that Gary at least gets it.

"Right, I can have my own feelings," I echo.

"Is that because she's anxious and nervous, or is that because she's a woman?" Ben jokes, trying to make light of the situation.

Gary clasps his hands in front of his face. "Because this is a big time," he says.

"But you know what I'm saying," Ben replies.

"We've been traveling a lot these past couple of weeks. I haven't been home," I say.

"It's been a lot, and it's wearing on me. Rushing from place to place, being home for three or four days, then getting on a bus. I love the time we have together, and I'm so grateful, but it's all just been so much," I say. I feel bad for complaining, but I'm just so tired.

"There's probably a lot of mental exhaustion for you and Ben," Gary says.

I nod, agreeing.

"You just have to be present with each other—it's too difficult to look into the future," Gary says.

"That's my only option," I say.

"That's a very smart answer, by the way. Very smart, very intelligent. It is. Ben can get negative about it," Gary says.

"I would just rather suffer the disappointment sooner rather than later."

"That gives so little hope," Gary says. "That means that you don't believe in Mia yet. It's going to take some time. This is why you're going to be apart for now. This is why you have a long-term relationship. Probably both of you have huge trust issues, you know what I'm saying?"

He sits back in his chair and tilts his head at us.

"This is what God gave you right now," Gary says. I'm surprised at how spiritual he's getting.

"I know what you need," he says, turning to Ben. "You need somebody to prove that they're never going to go away. But that's not because you're going away, that's how it's always been. Because of your dad." Gary looks back at me.

"So, don't pay any attention to him," he chuckles. "Let him talk. He needs to present himself a certain way. But be who you are."

I smile back at Gary, feeling more secure. Finally feeling validated for my feelings without Ben knocking them. I wish he could understand how hard this is for me too.

"She'll make her own decisions. She made a decision that you were worth it. Do you get that? Why would you want to take that away?"

"I feel like everything is being taken away," Ben says. "Everything."

"You have something, probably for the first time in your life, that's really genuine, right?"

"Now it's all being taken away," Ben says, shaking his foot, unable to sit still.

"No, it's not. And if you look at it that way, you'll be angry, or hurt, or sad. This is what the two of you have to go through right now. You're not being taken away eternally. You're going to build something more," Gary reassures him. "So, this can be the foundation for a stronger relationship."

"With all these places she travels—it's a different restaurant every night. She's going to make connections with other guys and other people. That's in my head. Someone else is going to see how amazing she is," Ben laments.

Gary nods intently.

"He's in a vulnerable spot. He feels that everything is in your hands. I think you're going to be working on trust. I think you both had some trust issues with people in the past and you probably need to feel some control."

I love Ben, but there is a part of me that cannot fully commit to him. There is no way I can tell him in this moment that I will stay with him forever. I feel restless. I want to go home.

"I think we're just going to try to move forward," I keep saying. I don't know what to do other than take one day at a time.

Grief

CHAPTER 17

BEN HASN'T PACKED A THING, and he's going away in three days. The woven Southwestern comforter his grandmother gave him is still crumpled across the unmade bed. The turquoise ladder stands upright near his closet with a row of worn-out belts hanging from it. The pajamas he got in Banff are strewn across the floor.

Terry is staring aimlessly at the TV. I know she'll be the hardest goodbye for Ben. Right now, it's the calm before the storm. We're waiting for his family to come over with boxes.

Margot, Ben's mom, pulls the screen door open. She's carrying two giant grocery bags.

"I thought we could have a working lunch, sweetie—eat while we pack," she says, bursting in and making her way to the kitchen.

I already feel sensory overload as she unpacks cold cuts, bread, potato chips, and iced tea, dispersing the deli meats onto paper plates in an assembly line on the stove and kitchen counter, rolling up a piece of turkey for herself. She looks like she hasn't eaten or slept in weeks. And I know she won't until court—even after that.

Adam and Tracy come in looking hesitant, like they're unsure of what they should be doing. They're carrying unmade boxes. The energy of holding a smile through all of this feels excruciating. I wonder if anyone can tell that I'm unraveling. Part of me wishes I were home. I just want to go home.

I don't even know where to start. I'm so overwhelmed. But Ben needs me. That's enough to light a fire. I toss my hair into a ponytail, roll up my sleeves, and grab some newspaper to start wrapping Ben's photo frames. I start with a picture of a family trip to Whistler, then a photo of him and his dad at his high school graduation. All of his childhood memories will be boxed up, stored away. Ben still has a few books from college, DVDs, and old phone chargers.

"Do you really want to keep all this, Ben?" I already know the answer.

"Uh, yeah, just put it all in a box. Everything still works."

We sort through his desk drawers, rifling through receipts and his old badge from the lottery app office. His closets are still packed with sweaters and dress shirts.

"Just keep it all," he says, fidgeting around the room. I can tell his mind is wandering again. He's not present, and I know I need to just take control and figure out his packing as fast as possible so we can enjoy the last few moments we have together.

Margot keeps rummaging through Ben's closet. I taped boxes together, waiting for her instructions. She's in full-on mom mode.

"Ben, do you want to keep these old car magazines?" she calls out. He's now playing video games in the other room with Adam.

I know Ben is just dissociating from all of this, but I wish he would snap out of it and help. How can he not see that I am so overwhelmed? It's so much, and I'm slightly angry at Ben's blatant disregard.

I start to throw them away when Ben's mom says, "Let's wait and see if he wants them."

It's going to be a long day, especially since Ben keeps disappearing.

"Yeah, just keep them all," Ben yells out from the living room. Great. None of this stuff matters. I wish he could see that. But to Ben, it's more than just stuff. I imagine he wants to come home to something that's his.

I'm dreading the moment that I'll have to say goodbye, but I'm also exhausted by his family and the mental gymnastics my brain is doing, thinking about the future, packing for my boyfriend to go to prison. I'm angry that he's not helping me. I can't wait to get home. I've spent more time with his family than my own this year.

When I told my mom about Ben's plea deal, she was in slight shock. She said what he did was wrong and that I shouldn't have continued to date him. That she wasn't going to let me derail my life for a man. I keep replaying the refrain in my head. I reassured her that this will be the end. When she texts me, "Are you okay?" my eyes well up with tears because she's the only person who has asked that question all weekend.

My makeup bag is the only thing left on the dresser. I stuff it into my duffel. Ben comes in and wraps his arms around me. He sinks his head into my arms, the smell of his woodsy cologne intoxicating, taking me back to Hotel Sole, where we first met. Careless nights driving around, eating oysters, and drinking expensive wine. The freedom to do whatever we wanted to. I can feel Ben's tears against my neck, but I can't cry. It's not because I'm trying to be strong; my mind and body are just in a state of shock. I've never dealt with real grief before. Ben is my first real love. Letting go is going to be excruciating.

"The hardest part is having to leave you," he says, sobbing into me. "I don't care about anything else. I love you so much." He's breathing heavily. I run my fingers through his hair, trying to comfort him. He's breaking my heart. I hate to see him hurt. I wipe his tears. The day we didn't want to come is finally here.

How did we get here?

Ben's lawyer is running five minutes late, but his assistant, a young man named Ryan, waits outside his office.

"We can just start inside. Ed is just getting off a flight and will be here any minute," he says, gesturing for us to come in.

"This is my girlfriend, Mia," Ben says, introducing me.

"Nice to meet you," Ryan says, shaking my hand with a firm grip.

Ed's office is filled with law books, shelves upon shelves neatly stacked. We sit down at a long wooden table—Ben and I in black leather swivel chairs, Margot at the head.

Margot shuffles through a folder with character letters she's collected from friends and family. His rabbi wrote a note about the community service Ben's been doing. His AA sponsor wrote about how Ben has stayed sober and attended meetings twice a week, and how he's sure that Ben will positively contribute to society once his sentence is complete.

I sip anxiously from my Styrofoam coffee cup, burning my tongue.

"So, the good news is, it's very unlikely that there will be press. It should be a quiet settlement," Ryan reassures us, clasping his hands.

"Oh, here are all the letters I emailed Ed. I printed them out for you both in case," Margot says, handing them to Ryan.

"Great, thank you," he says, lowering his glasses.

"Ed will take a look and pick out some of the most compelling ones that speak to Ben's character and then write up a few words for the judge. This will really help."

A short, older man with gray, slicked hair comes through the door—Ed. He looks tan and relaxed. He's a bit dressed up for a Sunday, but I'm sure he spends most of his days in suits.

"Sorry to keep you waiting," he says, placing his briefcase on the table. He sits down and crosses his legs and arms. He looks at Ben before acknowledging anyone else in the room.

"How are you doing?" he asks, pulling out a cloth to clean his eyeglasses.

"I'm okay," Ben answers. "I brought my girlfriend, Mia." I get up to shake Ed's hand.

"It's nice to meet you," I say.

"Pleasure. So, where were we?" Ed looks over to Ryan.

"I was just going over the expectations for Tuesday with Ben. It should be a fairly brief process, no longer than an hour or so and a quiet courtroom. It's unlikely the families will be there, and the press hasn't been tipped off, so that's good. The DA will read the charges and go over the findings from the investigation. Then Ed will have a chance to read from the letters. After that, the judge will ask how you will plead. You'll look him in the eyes and answer. It's important that you appear remorseful and that you fully accept responsibility. If you don't, he'll reject the plea deal, okay?"

Ben looks withdrawn, his skin so pale. He's exhausted. I can see the bags under his eyes. He's numb, we all are.

"I will, I can assure you that," he answers.

"Okay. Then they'll take you into custody, and you will have a moment to say a few words if you want to."

"Yes, we wanted to talk to you about that," Margot says. "I was hoping to bring Ben in tomorrow so you guys could practice the statement before the trial."

Ben shoots a death stare at his mom. She's trying to micromanage his prison send-off.

"Monday? I wasn't aware we were meeting on Monday before court. I assumed that's what this meeting is for," Ryan says. "But Ben, if that's something you'd like to do—if it'll make you feel more prepared, comfortable, I'm certainly happy to sit down with you for a bit." Ed nods.

"No, that won't be necessary. I've prepared my statement, and we don't need to drive all the way back out here again," Ben says, looking at his mother.

"Okay then. So, after the statement, they'll put you in handcuffs and take you to a courthouse cell, where you'll wait to be transported. You could be there for a few hours. Make sure you bring a change of clothes and sneakers you don't care about. You may not get them back."

My body tenses. Margot's face is completely blank. I'm shaken by how casually they're running through this prelude to prison, like he's reading from a script he's memorized. How is this real life? How is no one crying right now?

Ben looks serious, but not worried. I'm picturing him in handcuffs, and I can't bear the thought of seeing him dragged out of a courtroom. I'm so glad I'm not going.

"Will we be able to say goodbye to him before that?" Margot asks.

"It depends on the judge. Usually, once he's taken into custody, he goes straight away. It's unlikely, but it all depends on how the plea deal goes. You might be able to give him a quick hug, but I would make sure you say your goodbyes before entering the courtroom," Ryan says.

"Will they feed him back there?" Margot asks, her voice shaky.

"Yes. It will be something basic, like a bologna sandwich, but they'll feed him," Ryan assures her.

Margot looks white. She's kept it together this far, but I can sense her starting to unravel. She's so used to being a support. Her eyes are heavy with tears.

The room is silent. Ryan hands Margot a box of tissues, smiling politely. I wish the lawyers would break their professionalism to comfort Margot. To be as devastated as we are. Everything is happening so quickly. None of this feels real. The lawyers, the courtroom jargon, the play-by-play of how he'll plead and what happens when he goes into custody—it's all so unfamiliar. I can't even fathom what life will be like for Ben on the other side.

Ben reaches for my hand under the table. I swallow this temporary comfort like a painkiller.

"I'm okay." He can read my nervous body language. "It's going to be okay," he assures me.

I give him a robotic nod.

I fantasize about moving forward. The end of us I always knew was coming is here. But the pain of Ben's absence eclipses my roiling emotions. Would I be selfish for abandoning him? He's scared. I know he's scared.

My foot is shaking, legs crossed, our hands still clutched. I want this to be over. But I know it's only just the beginning.

It's my last night with Ben. I'm standing naked, my feet on the cold tiles of his bathroom floor, waiting for him to shower with me. The steam warms my bare skin. I don't mind this moment alone. I'm so drained from the weekend. The smiling and constant interactions with his friends and family. The draining session with Gary. The packing. All of it just leading up to this excruciating moment. I'm trying to be here for Ben, but part of me is longing for this to all be over. For a sense of relief.

Ben asks me again if I want to come to court. I tell him I can't bring myself to be there when he surrenders. I can't put myself through that. I can't watch him being taken away in handcuffs. I know that image will scar me forever. I'd much rather we say goodbye on our own terms.

He makes his way into the shower and hugs me for a long time. I can't tell if his face is wet from the shower or his tears. I can't cry anymore. I'm spent. Our wet bodies intertwine like that first summer night. Things are so different now. He kisses me over and over, and I realize this is the last intimate moment we'll have for a really long time.

It's Monday, the day before Ben goes to court, and my flight out of Boston is at 11 a.m.

Margot pulls up in her Lexus. I realize I'll never see Ben's apartment again. Terry will be with Margot, so when I come back to visit, I'll get to see her. She'll be a sweet reminder of Ben. I pet her and give her a hug goodbye.

Ben holds my hand in the back seat. We're silent most of the way. This is the hardest goodbye I've ever had in my life. We pull up to the airport. Tracy and Adam give Ben a deep hug. He and Tracy say goodbye and walk off to give us a moment alone.

Ben pulls out a marble stone that one of his friends from AA gave him. It's something he's held in moments of stress or weakness. I'm trying not to get emotional, but it's so hard. My tears wet the collar of his jacket. I don't want to let him go. I can feel the separation anxiety already setting in, but I'm embarrassed to show my vulnerability in front of Adam and Tracy, especially since they both seem stoic.

It's cloudy, and I stare at our shadows between the doors. Then I look back up at Ben and give him one last kiss. I tell him to call me later. I put the stone in my pocket and look for Tracy and Adam in the security line.

I got my first letter from Ben. It's stamped with the address of the Walpole prison. I feel shame and comfort holding the envelope in the lobby of my apartment building.

Ben's last meal before court was a bowl of microwaved oatmeal. He told me he couldn't stop thinking about me on the drive. How perfectly compatible we are. The words are like dopamine to my brain. I'm addicted to his affection, his desire for me. To being loved.

He says the thought of seeing me soon is helping him stay calm. It brings a pit to my stomach. The thought of going to a prison fills me with dread, then grief for life without Ben.

The judge settled on seven years. Ben didn't show any emotion. He just stared vacantly at the courtroom floor. He signed the documents and pleaded guilty. The judge asked him whether he accepted responsibility. Whether he understood what was happening.

"Yes, sir," he responded, in handcuffs.

"Through all this, I had you," he told me. "My life is meaningful because I met you. I know you'll always be there for me."

The assumption makes me feel uneasy. Ben began sobbing when the victim's attorney talked about the husband who lost his wife waking up in the morning to an empty bed. How he lost his best friend. His travel partner.

"All I could think about was you," Ben writes.

"At that point, I knew wholeheartedly I want to spend the rest of my life with you," he tells me.

"But the pain of knowing I no longer have control, of being able to see you when I want. To kiss you. To make you laugh. For the next seven years, I can't do any of that," he writes.

Then he read his statement. His remorse is "incalculable." He said he'll accept the consequences. That a day won't go by that he won't think of this loss. The pain that he caused.

When he was taken into custody, he winked at Margot to let her know he was going to be okay.

"We both know that did nothing to reassure her," he writes.

⚐

My phone hasn't vibrated in hours, and I'm compulsively checking for a call or text from Ben. I'm so used to hearing from him frequently. I self-soothe by scrolling through his old text messages.

I find the thread Ben sent me moments before going to court. It's a photo from our first New York date at an Italian restaurant on the Upper East Side.

Me: I love you so much. You are everything to me. I'll always have you in my heart.

Ben: My heart is so heavy, mostly because of how much I love you.

Me: This is only temporary. And we need to remember that.

⚐

Ben sends another photo of us in bed, me in a black turtleneck, him in his Henley gray sweatshirt. We're both smiling, so happy in that moment.

Me: You are everything I've always wanted. You have shown me so much love.

Ben: I will only love you more.

The last message I sent was a heart. It may have been the last thing he saw on his phone before turning it off.

I'm in bed, sobbing. I send Ben a text I know he won't see. But I'm comforted by this gesture, like replaying a voicemail from a dead loved one.

"I love you," I write.

This is a pre-paid call from. Pause. Ben's voice.

Ben. Cohen.

His voice is stern and monotone.

Operator: An inmate at. Abrupt pause. Massachusetts Department of Corrections.

It sounds like a woman robot.

This call is recorded and monitored. To accept this call, press 1.

I press 1. This process is so foreign, but I'm reeling at the thought of hearing Ben's voice.

Beeeeep. Thank you for using Securus. You may start the conversation now.

"Mia?"

My heart spikes hearing his voice. He's there. He's okay. He's calling me.

"Ben! Ben, where are you? Are you okay? I got your note. How were you able to send that so quickly?"

"Yes, yes, I'm fine. Everything is okay. I'm at a state jail, waiting for them to figure out where they'll send me. Ed is working on getting me into a facility in Franklin. It's a medium-security prison, but it's supposed to be a safer one," he says.

I'm trying to follow his words, but all of this is so surreal. I know our conversation is being recorded, but I'm too happy to care. "Ben, that's so good. That's great news."

"It will be, yes, if Ed can get that approved. He's trying to speed everything up. This place isn't somewhere you want to stay long," he tells me. He sounds tired, but okay. Like it's not total hell. He's just going through the motions to get to what's next.

"Do you feel safe?" I ask.

"Yeah, yeah, yeah," he says in a quick staccato, like others are listening. I know he needs to keep it together.

"Are you sure?" I need his reassurance.

"Yes. I miss you," he says.

"I miss you too."

He tells me to keep my phone with me because he only has one window a day. If I miss the call, we won't be able to talk. I ask him if he needs anything, and he just says to tell Margot that everything is fine. Then he asks me to grab a pen and paper and to write down his inmate number. I'll need this to register for emails.

M220896. I have to memorize it.

"I can't wait to see you again," I say, not knowing when or where that will be possible.

"Hopefully, soon."

CHAPTER 18

BEN HAS RELOCATED TO THE Franklin facility, and I can hear the relief in his voice when he calls.

His money finally cleared, so that means he's able to buy clothes, actual clothes like blue jeans and sweatshirts and a winter coat, and packaged food that isn't inedible. He misses good coffee the most. He says I spoiled him with La Colombe and Balthazar. But, of course, with his engineering brain, he figured out a way to make cappuccinos in prison. He calls them "sinkachinos" because he uses instant coffee and mixes the powdered creamer with hot water from the sink.

He's started selling them for fifty cents each, which is probably the equivalent of what you'd pay for a tall at Starbucks in prison money. He swears they taste disgusting, but the guys there love it. It's the closest they're going to get to a fancy coffee. He's figured out how to make other things he can't buy. I joke that he should start an inmate chapter of Goop. Before he was able to buy sneakers, he cut up a toilet paper roll, laid it down flat, and duct taped it to his socks to make slippers. He told me that the guys in there also figured out how to make cheesecake. Ben said they saved up cream cheese packets from breakfast for weeks, then crushed up Teddy Graham cookies from the vending machines to make the crust.

"It's not Junior's, but it's actually delicious." Ben laughs.

He's trying to figure out a way to make a mattress pad because his is so thin. It barely gives him any support, and his back hurts. He ordered two more pillows and dissected the fluff and stuffed it into a blanket that mimics a pillow-top mattress cover. He's lucky that his mom is helping him pay for things. I can't imagine how most of the inmates get by without support.

He tells me about the different job options he has. There's a program where inmates help train dogs. Some work in the commissary and serve meals. Others have cleaning duties, like mopping the visiting room. Others work in the garden. Ben assures me it sounds a lot more exciting than it actually is. I believe him.

There's also a volunteer who teaches yoga once a week.

"Did you learn any new poses yet?" I ask. Ben can never remember the names, and I find it hilarious to try to talk him through the movements. "How about pigeon pose?"

"Is that the one where you're crouched down on the floor?" he asks.

"Sort of. You're like hunched over one of your legs, and the other is tucked in," I try to explain.

"No, I don't think so."

"Oh, how about goddess pose?"

"What's that one?"

"It's when you goal post your arms out and spread your legs wide out on the mat."

"No, not that one," he said. "We did warrior two, I think. I like that one. The one with your arms spread out like a ninja."

"Yes, that's warrior two!"

"It's hard to hold that pose for long. My arms are killing me."

I smirk into the phone. Ben always makes fun of my girly workouts, and I'm thrilled that he's finally seeing that yoga is no cakewalk.

"Oh, and if you think warrior two is hard, what about *chaturanga?*"

"Chatter-what?"

"Chaturanga! It's like a push-up, but harder. You start out in a plank pose and hold it then you lower down with your elbows tucked in and sweep your chest in front and up."

"Hmm, no I think I'll just stick to push-ups," Ben says.

"I like corpse pose," he says.

"Me too, that's the best one, that and happy baby."

Ben bursts out laughing. "What the hell is happy baby? Is that an actual pose?"

"Yes! And you've done it before. It's when you grab hold of your feet on your back and sway back and forth. It looks funny but feels so good."

Ben gets a kick out of this. "Who's my happy baby?" he says like he's talking to Terry.

God help whoever is listening to this recording. We both lose it, laughing harder and harder at the idea of him doing happy baby in prison.

I'm picking through the racks at the Upper East Side LOFT, looking for an outfit to visit prison. Can you fucking even? What a humbling moment in a crowd of stroller moms. I'm visiting Ben for the first time this weekend, and I've read through the dress code three times. It's specific.

Shoulders must be covered, and women can't wear "revealing or see-through tops." Two easy enough rules. But then it says no jeans. No pants with zippers and no short dresses. So maybe I can get away with a jogger? But the pants can't have a string on them. I browse through V-neck striped tanks and T-shirts, debating whether or not the cut is too revealing, not that I have anything to show. Everything looks matronly. I know I'm going to a medium security prison, but I still kind of want to look cute for Ben. It feels pathetic. I haven't seen him in three months.

I wonder if this chambray dress would be allowed, but I know I'd feel uncomfortable wearing a dress. I need to pick something out before the bus leaves at 7 p.m. This situation is almost comical. I settle on a denim button-down shirt and call it a day, racing home to pack my suitcase and

Uber to the Bolt Bus. It's the cheapest way to get to Boston, and the longest. In these uncomfortable moments, I can't help but question why I put myself in these situations. I hate this fucking bus. Every mile is a reminder of how hard this relationship with Ben is. How hard it's always been.

I put on Mahler and try to relax. The soothing, classical music always makes me think of Ben and the time we snuck into the Boston Symphony Orchestra. We pretended we were accompanying an old couple and managed to get past the guards. We found seats three rows from the orchestra, and when the lights started to dim, we knew we'd pulled it off. We both sat there in awe, Ben's hand in mine.

My only preparation for prison was *Law & Order: SVU*. Ben's facility is nothing like it. You might think you were at a DMV with barbed wire, except you can't wear jewelry or bring in a cell phone.

When you get in, you pick a number, like at a deli counter. It's important that you pick a number first thing, because that determines how quickly you'll get in. Then you fill out a piece of paper. Luckily, Margot helps me through this intimidating process. She fills out the form, and I see her write "fiancé" down. She says it might give me more pull in the visiting process since I live out of state.

The fluorescent light shows how much Ben's mom has aged. The wrinkles on her hands, the crow's feet creeping on either side of her eyes when she smiles. She's convinced herself that this is all normal; it's the only choice she has. This is her life now, and it's becoming mine too. She would do anything for her son, and she knows he only wants to see me.

I walk over to where the guards sit behind a glass partition like conductors behind a ticket counter.

I put my cell phone and wallet with my driver's license in a locker. Ben's mom gave me a plastic card for the vending machines inside the visiting room. Ben is always starving, and the visits are his chance to get whatever he wants to eat, a taste of the real world.

"Eleven, twenty-one, thirteen, seventeen, twenty-two… Hernandez, Austin, Yu, Valero, Cohen," a heavyset woman calls out. We all rush to line up, proceeding to a back room where we're searched and walk through a metal detector. The process is quick. I try to keep up with the veteran visitors who know the protocol. There are wives of lifers, people who committed murder. They are frail and older-looking, like someone you'd expect to see sitting in a park or at a nursing home. There is a mother and three kids visiting their dad. Seeing all of these normal-looking people gives me a sense of relief. I feel less ashamed for being here, for loving someone who made a mistake. I wonder how long these women have been coming here and how they pass their time. They make this all look so routine. I wonder if I'll be able to stay with Ben for as long as they've stuck around.

We carry our visiting slips and take off our shoes, placing them into a yellow plastic carrying tray. We line up barefoot on the cold white tile. I give the female guard a weak smile when it's my turn to walk through the metal detector. She seems to recognize the other wives and girlfriends around me.

The buzzer immediately goes off when I walk through. I can feel myself turning red, thinking I did something wrong. The alarm is so loud.

"You wearing a bra with underwire?" a female guard asks. Shit. I forgot that's part of the rules.

"Yes," I say. "I'm so sorry. I forgot."

"Sign the book," she says, seemingly unfazed, motioning toward a marble composition book. I scribble my name and the date quickly.

"Empty your pockets for me," she says. I do it.

"Turn around. Hands up." I follow her commands, like a game of Simon Says.

"Feet up," she calls out. My back is still turned away from her as I lift my bare feet off the ground so she can see what's under them.

"Turn around," she instructs, then pats me down, her hands running along my waist, the outsides of my legs. This is more intense than a TSA pat-down.

"Flip your hair for me," she says. I tussle my straight brown hair to show her that there's nothing there.

"Open your mouth," she instructs. I feel like a sick patient being examined by a doctor. "Under your tongue." She gazes inside my mouth like she's looking for a cavity filled with cocaine.

The search is finally done, but my heart is still thumping with the uncertainty of what the visiting room will be like, what seeing Ben will be like. I quickly put my sandals back on and follow the rest of the group down a hallway. Another guard stamps my right forearm as we wait for a steel door to open. Outside, there's a courtyard that leads to the visiting room. There's a garden lining the path with sunflowers and marigolds growing along the walkway. I'm surprised to see so much beauty in this dark place. It gives me a sense of calm, like maybe this won't be so bad.

Two guards sit on a raised bench that looks a bit like a judge's area in a courtroom. We give them our papers. One of the female guards must be around my age, twenty-six or twenty-seven, maybe. She's pretty even in the unflattering blue uniform. She doesn't look at me when I hand her my slip. The visiting room has rows of plastic chairs lined up in a big V shape. It's so when you sit down, you are visible to the guards, almost looking right at them, Ben later tells me.

There are three vending machines lining the back wall. One has chips, Clif bars, candy, and a soda machine. On the far left, there are instant meals kept in a refrigerated machine. Ben loves the frozen bacon cheeseburgers, a far cry from Shake Shack but the closest he'll get to the real thing for a while. I notice a painted mural in the right corner. It's a painting of the Boston skyline and the Zakim Bridge glowing at night across the Charles River. It's a backdrop for families to take photos in front of. There's a small flat-screen TV next to it and a kids' area with a miniature plastic table and chairs with coloring books.

I take a seat, my eyes glued to the entrance. Ben and I have been talking on the phone every day, but it's so different now because I can't text him whenever I want and our time is restricted. I think about us dancing on our first New Year's. It feels like yesterday we were sleeping in my tiny bed.

He's wearing a gray sweater and matching pants, talking to one of the guards. Our eyes lock, and I can feel my pulse speed like a racecar. My mind immediately relieved that he's okay. He's continuing to work out, and it shows. I wrap my arms around him, and we hug for as long as we can. His clothes smell like vinegar and the familiar scent of his warm skin. Ben takes my hand and escorts me to two empty seats, looking up at one of the guards for approval to sit down. He doesn't let go of my hand.

"I missed you so much," he says, his voice choking up. His eyes are swelling with tears, but he's trying not to let his sadness show. He's worked so hard to maintain a tough persona, a layer of defense that's crucial to his survival.

There's such comfort in having him so close after months apart, even with a bunch of strangers. Ben has a new buzz cut. Someone gave it to him with a pair of disposable razors.

He's tan from running outside and playing softball with his new prison friends. It's easy to remember why I fell in love with him, even sitting right here. I'm so physically drawn to him.

Ben and I talk about my job, how I've landed a few profiles. This year started off as a train wreck being separated from Ben, but professionally, it's been picking up.

Ben is sad because Terry has cancer. This is a cruel fucking world. She was going to get chemo, but it's unclear how long the dog has to live after developing a tumor. The doctors say it will probably be six months to a year. Aside from me, Ben loves Terry more than anything. Now he's going to lose her.

"I just feel like I'm losing everything," Ben says, holding back tears.

"Ben, no. Don't say that. How could you say that? There are so many people who love you here. I love you. You have me."

"I know. And I love you too. I'm so lucky to have you."

"We'll get through this. We don't even know what the odds are for Terry just yet. You can't jump to conclusions."

"I know," he says, rubbing my back.

There are so many rules in this place. I'm afraid to sit the wrong way, or laugh too loudly, or make the wrong gesture. The one silver lining is that I get to hold hands with Ben. Something I never thought would be so meaningful.

Ben feels the same way, and he doesn't let go.

I thought spending five full hours in a room with Ben might feel like a long time. Especially since we can't leave or really get up from our chairs. But the visit flies.

I find my mind dissociating from the surroundings, like we aren't in a prison. I'm all consumed in conversation, drowning out the noise. The other inmates. Like it's just us. Like before.

When the visit ends, Ben hugs me. And when it's over, I feel at ease, knowing that he's okay. All of this is daunting, but maybe it won't be so bad.

On the bus ride back, I have a sense of whiplash. The thought of having to go back to my job, my real life outside of this obscure, sad, secret bubble.

My mom, Lauren, and Eva are the only ones who know Ben is in prison. I never told my other friends. Or colleagues. I told them I've distanced myself from Ben because it's too hard for him to commit. I blame it on the long distance, say it's too complicated to discuss, and they don't pry.

"On my way back on the bus," I text Lauren. She already shares my location anyway, but talking to her brings me comfort.

"Okay, sis. How was it? Are you okay?"

"It was fine. It's really not that bad. Ben is okay. He looks really good. Just a long trip."

"Okay, good. Love you," she says.

I call Eva. I need someone to talk to on this two-plus-hour bus ride.

"Oh my god, how was it?" she asks. I sugarcoat everything. Even though Eva is my best friend, I still have this fear of judgment. I have to make it seem like everything is fine. Like this situation is a lot more normal than it seems.

"So, it actually wasn't bad. I mean, yes, there is barbed wire, but it really feels like you're waiting to go to the DMV."

"Really? Wait, but was it so scary?"

"Honestly, no, it just feels like you're in a room with normal people. I mean some of them have been in there for so long, for crimes they committed when they were teenagers. Ben has met a lot of them, and they seem like completely different people. Like so remorseful and just made a mistake. It's really sad to see the guys with their kids. It must be so hard."

I fear that I'll lose Eva's interest. I wonder if she thinks I am insane for even going.

"That's so sad. I can't even imagine." She sounds sincere. "So how was Ben? How's he doing?"

"He looks so good, and I mean, he seems to be in good spirits, all things considered."

"That's great. What does he do all day?"

I try to make it sound like Ben is in an easy, campy prison. Like it's not as scary as on TV.

"I mean, these guys don't have it so bad. Like, he works out a lot. And they have people who garden, and like, they cook. Ben told me he made a cheesecake. And they do yoga."

"Oh my god. Stop it—yoga? What? How?"

"Yeah, they do it in the yard."

"Okay, I love that for him," Eva says.

I gloss over when I'll see him again. Keeping it open-ended, like Ben's mom isn't already texting me asking if dates in August work. I feed into her urgency and respond without taking a minute to look at my schedule. "I think so!" I say, just to get her off my back. I should look at my calendar first. I wish she would give me space. I'm grateful to at least have Eva to talk to, even if I stop myself from being fully honest about how daunting all of this is.

"That's so good. I mean, see what happens. I know it's hard—seven years is a long time. You should, you know still try and put yourself out there," Eva tells me.

I wonder what she's really thinking, but I'm grateful for how gentle she is. She's such a good listener.

"I know. I will, that's the thing. There's no way I can keep things going for that long. It would be too much. It's just a lot," I say.

I still have hours on this bus. I pull out a mini bottle of cheap pinot noir I got from a gas station and a cookie, relishing the fleeting comfort of something familiar in this shitty moment.

I love Ben, but I still feel like I'm being pulled in two directions. Stay or go. Stay or go.

CHAPTER 19

HAVING ONE FOOT IN BEN'S world feels like quicksand, but the thought of losing him pulls me in deeper so that only half of me feels fully present here. Half of my heart is anchored with him.

When I arrive at Second Avenue Deli, Dylan, a match from a dating app who I've been out with three times, is already at the table, scanning the menu.

He hesitates before leaning in to hug me hello, smiling with his almond-shaped eyes. He actually looks like a grown-up version of Ben, with his dark brown hair with silver strands, a bigger face, and a more pronounced jawline.

I arrive ten minutes late, punctual for me. We joked on our first date that he is always a half hour early. When we met at a wine bar in the West Village for our first date, Dylan was quiet but charming. He trusted my judgment in wine pairings, so I ordered us a flight of Chablis. My confidence came with ease because deep down, I don't care where any of this really goes. The voided expectation makes it easier to be fully myself.

Dylan has a more relaxed vibe, with a white T-shirt under an unbuttoned gray plaid shirt and slip-on Vans. I can feel his eyes analyzing my body, a black bodysuit tucked into high-waisted black jeans that fit so well I no longer need a napkin security blanket to hide parts of me. I feel awkward when Dylan's gaze lingers, not used to the attention on my body, a walking shadow of myself.

Our towering pastrami sandwiches arrive. We bonded over our love of Jewish delis on our first date, a safe surface-level hour or so of him telling me he works as an engineer for a startup, and me telling him the last time I had a pastrami sandwich was at The Polo Bar with a martini during an interview for my food column. He talked in short sentences, letting me lead most of the conversation. He's handsome, with quirky freckles of personality, like his love of house music and Brooklyn raves, his abandoned dream of being a DJ.

He blushes when I flatter him, fawning over his love of museums. I tell him about the cookie at the Whitney Museum. He says he'd take me to Untitled for dinner if I wanted to. His company is a sweet escape, and I selfishly keep saying yes to his dates, letting him buy me dinner and hoping chemistry will spark, but it hasn't so far.

I take small bites of pastrami. My appetite is waning, and I can barely make it through half. Ben celebrates my progress at the gym and how clean eating will help. My mind starts registering delicious food as a sin. I feel guilty for eating more than I should. I tune out most of the conversation with Dylan but find a thread about his closeness with his brothers endearing.

He shows me a photo of him and one of his brothers in a blow-up pool on the balcony of their old high-rise Upper West Side apartment, big smiles across their faces. Something about the boyish charm of that picture takes me back to the first night I heard Ben laugh at the sushi restaurant in Sag Harbor. And suddenly, I'm sinking into the unbalanced happy sadness of this moment.

"I've been contemplating moving to LA," Dylan tells me. "My brother lives out there. He's a food scientist. He moved there after our mom died."

"Oh, no. I'm so sorry. When did she pass away?" I ask him.

"It's okay. Just a few months ago. It happened really suddenly. One day she had jaundice. Her skin turned yellow. We found out she had pancreatic cancer," he tells me.

I ask him questions about how it happened, why they couldn't do more for her. He tells me they tried everything. That it was too late. That one day, they were on a trip to Bermuda together, and the next, he was taking bereavement leave.

"I'm so sorry, Dylan. That must have been so hard for you," I say, gutted by the unexpected turn this conversation took.

My sadness goes from a wave to a riptide hearing Dylan talk about his loss, and even though his emotions don't show it, I can feel his sadness with mine so deeply.

"Yeah, she died a few months later. It all happened in less than six months."

The heaviness of this moment consumes me, like I could cry onto my pastrami because I realize that neither of us has the capacity to love right now, just that we both so desperately need it.

"Do you think you'll move to LA?" I ask Dylan.

He tells me he's not sure. He talks about considering finding a new job. Maybe working with his brother. He pays for dinner and walks me home. There's no reason why I shouldn't sleep with Dylan, but I have no desire, and he's too respectful to try.

We kiss outside of my apartment, and I can feel his smile, a half-moon on mine, our shadows exposed in street light. A temporary calm from waves of grief. Eventually, we become strangers again.

Ben's sister Tracy and her fiancé Adam got married last month, and I went to the wedding alone. I got my hair and makeup done, put on a navy gown, and watched them walk down the aisle, feeling the weight of my grief with their happiness. It crushed me with every smile. Could none of his family tell I was screaming through our small talk? I must have a brave face.

Ben wanted me to be there for him, but it was so painful to celebrate without him. And I felt weirdly out of place, like a victim or a martyr. His family didn't know how to act around me. It was like they thought it was noble, but they also felt bad for me. I felt bad for me.

Ben's uncle slow-danced with me. It was the sweetest thing anyone did for me that night. It made me feel happy in that moment, and then so fucking sad. Ben called, and I put him on speakerphone to talk to his cousins. I drank a lot of champagne. I talked about work because it was the only shield I had, the only way to show that I wasn't a completely sad loser.

At some point, I had to walk outside because I couldn't breathe. I felt like there was a giant crushing my lungs. My skin got really warm, and I started to feel dizzy and shake. I tried to find a quiet place where no one could see me. I started doing the deep breathing exercise we learned at that meditation, and eventually, it passed.

Ben has a way of being so convincing, guilting me into doing things that I don't want to do. I don't want to be here. Now he wants me to go to his sister Alana's wedding in November, to represent him since he can't go. But I don't want to. This time, I'm saying no. I write him an email:

> Ben, I love you, but there are times when I feel trapped in this relationship. I don't want to plan ahead. And I don't want to commit to anything. I want to do things on my own terms, and I want the freedom to do what I want. You're expecting too much from me, and I don't have anything else to give.
>
> These expectations are being set for me, and they're too much for me to take on. It's selfish of you to expect me to attend all your family events. I can't be your girlfriend and your proxy. The future is so uncertain, and you're putting a lot of pressure on me.

Every chair at the airport food court is full, and I follow Lauren as she weaves through suitcases, people hunched over laptops, and loud family groups, determined to snag us seats so we can eat before our flight to Italy.

"Just hover," she says, her oversized Louis Vuitton bag resting on her suitcase. "Someone will get up."

A couple offers us their table in seconds, and Lauren gives me a "told you" smile, opening up a bag of Cape Cod chips. Lauren and her zero fucks attitude never cease to amaze me, and I get the most joy out of watching her in action.

Work has been crazy, and it's been weeks since I've seen her, so this travel story I'm writing on the Amalfi Coast is the perfect escape. I feel grateful that the career I built has allowed me to go somewhere I've always dreamed of. I feel most like myself when I'm traveling alone, and with Lauren. I relish the independence from Ben, feeling like myself for a moment again.

Lauren agreed to take a few days off work and to buy a plane ticket to tag along with me on one condition: she didn't want to talk about Ben the whole time. At first, I felt hurt, but then I realized that it's easier to not talk about him.

Today might be the best day of my life. I'm on a boat in Capri with my sister and a driver named Luca. He's pouring Lauren and me champagne. The prosciutto di Parma is a salty euphoria on my tongue. It's paired with the freshest slice of mozzarella and tomato I've ever tasted. The olive oil is divine. It's *aperitivo* hour, and I'm gazing out at the cliffs of Capri, feeling pure bliss.

The story I've been assigned is about wine on the Amalfi coast, and we're enjoying some downtime between vineyard tours. My phone doesn't have service, and it's the first time in a long time that I feel fully like myself.

"Come on. Jump in! The water is amazing," Lauren says, pressuring me to dive into the Mediterranean. I don't need much convincing. I plunge in, feeling the cleansing saltwater soothe my skin and crisp sea salt air. This place is paradise and the escape I needed. I feel like I'm living my life again.

Luca, the boat's captain and bartender, made us each an Aperol Spritz. It tastes sweeter than the ones I've had in the city.

"I wish we could stay here forever," I tell Lauren.

She nods beneath her oversized beach hat. The wind laps through my hair when the boat starts up again, and it's intoxicating.

I stare at an abstract painting of a woman with oversized lips and a massive forehead in the foyer of Adam and Tracy's Gramercy Park penthouse.

"This could put our kids through college," I remember Ben telling me. Adam's brother had been gifted Grandma M's famous painting as a wedding gift.

Ben insisted I go to their housewarming party. I told him I wouldn't unless Eva could come. And like a saint, she canceled her plans. With her vintage Fendi baguette bag draped over her shoulder, she joins me to meet the brother of my prison boyfriend.

I'm thankful to have her by my side so I'm not here solo like a widow.

It's exhausting having to carry myself alone. It feels like I'm missing a limb without Ben. Having to put on a happy face and act like everything is okay is getting more and more excruciating.

Adam pours Eva a glass of prosecco while I marvel at the wine refrigerator that fits perfectly into their marble island. I'm so envious of their lifestyle. Despite all of the chaos with Ben, they have continued building their lives, and I can't help but be reminded how stagnant my life feels.

I want this to be my life so desperately.

"How are you?" Adam asks me, handing me a glass. His tone is sincere, and it makes me feel both shy and comforted.

"I'm okay," I say.

"You know, this year has oddly been okay," I say genuinely.

"I mean, it's so sad. It's been really hard with Ben gone. I miss him. But there have been waves of happiness. But then days back here are hard. You know? It's just one day at a time."

"I get it," Adam says, taking a sip of his Macallan. He's not one to open up, but he's strangely the only person in Ben's family who I feel like genuinely cares to ask how I'm doing, and without an expectation that I'll be at the next event, or send Ben more letters in prison, or set a date for our next visit, like Margot pushes me to do. Adam isn't transactional. I feel more at ease around him.

I see Tracy's sister perk up when Eva tells her about her job in fashion. I'm just so happy I don't have to be here alone.

Matt is from New Jersey and ignites my sex drive for the first time since Ben left. I've been under him on my couch, over him on his, in daylight in his living room, his kitchen. His bed. My bed. Our physical chemistry is invigorating.

He's even more of an adult with his clothes on. He owns his apartment in Hoboken. He works in finance. He talks to me about investing in tech startups and wanting to buy more real estate. Life with Matt feels like cruise control.

He picks me up in the city with an iced coffee in the cup holder and tells me, we're "going on a food tour, well sort of."

He read a story I wrote on Anthony Bourdain's favorite restaurants in New Jersey. And an hour later, we're eating fried hot dogs in a dive bar together. I even order a beer, then spend the night at his duplex apartment.

Matt is the perfect distraction. He picks the right table at restaurants—sitting us next to the wood-fired stove at the best restaurant in Hoboken. Our conversations are sensual but never too emotionally deep. On another date, he makes me his grandmother's *kibbeh* recipe, a Syrian meat loaf I've never had. After, we're vertical on his couch, sipping the perfect red wine naked together. He makes my loneliness evaporate, pretending not to notice a missed call I get from Ben, twice, when we're lying in his bed.

He tells me he and his ex broke up. For a moment, I picture us living together in Hoboken. I think about the possibility of becoming a Jersey girl. On one night when he says he has plans with his guy friends, I don't overthink it when he doesn't invite me.

He grows distant eventually. Plans become elusive. I text him on a flight back from a work trip in London, and eventually he tells me that "someone from his ex's circle reached out." I'm shattered because I was starting to feel a real connection with him. For the first time, I felt like I could finally move on from Ben. I'm shattered that our fling ends just as I land back in New York. I dread being alone again. And my mind wanders back to Ben.

Ben has a lot of time on his hands. That's an understatement. He gets old magazines and has this newfound obsession with sending me cutouts of workout routines. He's been working out consistently at the gym and subtly mentions how attracted he is to fit women on our calls and that it would be cool for us to work out together, separately.

"Okay, follow this influencer on Instagram. You ready? Write this down. @FitForBreakfast. See how toned her arms are? And her ass is so perfect," he says.

"My body is never going to look like that," I say, visualizing the ripped physique. "No matter how hard I work out." It bothers me that Ben is trying to compare me to these unrealistic body images.

"Sure, it can—do what I told you—find someone at the gym who has a body you want to look like and ask them if you can follow their workouts."

"Ben, that's so awkward. That's not how it works."

"Yes, it does. I did that all the time. It's how I got all these routines. It was the best thing. I'm telling you. It'll work just find someone."

I put him on speaker as I scroll through my emails. He can always tell when I'm not paying attention.

"Mia," he snaps. "What are you doing? I can tell you're not listening."

"Yes, I am!" I lie. "I was reading about an assignment in Cannes to cover a champagne launch. How fun does that sound?"

I fantasize about sipping champagne and eating baguettes on the French Riviera.

"Mia, you know it's that much harder to watch what you eat on vacation. You have to be disciplined," he says.

"Ben, I don't go away that much. And when I do, I'm going to savor these once-in-a-lifetime opportunities."

I've truthfully never cared about counting calories or working out. I love my appetite. And I'm excited about food. Why shame me for that? It's my passion and my job. It feels like Ben is planting these unwarranted insecurities in my head.

"I think working out can be something we do together, separately—please do this for me?"

"Okay," I say, to get him off my back. I know he doesn't get to talk much, so I try to go easy on him. But he can be annoying, even in prison.

Lauren slaps my hand when I reach for the phone at the dinner table. Ben's constant reminders about working out have rubbed off on me. For the first time, I'm obsessing about my weight. I hardly have an appetite. Ben has called twice already since I came to visit Lauren. He's hounding me about helping him google answers to his history homework. I'm thrilled he's learning in there, but he makes me feel guilty when I don't drop what I'm doing for him.

"Mia, we're having dinner. That's rude!" she says, mid-bite of the chicken scarpariello our mom made.

"Leave her alone!" My mom comes to my defense. She may not agree with my long-distance situation, but she knows how much I care about Ben, and she can tell how hard this has been on me.

"You made me miss the call. Lauren, he only gets so many windows a day to talk!" I say.

"Okay, but you're with your family right now. That's rude. He's got plenty of time in there. I'm sure he'll call back," she says, trying to make light with her token sarcasm. I refrain from calling her a hypocrite for scrolling through her phone moments earlier.

Even though Ben and I talk a lot, I still hate to miss a call.

My mom plops a second spoonful of ravioli on my plate.

"Mia, I think Ben is a little controlling, don't you?" Lauren says, waving her garlic bread. "He calls, and you jump. It's okay to live your life, you know?"

"He's not controlling. If anything, he's supportive. He's always there for me," I say, forking a ravioli.

"I don't know. Even before prison, he had these tendencies. He always had to have a coffee—he had three when he was here. It's like he replaced the alcohol with the caffeine. And he is so insistent you do everything he says. You don't have to jump through all these hoops," she says, then encourages me to keep going on dates.

She doesn't get it. Yes, Ben can be a little much, but she doesn't see his sensitive side like I do.

"And then how many times are you going to have to visit him in prison?"

My mom gives me a nervous stare.

"I told you I don't agree with any of this," my mom says. "You need to let me know if you go—if you go visit him. I want to go with you. Tell his mother I'm coming. I don't want you going alone."

"Mom, it's okay it'll be fine. I don't even know when I'm going," I lie. "But thank you. That means a lot."

"You're my daughter. It breaks my heart to see you going through this. This is the last thing I want for you."

"Mom, it's really okay. He's doing great there. He's okay. I'm okay—we'll see what happens."

I shift the conversation to the brighter subject of my potential Cannes work trip. It's exhausting having to defend Ben with forced optimism. I think about having to quietly sneak away from the bar at Carrie's twenty-seventh birthday last weekend. I couldn't miss his call, but I didn't want our friends to know I was still talking to him, and from prison no less. Then he got mad at me for rushing him off the phone. I can't win.

I find a thick letter in my mailbox when I get home. I romanticize the letters, despite being terrified that my neighbors will see the correctional facility stamps. I smile at the hand-drawn heart on the seal.

Inside is a note telling me how much he misses me, and a pile of magazine cutouts with workouts from old fitness magazines.

I'm on a boat in Saint-Tropez, touring the South of France. The lavender fields and zippy roads through Nice and Cannes and Monaco are a nice distraction from Ben.

I've been freelancing for travel publications to keep sane and am so grateful for my career right now. My friend Henry, a writer for *Vogue*, is also on assignment.

We ditch our champagne glasses and dive into the navy waves. I tread water on the seawall in disbelief that I'm here, but I'm also anxious about how I'll navigate Ben's calls in front of Henry. He's in a blissful bubble of glamor and fashion parties, out with designers nearly every night in New York. He would never understand Ben's situation or even empathize with it.

I worry Henry will get suspicious, wonder why Ben always calls me and why I always rush to pick up. I try not to let it get to me.

Henry is back at the dock, staging a photo shoot for us.

"Don't be so stiff!" he says, uncrossing my arms. "Put your glasses on and look away from the camera."

I can feel my shoulders hiking up. This feels unnatural for me. I'm so insecure in my situation with Ben that it's beginning to affect my confidence, which always came effortlessly with friends and certainly in my professional circle. Even in my new toned body, I feel like an imposter.

"Pretend you're laughing!" Henry commands. "Walk toward me. And don't smile so big."

I refrain from showing my teeth.

The result, shockingly, is a perfect photo. It looks like the aspirational me.

"Okay, you really nailed the shot," I say. "I look so glam."

"Right?" Henry says, trying to figure out the perfect caption. "Should we go with—Cannes do?"

I'm still staring at the photo. I look so carefree and happy. I have a fleeting sense of validation from the way my body looks, but I still feel so unlike myself.

My noticeably chiseled arm. A flat stomach. I look great, but I feel like the worst version of myself. I wonder if Henry can tell I'm hiding something. Like a part of me isn't here. Half of this is an illusion, masked in my red Parisian sunglasses and the $300 swimsuit I can't afford.

"Um," I say, trying to give him a caption as currency for taking this perfect photo.

"Why not… Catch me if you Cannes?" I suggest.

"Okay, and this is why they pay her the big bucks." He jokes with a smile.

I'm in a daze of delectable Camembert, and like clockwork, Ben calls, a reminder of how he'd likely police my portions.

I answer, frantically lowering the volume on my phone so Henry can't hear the pre-recorded prison pleasantry.

"I'm just going to take this," I say, regretting my word choice like it's a business call at 10 p.m. I feel the abruptness of my exit follow me, hoping Henry will just scroll through his phone in my absence.

"Hi, honey," I say. "I was just at dinner with Henry."

"Oh, *oui?* Does Saint-Tropez have that certain *je ne sais quoi?*" Ben says in a cheesy accent that gives me more cringe than charm.

"It does," I respond.

"You're being fake. I can tell. Like you aren't listening to me."

How is it that he can tell I'm anxious or trying to rush him off the phone just by the tone of my voice?

"Ben, no, I'm not!" I say, rolling my eyes.

"Yeah, you are." He loves taunting me.

"Ben, I'm having dinner with Henry. I can't talk long. It's rude that I left so abruptly."

"I want to meet him. Put me on speaker!" Ben says, dying to make a cameo in the south of France from a prison in rural Massachusetts.

"No."

He knows that I don't want anyone I work with to know about us. He's quiet, like I hurt his feelings.

"I told him about you—I just told him you live in Boston and that I want him to meet you one day. Maybe he'll write about our wedding in *Vogue*," I offer, pandering to his ego. Ben loves the idea of being famous.

He doesn't buy it.

"No, come on. Put me on speaker! This will be a way to come out of your shell and stop caring about what other people think. Come on, please, Mia. Seriously, I am so bored in here all day. All I want to do is have a real conversation that's not with my mother or Grandma M, to talk to people like a real person. I'm like a monkey in here. Why do you make it so hard?"

I let out a long sigh. His guilt trip is working.

"Okay, fine."

Henry never met Ben before prison. We're close industry friends, but our friendship is still relatively surface-level, so it's not unusual that they wouldn't have met. As far as Henry knows, we're in a long-distance relationship.

"Henry, you remember I told you about Ben, right? He's in Boston. He just wants to say hi!"

"Hello, sir," Henry says, combing a hand through his perfectly curled brown hair.

"Hi, hope you both are having fun out there—no French kissing!" Ben says, I can hear him laughing at his own joke. He knows Henry is gay but always feels the need to mark his territory.

"Oh my god. You are so corny," I say. "Okay, sweetie. It's getting hard to hear you in here," I lie.

"Why don't you try me in the morning, okay? Sound good? Love you too." I hang up before he finishes saying goodbye, anxiously trying to beat the operators from cutting us off before 10:30.

"It's so cute that he insists on calling you. Like, on the phone," Henry says, half making fun of me.

"It's like, so flip phone era of you."

I laugh it off. I still feel insecure, but I coyly play it off.

"Oh, Ben is so old school. It's sweet actually. He loves a phone call, especially when I'm traveling. He just has to hear my voice. I felt bad I missed his call before, so I had to answer."

Henry nods, his attention span diverted to a Ralph Lauren ad for a sample sale on Instagram.

"Well, that's sweet," he says, slightly condescending. "How did you two meet again?"

"The Hamptons," I say, hoping our origin story will convince him that Ben is legit.

"Well, is he going to move to New York or what? You obviously can't move there—that would be, like, media suicide," he says.

"Oh, yeah," I say. "Definitely—he wants to. He just. Well, he…" I can hear myself fumbling for a believable lie. "He just got this promotion at work. He works at his uncle's company, and he's managing a big team, and he needs to stay in this position for at least a few more years." I hope I'm selling it.

"What is the company?"

I can't tell if Henry is genuinely curious or just being polite.

"Could he not just transfer to New York or is there a satellite office?"

"I wish," I say, nervously playing with the olives in my martini glass. "I wish it were that easy, but we'll see. We're just taking it slow. You know, we're really not in a rush."

"Anyway, I'm buying us another round of champagne," I say, hoping he'll drop the subject.

I chug the rest of my martini so fast, I can feel the hangover headache already setting in. A waitress comes back with a tin of the finest Osetra imperial black caviar. Henry and I drape a greedy amount over our thumb and index fingers, like addicts of excess. The salty flavor of the ocean baptizing my palate. And suddenly, the night is reborn.

"This is better than coke," he says.

CHAPTER 20

I GET TO FIRST AVENUE and see a girl layered in a puffer jacket and gloves already lined up near the bus stop.

"This is the 7 a.m. to Boston, right?" I ask. She smiles, nodding. The sun is rising over the East River.

I've been dreading today and all the hurdles I have to go through before I finally get to see Ben. I put my headphones on and try to zone out, but I can't stop thinking about what Ben will be like, if he'll look different since I last saw him. It's been six months.

I've been through a lot this week. My mom can't bear the thought of me having to see Ben in prison, but she's rational enough to know that I love him and it isn't an easy situation. Lauren listens, but I know deep down she doesn't support any of this. It's a lot to keep inside, and I wish I could be more open.

Even Eva, who has been my rock up until now, doesn't really understand. She listens, which is more than I can ask for, but I'm self-conscious that she's judging and wondering why I'm still engaging in this relationship. Why I'm putting myself through all of this pain.

When Margot and I finally get to the prison, there are already about twenty or so women waiting for the first group. I quickly grab my number, thirty-seven, scribbling my name, Ben's, and his inmate number on the paper, and bring it to the window with my license. We still have about an hour or so to wait. I don't recognize any of the guards from my last trip, but one of them greets Margot with a familiar, "Hi, Mrs. Cohen," when they see her walk in with Terry, bending down to pet Ben's dog. She's grown weaker from the chemo but is still walking, which Ben says is a blessing enough.

I still can't believe Margot got her trained to be a service dog just so Ben can see Terry in prison. I decide to stand, flipping through an old issue of *Bon Appétit*. I know I won't be on my feet much today. I escape in the pages of tarts and soufflés and read a trend story on how the cruller is the new Cronut. I don't have much of an appetite lately.

Finally, they call my number. My bra goes off in the metal dictator again, but it's not as daunting as it was during my first visit. I sign the book. Margot waves to me, mouthing that she'll be out front at 8 p.m.

This time, there are dogs sniffing us for drugs, which means that something bad must have happened recently. We make our way through the garden again; it's now covered in snow. Now it feels more like prison.

I hand the guard my paper, and he prompts me to have a seat until Ben comes out wearing a black T-shirt that says, "Project Youth." It's a seminar he's been participating in where he talks to kids about his accident and the lessons he's learned. His hair is shorter, more like a crew cut you'd see on a marine. He hugs me for a long time, and I can feel how much more muscular he's gotten since my last visit.

"I missed you so much," he says, kissing me and holding me close. I can feel my shoulders lower, tension releasing from my body in his arms. We're allowed to kiss hello, but if you linger too long, a corrections officer will reprimand Ben.

"Hmm, want to sit back there?" Ben asks, motioning to a row near the windows and coffee machine. I nod and follow, still in awe that I'm actually with him, holding his hand again like we used to.

It's December 1st, and they've already decorated for the holidays with "Merry Christmas" signs, cheap tinsel, and a giant eight-foot Christmas tree near the photo station. They even changed the painting landscape to match. It actually looks really nice.

It's almost 1:30, and Ben is starving. He tells me his vending machine order.

"Ready? Can you get me a double cheeseburger, chicken Caesar salad, a strawberry Chobani, a chocolate chip Clif bar, a Rip-n-Dip, and an apple juice?"

"Oh my god. How do you eat all that?" I say, forgetting that the food in there must be so awful. Of course, he's starving. Thank god Margot filled up the cards with forty dollars. I swarm the vending machine like a vulture, scouring for the double cheeseburger. If you don't get to it early, they sell out.

I find everything but the chicken Caesar salad. Then I microwave his Rip-n-Dip. It's a weird calzone-looking thing that comes with a sauce that's allegedly marinara.

Two other women and I wait around the microwave.

"How do you cook this thing?" I ask, fumbling with the wrapping.

"I usually pop that in for about a minute and ten," says a woman with a blonde bob, who must be in her fifties or early sixties.

"It helps if you put a plate over it. It makes the edges a little crispy," the second woman, a nice Spanish lady I met in the visiting room, offers.

"Ah, good idea," I say, reaching for a paper plate. "You know, this honestly doesn't look so bad." I find comfort in our mutual roles.

"Yeah, they got a bunch of new food items in this month," the blonde woman says.

"I don't eat it, but he loves it," the woman says, chuckling. I find comfort in their solidarity.

I remember Ben pointing to the blonde woman earlier. Her husband was the subject of a crime show on TV—for money laundering, or something. Ben wants me to interview him over the phone for an exposé piece I could pitch. I actually considered it.

"Yeah, my husband gets it all the time. Make sure to peel off the paper over the sauce so it warms up," the Spanish woman says.

I come back with four plates of food and an apple juice for Ben.

I can't get over how good he looks. His pecks are defined with rock-solid muscle. He flexes his stomach for me, and I can feel the six-pack beneath his shirt. I run my fingers through his new buzz cut. He tells me how painful getting a haircut is here because it's a straight-up blade on his head. He points to some of the scabs. I still think he looks handsome.

"See that guy with the long ponytail in the white T-shirt?" he says, pointing out a middle-aged man. He's walking toward a woman sitting by the guard's booth. "That's my roommate. He hasn't seen her in over ten years."

"Who is she?"

"I think it's his ex-wife."

It's difficult for me to watch two people reunite after so long. I can now empathize more and more with the people in here. I no longer see them as just criminals, but rather as people who made mistakes. Those mistakes cost some of these people the rest of their lives.

"What did he do again?"

"Strangled someone to death," Ben says nonchalantly. It makes me a little uneasy.

"Oh my god." The old man looks so gentle.

We watch him and the woman hug for a long time. Ben tries to wave his roommate over, but he doesn't see him.

There aren't as many kids in the visiting room this time. It's mostly wives and girlfriends and adult family members.

"See those two over there?" Ben points to a man who looks like he's in his late thirties or forties sitting next to an older woman and man.

"They're father and son. They've been in here for over twenty years. Tony and I prank each other all the time. He threw water on me when I didn't wake up to go to the gym on time today," he says.

"He's been here for twenty years already? He must have been a teenager when he came in."

I can't get over how young he looks. His hair is buzzed like Ben's. He's handsome.

"He was. He was in the mob, and something happened. Someone was trying to kill him."

"So, what happened?"

"His dad took care of it."

"What? So, the dad killed the guy for his son?"

"Yes, and now they're both here."

"Forever?"

"Yup."

The whole thing feels so surreal, like stories you hear about on TV.

"At least they're here together."

My mind tries to make sense of their life sentences. I can't even fathom it.

"Want some?" Ben asks, cutting into the Rip-n-Dip. Maybe I'm just starving—I hadn't eaten since early morning, but it actually looks good. It reminds me of the pepperoni rolls my dad used to make.

"Sure, that actually looks good."

"It's new. I haven't tried it."

He cuts into it with a plastic fork and knife and dips a little piece into the sauce.

"Wow, it's so good." I laugh, already feeling guilty about the calories. "It's like a pizza bagel or something."

"Yeah, it's not bad. I've seen a lot of the guys get them, so I wanted to try it," Ben says.

"So have you been cooking back there?"

"No, it's a pain in the ass. You have to reserve a time slot and book the hot plate, and by the time your day comes around, you might have something else going on, like the gym or library, so it's not worth it. Every week, one of the guys will buy food, and someone will cook it up, and we all eat."

"Aw, that's nice. What do they make?"

"It's nothing crazy. Usually rice and beans; we've had a lot of chili."

"What about pizza?"

"Yeah, sometimes they make pizza. I have a leftover package of clams I'll eat later tonight."

I cringe at the thought.

"There are so many things that will be banned from my eating list when I get out of here."

"Like what?"

"Hot dogs. I can't ever have hot dogs again. They've ruined them. We have them like every week. Chicken pot pie, none of that. No stew of any kind."

"Wow, it's all that bad?"

"Yeah, I'm just sick of it."

We're both silent for a few minutes. I lose track of how long we've been sitting.

"I love you," I say.

"I love you too," he says, choking up a little. He seemed a little guarded during the first hour, like he was trying not to get emotional.

"I don't know. It's just, I love seeing you here, and I'm so happy you're here, but it's so hard because I don't want you to leave."

I just hug him, holding him to my chest for a few minutes. I'm too exhausted to cry, but it's hard not to. I try to stay in the present. I wrap my hand around his and hold it.

"Do you want to hear my Project Youth speech?" he asks.

"Yeah, you read it to me already."

"I added in a lot of new things," he says.

"Okay, yeah, I want to hear it."

By the end of it, Ben is teary-eyed. He has to give this speech every Thursday and Friday to a new group of high schoolers and college kids. It must be so hard for him to relive the accident, over and over again.

I ask how he manages, and he says, "This is my life now. This is my story."

"I'm so proud of how you're handling all this. I really am. I think you should really think about coming up with a program yourself. People need to hear this," I say.

"I know. I've been thinking about how I can. I really see myself speaking about this; going into schools, doing talks."

I hug him. He smells like cologne. He says he used a magazine sample.

We only have an hour left, barely that. I glance around the room and see couples playing board games like Scrabble or Connect Four. There's a football game on in the background, but only the guards are watching. It's so easy to be present with Ben. He's the only person to fully see me. I'm able to be vulnerable with him. To be myself. It's one of the reasons I can't let go. I'm so attached to the feeling of calm I've grown to associate with his company. His presence. He makes me feel less alone. I'm addicted to our emotional connection, even when it's unstable at times.

I wish time could stop so I didn't have to feel the pain of leaving without him. This type of concentrated connection could be therapy for so many couples who take each other for granted.

In that last hour, Ben and I laugh. And cry. And sit quietly just staring at each other, my forehead on his. We talk about what we'll do when he gets out. We fight about the kind of Christmas tree we'll get. I insist we chop down a real one upstate, and Ben jokingly refuses to deal with the cleanup, insisting we get a really nice fake tree.

"I'll get us the most expensive, real-looking fake tree there is," he promises. It's 7:30.

"I can't believe how quickly that went," Ben says.

"I know, it feels like I just got here."

Ben and I finish a pack of fruit gummies, and I throw out the last of the trash. I hug him so hard. It feels like we can both just get up and walk out, and for a moment, I forget that he can't come with me. That's the hardest part.

Margot picks me up. I'm starving, and normally, I try to be polite, but I have to let her know. Luckily, she's taking us for Chinese. I'm not taking a train until tomorrow morning.

"You first," I say. The wind is so strong, I have to pry the glass door to Empire Hunan open.

"How many?" the familiar host asks.

"Just two please, not for hibachi," Margot says.

"What kind of appetizers do you like? Order whatever you want," Margot insists when we sit down.

"Oh, I'll eat anything. I'm really not picky."

"You have to pick something. Whatever you want—dim sum, lo mein, a ginger salad, wonton soup?" she says, reading the menu out loud. "I don't care."

I know Margot won't relent until I pick something.

"Do you like gyoza?" I ask.

"Are those dumplings? I like dumplings. Are they fried? They could probably do steamed if you don't want fried. I know it doesn't say it on the menu, but they'll do it."

Of course, I wanted fucking pan-fried. I just left my boyfriend in a medium-security prison. I'm too tired to insist.

"What kind of entrees do you like?"

I browse for the most basic thing on the menu. I remember Ben told me he got food poisoning here once with his sister, but he kept coming back because it's the only Asian place in town. I look for a chicken dish. Chicken teriyaki. Perfect. No one can fuck up chicken.

"I think I'm going to get the chicken teriyaki," I say.

"Oh, I've never had that before, but it's probably big enough for us to share, right?" Margot asks.

Jesus Christ, no. I don't want to share this meal with you.

"Yeah, that's fine," I say.

"Do you want white rice?"

No. Brown.

"Yes, that's fine." I'm trying to make this order easy so we can get out of here fast and I can finally sleep. We order, and the waiter comes back with our steamed dumplings.

"Oh, maybe we should get a second dish," Margot says. Obviously. "Can we see another menu?" she calls out to the waiter. "Go ahead. Pick out another dish. What else do you like?" she asks me.

I'm so exhausted by this point that I can't even finish a sentence, let alone pick a dish that both of us will like. I keep trying to be agreeable but realize I'm using a saccharine tone. I wish she would just pick something and stop making everything such a process.

"Um, I like any kind of chicken."

"Another chicken dish?"

There's no reasoning with this woman. She likes to make it seem like I have a choice.

"I love General Tso's," I suggest finally, my voice less accommodating.

"Oh well, that's fried," she says.

"Margot," I snap. "I'm really okay with this dish that I have. I'm not that hungry. It's late, please, you pick."

The chicken teriyaki finally arrives, and it appears to be edible. Thank God. I shovel two heaping spoonfuls of rice onto my plate and serve Margot a few slices of chicken. I savor the first bite of real food I've had all day.

"So, how's your mom doing?" Margot asks between bites of chicken. I can tell she's about to meddle.

"She's good," I say. "She's probably at my sister's." I hope she'll leave it at that, but I know better.

"Does she know you came up here?" She keeps going, like a wind-up doll.

"No, she doesn't know," I say, trying to prepare a reason. "I just figured it was better if she didn't." I can see her eyes widening like she's trying to make sense of what I'm saying.

I don't want to talk about my family. It's already exhausting trying to explain the situation to them; I don't want to explain their reactions to Margot. I'm so sick of having to manage everyone's emotions. It's like walking around ten thousand fucking land mines.

"I don't know how much Ben told you, but we actually got into an argument over this. My mom is so supportive, and she loves Ben, but she just doesn't feel comfortable with her daughter going to prison." I say, folding my napkin for no reason.

"And I honestly don't blame her," I say, reaching for a sip of water to let Margot process.

"Oh, I had no idea, no Ben didn't say anything—he doesn't like to bring up anything personal between you two," she says. I know she has to be lying. Ben tells his mother everything—everything—even when I tell him not to.

"You know, I don't like to get in between you two, but I let my kids make their own decisions. You know, I would never want to play God—I just wouldn't want to be to blame, you know, if something ended up going wrong," she says.

I can feel the palms of my hands starting to clam up; an anxious jitter runs through me, and my entire body starts to shake. I feel uncontrollably angry. Whatever appetite I had is gone. Here we go, another fucking lecture. Is this woman seriously going to do this now? After I had a fourteen-hour fucking day.

"You know, if this were Alana, and let's say, she was in this situation with her fiancé, and he was going away for something—I would never try to tell her what to do because I know how much she cares about him," she keeps going.

I can feel my body tense more and more, and my heart starts beating faster. Pure rage. I try to take a deep breath.

"I would just try to be…supportive to her, you know?"

I nod and smile like a mad person.

"I mean, let's say they were dating for years, and he was a good guy. Of course, I would be devastated, but I'd know how much she cared about him."

I can no longer process the words coming out of Margot's mouth. I just watch the lines on her face expand and contract. This woman is really trying to tell me she'd be supportive if her only daughter was dating someone in prison?

I know she would do everything in her power to ensure the exact opposite. I can picture her lining up single guys she meets in the grocery store or at the beach—hell, she'd probably bribe them if she had to—to distract Alana from dating a criminal. What really sends me over the edge is how selfish she's being. She wants the best for her son, that I know, but

I'm not a fucking rag doll she can throw around and adapt to this fucked up situation.

"I just wouldn't want to play God," she repeats. She nibbles on the fried noodle chips. She's even inconsistent about her fried food habits.

"You know, like what if they really are meant to be? I would never forgive myself if I was the one who discouraged her."

I feel my chest starting to close up, and I start to gasp for air. I realize I'm having a full-blown panic attack at the table. I keep hearing the words, "I just wouldn't want to play God," repeat over and over in my head until I finally lose it.

The words come out of my mouth like wildfire before my brain can process what I'm saying. It's one of the few times in my life where I explode with exactly what I'm thinking, unfiltered, without sugarcoating a word.

"Margot, stop. *Please stop,*" I say, raising my voice octaves louder than I should in a dining room. A woman at the table next to us looks up from her plate.

It startles Margot so much she looks like she's choking on her soup.

"Don't say that. You cannot possibly say that. That's not fair. None of this is fair. Don't you say for a minute how you would react in this situation. You can't. My mother has been beyond supportive—my whole family, for that matter, especially given the circumstances." My voice is trembling now, and I'm talking so loudly the couple next to us can't help but stare.

"My mother has been beyond supportive, and of all people, you should understand. She sacrificed so that me and my sister can have everything. And we do. I do. I have everything I ever imagined possible. You know she loves Ben. She loves him like a son, but it destroys her that her daughter is in pain."

I'm sobbing into my shitty suburban teriyaki.

Margot looks like she's on the verge of tears too. The wrinkles in her crow's feet show her age in the light; her faded light-pink eye shadow glistens at the corners of her eyes.

"I try to make it seem like everything is okay, but it's not. I know that I don't show it, but I shouldn't have to. This year has brought so much pain, and it kills my mother to see me go through this, the trauma of all this, because it's exactly what she's been trying to protect me from her whole life."

There is a brief moment of silence for the first time that whole night. Our meals are cold.

"I had…" Margot says, slowing down and choosing her words carefully. "I had no idea. You've never said anything."

"I shouldn't have to, Margot. How could you not know how much this has weighed on me, on my whole life? How could you be so blind? This is not what I want for my future," I say, looking her straight in the eyes, still shaking. But I'm proud of standing up for myself.

"It's not easy for me to come up here. It's not easy for me to walk into that prison. This has taken a lot out of me, but I do it." I'm holding back tears again. "I do it because I love your son."

Another moment of silence fills the air as she sits with her head down like a scolded puppy. I want a drink. No, I want to sleep for a long, long time. And just to spell it out precisely for her, I finally utter: "I am not okay, and I am in pain."

Now Margot is sobbing, so much so that the waitress silently slips her a paper napkin before disappearing into the kitchen. The other nosy dinner guests finally turn away to give us some privacy, but it's too late. The show is over. Everything is literally out on the table.

Margot pats the corners of her eyes with a napkin. Her mascara is running.

"I'm sorry, Margot. I didn't mean for that to happen. I just had to let you know; none of this has been easy for me."

"I'm so sorry, sweetie. I should have known. This is my fault. Of course, it's been hard, and I want you to know that your mother has been supportive, of course she has," she says.

I know she's about to backpedal on everything she said. I want to believe she means it. How could she not realize how insensitive she's been?

"You're right. It's unfair for me to say those things," she says.

I know her intention is to protect Ben, but she crossed the line. I'm still shaking, coming down from the rush of anger that consumed me.

All I wanted was dinner and a little bit of Zen after the anxiety-ridden day in prison. Now I just feel fucking awkward sitting with this woman who isn't even my mother—or mother-in-law, for that matter—in a claustrophobic suburb. I want to go home. I want my own mother.

"You're not going to finish the chicken? Oh, I hope I didn't ruin your appetite," Margot says, trying to smooth things over like she always does.

Of course, I wasn't going to finish the fucking chicken. Then she has the audacity to whisper with remorse, "Please don't tell Ben."

Ben is the first person I will tell. Oh, I am going to kill him for making me spend another weekend with his mother. I've told him so many times that I just want a hotel. I just want to pay my own way. "Let me be independent." But he insists I spend time with his family like a broken record. This is the last time I sanction myself to this prodding.

The rest of the night, Margot does the exact opposite of what I need. Ben has told her not to come in if my door is closed, but of course, she doesn't listen. I've never wanted to chase a handful of Xanax with a bottle of vodka so badly in my life.

"You know, I'm glad you were so honest with me," she says. "I don't want you to be afraid to tell me anything. This hasn't been easy for anyone, and I guess my way of dealing with it is to keep focusing on one day at a time. But I realize not everyone deals with it that way."

I just nod and agree. I have nothing else to give. It's too late to text and bitch to anyone. My sister will yell at me for being there in the first place. Eva is probably sick of hearing me complain. I just want to be alone and cry. But Margot has an insane way of making amends.

"Oh, I have to show you the photos of Terry's cancer before they remove the tumor." She leaves the room for a moment, and I briefly consider grabbing a pillow to scream into. Instead, I take a deep breath and try to calm my nerves.

"Oh wait, I brought you a little something from the outlets," she says, leaving the room again. Even Terry looks exhausted from all the commotion. Margot returns holding a dark gray, long-sleeve V-neck shirt from the Gap. It's so basic, but exactly something I'd pick out for myself.

"Thank you, Margot. You didn't have to do that. This is so my taste," I say, holding the shirt up to my stomach.

I feel like I yelled at a small child. Despite our dinner fiasco, I know Margot's heart is in the right place. I know she cares about me, maybe even loves me like a daughter.

"I'm glad you love it," she says, smiling.

I don't want to be rude, but since Margot can't read social cues, I know I need to be blunt. I get back into bed.

"Does the TV work?" she asks, playing with the remote. I sneak a glance at myself in the mirror. My dark circles are alarming.

"Oh, I don't know. It's fine though. I only put it on for the extra light at night. I don't even watch it," I say.

She's still fiddling with the remote, so I get under the covers. She still won't take the hint. "Margot, don't worry about it," I say. "It's fine. What time should I set my alarm for?"

"Well, I thought we'd get breakfast at the diner at 9 before you leave."

"Perfect," I say. "I'll set my alarm for 8."

"Okay. Are you sure you don't want me to try and fix your TV?" she says.

"No, it's really okay. I'm just going to go to sleep now."

"Okay," she says, in her chirpy voice. "I'll let you sleep. Goodnight, sweetie."

"Goodnight."

I try some breathing techniques, and my body eventually surrenders.

I dread walking down the halls at work. Everyone knows me as a ray of sunshine, but I am absolutely dying inside with every "Hey!" "How are you?" "Sounds good!" "Great!" "Will do!" I've muttered over the last few months to avoid talking about my personal life. I'd have to unravel this whole, excruciating story.

"How was your weekend?" Leah asks.

"It was good. Just visited some family upstate. Nothing too exciting," I lie. I wonder if she can tell. This conversation is making me anxious. I don't want to be here. Why are we working so close to the holiday? I politely return the question and walk to the bathroom so I can have a moment to collect myself in a rare span of silence. I wonder if anyone can tell how much I'm faking. I wonder if anyone can see the sadness beyond my cheery exterior. I am drowning.

"Great dress," another colleague tells me as I walk out of the bathroom. I glance down at the leopard print cotton knit dress that's now too big on me.

"Thank you! Zara! Thirty dollars—I got it a few years ago. It's such a great staple. I'll send you the link."

If she only knew that the last time I wore this was at a prison.

"If only it weren't so taboo to start a podcast called *Cabernet and the Clinky*," I joke to Ben, on our recorded call that night, taking a long sip of my Josh Cab Sauv. Crumbs from my chocolate are scattered on my nightstand. I've given up cleaning them. I have no one to impress these days.

It makes us both laugh, at least. "Pitch it to Spotify!" he jokes.

"Hey, did you get those sunglasses I wanted? The ones I sent you from the magazine clipping?" he asks.

Ben now flags items he sees in magazines for me to buy so that he can come home to everything he's missed. It's a way for him to feel like he's still living his life, that people still think of him as a human, not a prisoner. But no, I haven't bought it for him yet. I can barely pay my rent, let alone invest in something that might be obsolete by the time he gets out.

"So, you didn't get them?" he presses.

"Ben, no, I'm sorry—I haven't had the chance, and I mean, you don't need them right now—why should I spend the money?"

"Spend the money? I had Margot send you a Venmo for Christmas gifts, didn't I? It makes me think you don't care about us. Like you won't be here to give them to me when I get out."

Oh, this is where this conversation is going tonight.

"Ben, you know I love you. I just—can you give me a break? I didn't get a chance."

"Whatever. It's clearly not important to you, or you'd have made it a priority."

"Ben, don't do this."

He hangs up.

He doesn't call me for a day, which leaves me feeling uneasy. Especially because I can't call him back.

Ben calls me the next day. He tells me he's sorry, that he overreacted. That he won't ever bring it up again. He writes me a New Year's card with fireworks colored in crayon, and he reads it to me over the phone:

"Knowing you these past two-and-a-half years has been a silver lining in a very tumultuous situation. But despite all the difficulties, all the people who tried to influence your decision about letting me into your life, you decided to follow your heart. Mia, your courage to follow your heart is what makes you so different from everyone else I've ever met. It has me head-over-heels for you. We don't know what the future holds, but I sure as hell hope that my future has you in it. Happy New Year, my lovely Mia. May this year be your best yet.

Love,
Ben."

Free Fall

CHAPTER 21

WORKING OUT IS THE ONLY time I don't feel pain. Sweat drips down my face. I'm in a 104-degree room doing burpees to the *Flashdance* song "What a Feeling." I've become obsessed with a hot HIIT workout class near my apartment. It puts your body through pure hell, but when you come out, there's this wave of euphoria I'm becoming addicted to.

"We carry children, we carry groceries—just five more burpees!" my instructor, a gay Broadway actor, encourages. I feel like I'm going to faint, but somehow, I keep going.

I'm starting to feel less and less like myself. When Leah left the newspaper, things started going downhill. The food section was cut. She got a job at a food magazine and said she'd hire me if she could, but I can't afford to wait.

Instead, I took a breaking news reporter role. I can finally afford my bills and student loans. But the pace of the news cycle gives me anxiety. It's too soon to quit.

The release I get from this class is the only peace I've had since Ben was here. I think about him joining me on the mat next to mine. I wonder if everyone is suffering as much as I am. You have to be a little crazy to be in a class like this. And hell, my jeans are starting to fit better. Ben sent me more magazine cutouts of low-carb diets. I don't need a diet. I've lost my appetite. Food isn't as exciting. He loves sending me photos of fitness instructors and their workouts. He compliments my progress and says I shouldn't be afraid to do more—to go twice a day. That I'll feel even better. I'm proud of myself for even committing to this one workout. I'm not doing it to look better; I'm doing it for the release. "In a few years, you can look like that," Ben says of the fitness-model pictures he sends.

But I'm not doing these workouts to change my body. I actually miss my curves. I miss my appetite.

Ben is already waiting for me. He looks so handsome in the gray V-neck sweater I love. I'm so happy to see him. I wrap my arms around him, and we hug for a long time. He kisses me in front of the crowded visiting room. I don't care about PDA like I used to.

"You look so good," he says to me. "Like, really good. I don't even think you realize."

"Thank you," I say. I hadn't noticed. I hate that his words give me more validation than my own.

We find two empty seats next to an older Asian man sitting with his granddaughter.

"Sorry to keep you waiting," I say. "The waiting room is the most crowded I've seen it in a long time."

"That's okay, baby," he says. "I've had a busy morning. I got up, had breakfast, and took my Spanish class, then I worked out, and by the time I finished, it was time to come see you. How was the bus ride?"

"It was okay. Yeah, not too long. I got up at 5. But I got lucky. No one was sitting next to me. I did that thing you told me to do: I put my headphones on and pretended to be sleeping so no one asks to sit with me."

"I told you it works!" he says, excited that I took his advice.

"We have to take a photo," he says, glancing at the backdrop. It's the same Boston skyline they had up before Christmas. Couples are already lining up to take their photos. "You want to?"

The photographer is a lifer, but he worked that digital Canon like a BFA photographer at the Met Gala. I wish I could post some of the photos he took on Instagram; they're that good. Who knew a digital camera had better lighting than my iPhone?

Ben had me scope out the vending machines before the rest of the prison wives and girlfriends got to them. I bought us a bag of Skittles to share. They were hard as a rock, probably past their sell-by date. We both laughed, feeding each other Skittles.

"Did you get my email?" Ben says.

"Which one?"

"You know, the one about the photos I want you to send me?"

I've never sent a "sext" in my life, mainly because I never felt like I had a body worthy of showing off. So, naturally, I refused to send Ben photos that would be seen by God knows how many people. All mail is photocopied before he gets it.

"Come on. You know I'm so turned on by you," he says.

I didn't realize that my arm is around him when one of the officers, a woman with short black hair, comes over to reprimand us.

"Oh, sorry!" I say. Ben doesn't seem to care. He reaches for my right arm and rolls up my sleeve, tickling it up and down like he used to in bed. It's good to be close to him again.

Ben tells me about the Innocence Project, a group that helps innocent people who are incarcerated fight for their freedom. I ask if there are men in there who have been falsely imprisoned, and he says there are a few in his block who claim to be. When I look around the room, I don't see villains. I see fathers, and husbands, and sons, and grandparents. Normal, everyday people who could love and feel and, maybe, deserved to have a second chance. What good is it being locked up in a prison for the rest of their lives?

"Do you see that guy over there?" Ben says, eyeing a man in his forties. "He's been here since he was nineteen."

"What did he do?" I ask.

"Killed someone. He doesn't even remember it."

This man has spent decades repenting for a mistake.

"It's not fair," I say.

"I bet you would never have thought that way if it weren't for my situation," he says.

He's right.

Ben tells me the time is going by so fast. A month feels like a day to him. He spends his days teaching some of the new inmates how to work out. He wants to work at his AA sponsor's company when he gets out. I tell him I have a colleague based at our Boston office who comes to New York sometimes, and joke about how I should just commute with him. Ben entertains the idea for a second, joking about how I should stay with his mother in Marblehead and commute twenty minutes into Boston and see how I like it. This turns into a familiar conversation about where he'll move after his sentence.

"I don't care where we live, as long as I'm with you," he says.

We only have an hour left of our visit, and Ben still has an uneaten cheeseburger from the vending machine. I microwave it for him and get him another apple juice. Ben scarfs it down. I'm still amazed by his appetite and how he hasn't managed to gain a pound, just muscle, since he's been here.

"I don't want you to leave," he says, pulling me in close.

"I know, neither do I," I say, thinking about the lonely ride home. I can't believe I'd been in New York only ten hours earlier. Maybe I was starting to feel time the way Ben did.

He masks his sadness by lightly kissing around my neck; he knows how ticklish I am.

"Ben! Stop it," I say, slapping away his hand. "I hate that."

"You stop it," he says, mocking me playfully.

I hate being tickled, and he knows it, but he loves getting a reaction.

"Let me see your arm," he says.

I cross my arms.

"Come on. Let me see it," he says.

He starts rubbing up and down my arm when I feel his hand grazing my chest.

"Ben, stop! What are you doing?" I say, pulling back.

"Come on. Let me do it," he says, insistent.

I'm literally being felt up in a prison visiting room. I keep telling him to stop. I keep saying no. Ben is so persistent, and no one is looking, so I just sort of freeze and reluctantly let it happen. I can feel his hand on my breast. I wonder if this is actually turning him on.

"Okay, that's enough," I say. "Seriously, stop it."

"Come on. Let me do it," he says again.

One of the guards abruptly rushes at us, yelling for Ben to come with him.

Fuck. Fuck. Fuck. Of course, they were watching us. I stay calm and completely still, which surprises me.

Five minutes pass, and Ben still doesn't come back. Fuck. What are they going to do to him? What are they going to do to me? Another few minutes pass, and the woman guard starts walking toward me. Fuck.

"You have to leave. Your visit's over," she says. "You're out."

I don't know what to do. I get up and quickly grab the photos we took. Ben's ID is still sitting on the chair. I give it to her. The entire visiting room stares as I'm escorted out of the room. I never get in trouble. This is mortifying. The guard walks me outside.

"What's going on?" I ask, my voice more frantic now.

"They saw something in the camera. Something inappropriate. You'll be getting a letter in the mail about it."

A cold, nervous shake overcomes me.

"I'm so sorry, I don't know what happened. We were just..." I was trying to catch my breath, trying not to cry, although I probably should have. Maybe she'd sympathize with me more.

"We were just joking around."

"I know, but our superintendent saw something on the camera. It came from the higher ups. The rules have gotten stricter. You can't have contact like that."

"I'm sorry," I just keep apologizing. I must look like a deer in headlights.

"It's just," I try to explain our situation to her. "It's just we haven't seen each other in months. I think he just…" I try to catch my breath. "I think he was just excited and didn't mean to do anything wrong."

"You have to leave. The visit is over," she says. She turns to go back inside.

"Will I be able to come back tomorrow? I came all the way from New York on a bus today, and I don't…I don't know where I'll go."

"I wouldn't try coming back tomorrow," she says.

The walk back to the main check-in feels surreal. I've never been so ashamed or embarrassed in my life. I'm afraid this will go on some sort of record. What if they take away my visiting privileges? What if this is the last time I ever get to see Ben? We didn't even get to say goodbye. The old me would have started bawling, but I can't cry. I just shake. Margot is waiting.

"What happened? Is everything okay?"

I must look like I just saw a ghost.

"No," I finally say.

"Something really bad just happened. They kicked me out of the visiting room. I didn't get to say bye to Ben."

"What? You're kidding. What happened?" she says.

"They said they saw something on the camera, something inappropriate."

Before I can even finish my sentence, Margot makes her way to the guards she knows at the glass window. A woman with short brown hair and a badge that says Rodney seems concerned. She makes a call, then tells us the new rules are much stricter than before. Margot musters up fake tears and says it must have been a mistake. She explains that I'm visiting from New York and I haven't been here in six months. This was my one visit with my fiancé.

Margot tries to drag emotion from me. "Don't worry, sweetie. It'll be okay," she says, almost commanding me to cry so the guards will feel sorry for me. But I just can't. I feel so overwhelmed and depleted, I can't even cry. If anything, I want to scream. Scream at Ben for humiliating me and making this happen. I just explain in a monotone how bad I feel, and that I hope Ben is okay.

"It was just a misunderstanding," is all I keep saying.

I'm furious at Ben. How can he be so stupid? If he had just listened to me, if he had just dropped it, we wouldn't be in this situation. He did this to himself. I don't blame the guards for ending the visit. It infuriates me how little self-control he has, even after everything.

My cell phone starts ringing. It's Ben. I walk outside.

"Hey, is everything okay?" he asks.

"Yeah, I'm with your mom now." It's freezing outside, and I don't have a jacket. I'm still shaking.

"Listen, it was all just a misunderstanding. They said they saw something inappropriate, but I explained to them that we were just joking around."

I know we can't talk about anything because the call is being recorded. And it could be incriminating for Ben.

"What's going to happen?" I ask.

"I don't know." Ben sounds like he's on the verge of tears. "They gave me a ticket and said I would have a hearing to discuss it."

"What does that mean? Do you think, do you think they'll let me come back?"

"I'm sure it'll be okay," Ben says, but neither of us knows what's going to happen. The correction officers can do whatever they want. They could take away contact visits, or worse, ban me from the prison altogether.

I'm getting angrier and angrier with Ben, at how selfish he was. I came all the way up here. He asks too much of me. I just want to go home.

One of the correction officers must have noticed I was shivering.

"Hey, are you okay? It happens. Don't let this get to you. They changed the rules, and it's stricter now," he says, making me feel a little less humiliated. I'm also startled by how human he seems.

"It's not that at all. We just haven't seen each other in so long. I really had no idea about the rules," I lie.

He seems understanding, like he's on my side. I think he even made a joke about keeping our hands to ourselves. I shake his hand as we leave, grateful that someone sympathizes with this hideous situation. Either way, it's not going to change what happened. I won't be able to come back tomorrow. That's the end of it. Part of me feels relieved to go home.

It's starting to get dark as Margot and I walk back to the parking lot. She keeps reassuring me that everything is going to be okay. And if it isn't, she'll take it up with the governor of Massachusetts, like she even knows him. I stop listening. I'm still so humiliated. I can't believe this is my fucking life.

The newsroom is fully staffed on Christmas Eve. It's like everyone is trying to outwork the next person. *Get me out of here.* I'm counting down the minutes until I can. At 3:50, I pack up, trying to strategically leave without anyone noticing. Fuck it. It's fucking Christmas.

"Okay, guys, I'm heading out to catch my train but hope you all have a Merry Christmas," I say. "I'm out tomorrow, but I'll be back on the 26th."

"Take care," I say, cringing at my word choice. When did I start sounding like an adult? I can hardly take care of myself.

Ben calls when I get into the elevator at Lauren's. I forgot I told him to call me at 6; he's right on time. Lauren hates when I'm on the phone with him. I answer anyway. The apartment is imbued with a humid fog. She's deep-frying octopus. I'm starving. There's half a plate ready, and I start mindlessly shoveling it into my mouth.

Ben says I need to conference in his grandpa down in Boca because they're about to light the Chanukah candles. I can already sense that Lauren is aggravated, and I give her an "I'm sorry" look, trying to convey that my hands are tied.

"Get off the phone, Mia! What the fuck are you doing?" she yells from the kitchen.

I want to kill her.

"Lauren, I told you I will be right off. Give me ten minutes," I say, slamming the door.

Lauren can be an angry person. And I must have set her off, because she comes storming into the room, grabs the phone out of my hand just as Ben's grandfather is singing the Chanukah prayer on speaker, and throws it on the ground.

"Enough!" she yells. "You just got here and you're on the phone with him? Why is he making you talk to his family, Mia? It's very weird. This is too much now."

I start sobbing.

"You just hung up on him! And now he can't celebrate with his family. Because he's in fucking prison!"

"We are your family," Lauren says. She looks furious. "He is controlling you. How do you not see it?"

CHAPTER 22

I'M HUNGOVER AT BRUNCH WITH my college friends, Carrie and Jade, and start to feel anxious when Carrie brings Ben up. "Mia, whatever happened to Ben? Do you still hear from him?" Carrie asks, mid-sip of a Bloody Mary.

I lie, and tell them we broke up months ago but still keep in touch.

I weirdly don't panic or pause. I don't want to hide him anymore.

"Yeah, every now and then," I say, keeping it vague.

Carrie's eyes widen a bit like she's surprised. I'm not surprised, because I haven't mentioned him to them in months.

"Did he ever end up going to jail?" Carrie asks curiously.

I still struggle with the embarrassment of saying, "Yes, he's in prison," but I spit out some version of that.

"He was waiting for the trial while we were dating and then ended up getting a plea deal. It's just been tough. He's such a good person, Carrie—you remember that day in the Hamptons."

"Yeah, he was very sweet," she says. "And so cute."

"I know. So anyway, he can't leave the state. He's in a facility," I say, wondering if they'll interpret that as prison. No one says the word.

"Have you seen him?" Jade asks.

I pause for a moment.

"Yeah, I have."

She looks surprised. Jade is from Bedford, not far from where the Clintons live. When Martha Stewart went to prison, it was a huge scandal in their town.

"Really? What's it like?" she asks, clearly fascinated.

"It's kind of like a DMV. There's food there too," I say, sugarcoating it inadvertently. It's just my nature to make life seem like everything's fine. It's less painful than facing reality. I realize how in denial I've always been about Ben's situation.

"How long will he be there for?" Carrie asks.

"That's the thing. He could be working at a real job next year if everything goes okay. It's just hard because we never really wanted to break up, but we kind of had to," I say, lying. "But he's been so understanding, and of course he doesn't expect me to wait for him."

"He basically says I can do whatever I want," I say, unable to share the truth.

"Honestly, it's kind of been the best five-year plan. I've been focusing on work, and we talk every now and then, and, you know, I can still date. I'm keeping options open, but it's hard. It's hard to meet people."

"I know. Well, honestly, I think that's so smart, and, I mean, in a few years, it'll all be done with, and it's not something that's going to hang over him," Jade says. Her optimism seems genuine.

Carrie agrees. I'm kind of surprised at how they react. I'm proud of myself for opening up, even if I'm not being fully honest. I've been so ashamed for the past few years. It feels like a weight was lifted off my shoulders just by talking about Ben like he's a real person.

"It was just hard because we really connected before he left. He was my best friend, and we would still be together if he wasn't in this situation," I say, trying to convince myself.

She keeps reassuring me that he'll find a job and everything will be okay. This will just be a small part of his life, and everyone will get over it. It makes me feel better. I believe her. I really do.

Ben calls me while I'm out, and some rap song is on, so I put my drink down and walk out of the restaurant. I'm excited to tell him that I've finally told my friends about us.

"Hey, can you hear me? I just stepped out. I'm at a dinner with Jade and Carrie. Guess what?"

"What?"

"I told them about your situation," I say, waiting for him to praise me for being so brave.

"That I'm in prison?"

"Yeah, and that we're still in touch. And that I've been to visit," I say.

"What did they say?"

"They seemed really supportive—and understanding. They said this will be all be behind you soon enough and that things will be okay."

There's a pause.

"Yeah, well, just because..."

"What?"

"Just because they seem like they're supportive doesn't mean they really are," he says.

Ben's mixed signals are exhausting. First, he pushes me to tell the world about our situation. How he wants me to stay in touch with his family and buy him birthday gifts to ensure him that I'm thinking about him. And now, when I finally have the courage to tell my world about him, he makes me question whether or not I can trust them.

I'm not going to let him get in my head. I opened up today, and that's a big deal for me. I was vulnerable with my friends, and even if they had judged, I'm still glad I did it.

Ben calls again later that night. He wants to know more about what I told Jade and Carrie.

"Nothing. I just breezed over our situation. I said that prison isn't so bad. And I embellished a little. I just said I could see other guys—just so it doesn't seem like I'm waiting all these years."

"Why would you say that though? Is that something you want?"

I can sense his insecurity, like that day in Gary's office.

"Ben, no. I just wanted to tell them about us without it seeming crazy that I'm waiting for a guy in prison for seven years, maybe less with your good time."

Now he thinks I'm cheating on him. He can be so infuriating sometimes. I tell him how easy it would be for me to do, and that he'd never know. I leave out the part that I already have. I never promised him I would be fully committed. Then I hang up the phone.

The next day, I wake up feeling anxious that Ben won't call back. I want to tell him that I didn't mean what I said, and that I love him and I can't wait to see him next week.

I'm getting a lot better at changing in public restrooms. I'm trying my best to balance on my sneakers so that I don't touch the disgusting floor in the handicap stall at the bus stop. I strip off my leggings and quickly slip on black elastic waist trousers. Jeans still aren't allowed. I need to make it to the prison before 11:30 when the doors open. I'm Ubering. It's just easier than dealing with Margot immediately. I don't even feel weird about it anymore. The ride is less daunting now too. Once we pass by the old motel and diner, I know we're close. The Uber driver says nothing as I follow along and track our route.

It's been almost six months since I've seen Ben. His lawyer had a meeting with the prison higher-ups and explained that it was all a misunderstanding. Ben had some of his visits revoked, but now everything is back to normal. And I'm excited to finally see him again.

I pass by the familiar suburban houses, the Patriots and Red Sox flags waving and Audis lining the driveways. This is such a nice neighborhood. Do they know how close they are to this place?

I see the blank strip of land leading to the barbed wire.

"I don't think I can go up any farther," the driver says as he pulls up to the gate.

"Here is totally fine."

"Is this where you want to be dropped off?" he asks, which I interpret as "are you sure you want me to leave you, a pretty young girl, at a prison?"

"I don't want to be here, but I have to," I say, a knee-jerk response. I hate that I think I have to justify why I'm here to a stranger. "Mind popping the trunk? Thanks so much." I grab my black duffel bag, the one I've taken on my work trips to Monaco and Saint-Tropez and Capri. And now here. Again.

I march up the stairs on a mission and breeze through the lobby to grab my ticket. I'm number 45. I hope that's the first group. I look for a locker. Why do they seem to be getting smaller and smaller?

A woman behind me is talking about how "he" only has one more year left. One more year, I think. That's nothing. What a breeze. I think about Ben's first year in this place. It was hell. It felt like we'd never see the end. But now that we're nearing the two-year mark, I realize how fast it all went.

The last few minutes of waiting are always the hardest. Waiting and waiting and waiting. They call in the first group. I'm grateful that I'll be able to hold Ben's hand. Originally, they revoked that as well, along with kissing. It made me so sad. So many people take holding hands in public for granted. I remember even feeling shy about it initially. Now I crave it. It makes me look at couples differently. I want to shake them and tell them to stop taking each other for granted. To hold hands more. To say I love you more. Thankfully, the rule has been lifted.

Ben looks so good in a short-sleeve T-shirt and jeans.

I can feel his chest against mine when we hug. His biceps are so muscular now he looks like he's gone out to battle and came home a grown man.

We kiss, and I have an acute sense of self-awareness. I can sense people watching after the last incident, but I just think about how good it feels to have Ben with me again.

He's wearing his yarmulke, I notice.

"When did you get that?"

"Tony left it for me before he moved to the minimum."

"That's sweet."

"Yeah, it is. I wear it every day. I don't ever take it off."

"That's so good. Your mom must be happy," I say. "How is Tony doing?" It must be hard for him to have lost his best friend in this place.

"He's doing really well. He just got out of the minimum a few weeks ago. I'm trying to get him an interview with Randy's construction company," he says.

"Do you think he has a shot?"

"You don't understand. Tony is going to make an incredible businessman. You should have seen him in here. He's so good at talking to people and getting what he wants. He was banging correction officers in here left and right."

"Really? No. Here? How? How did he not get caught?"

"The officers practically throw themselves at him. I don't know how he does it. He was banging this girl at the hospital unit at one point. The security guards would bring stuff in for him. Anything he wanted, he got in this place."

"Wow, that's nuts."

"Yeah, Tony is a smooth talker. He can convince anyone to do anything. That's why he's going to be good in business. So, I asked my uncle to give him an interview with some of the top bosses at the company, and he spent like an hour and a half on the phone with him."

"I hope it works out. Do you think the company will hire an ex-felon?"

"It's a private company, so they really can do whatever they want."

Ben always reassures me that he's got an in at the company because of his AA sponsor, and I've never thought twice about it. But I can't help but wonder. What if this company doesn't hire Ben because of what he's done, because he's a convicted felon?

Ben tells me that he's trying to send Tony a Casio watch. He gave him his before he left, and Ben wants to repay the favor, so he asked Margot to find one online and mail it to him.

"That's really sweet of you. I'm sure he'll appreciate that."

"Yeah, I mean, usually when people leave this place they move on. They forget about everyone in here. It's like this weird bubble. You can be best friends with someone and then never hear from them again. When people get out, they move forward and try to block this hell out. Remember my buddy, Tim? Haven't heard from him since he left. He was the guy I worked out with every day. Every single day."

"That's tough, to become so close with someone and then it's like they don't exist."

"That's just life here. You move on."

Ben wants to take another photo of us. He likes looking back on them. I joke with the camera guy, telling him to make us look good. He snaps a few photos with the Canon digital and shows them to us. The lighting is perfect, as usual. This guy never takes a bad photo.

"He needs to take our wedding photos," I joke, forgetting that he is likely here for life; though, I don't know why.

We're sitting back down, side by side, and Ben tells me he wants to buy me the real version of the ring we saw in Salem, that he asked his mom to take money out of his savings for it.

"I'm going to get you the ring you wanted," he says. "Seriously. Go online and look with my mom and pick it up with her, okay?"

"Ben, you don't have to do that. I don't want your mom spending all this money on me or thinking that I'm taking the only real money you've made in two years," I tell him.

"Mia, I told her this is how I want to spend it, okay? I know it's annoying to have to go through her, but it's the best I can do, and I want to get you the ring. So, if she asks you, show her the one you want."

I think about the ring in the Salem shop, how I thought it was a real David Yurman.

As messed up as Ben's situation is, I find comfort knowing that he loves me. That he can't leave me, especially here. And yet, I know I have to move forward. It's why I keep trying to date behind his back. But I'm still so emotionally invested in the fantasy of us.

"Get something you can wear every day and think of me," Ben says.

The next day, when Ben calls, I can hear the anxiety in his voice. Something isn't right.

"Something bad happened," he says.

"What is it? You don't sound right."

"I left my journal in the kitchen a few nights ago."

There's a long pause.

"Okay, and what happened?"

"I left it there, and someone found it. They read it, and they passed it along to everyone in the block. Everyone read what I wrote."

"What? You're fucking kidding me. This is something straight out of a movie. Ben, you're not being serious?" He's so good at pranking that I can hardly tell when he's being serious now.

"Mia, do you have any idea what I wrote in there? It was pages and pages about these guys. I made fun of them at some points. It's brutal."

I can tell he's mortified. It reminds me of the Burn Book in *Mean Girls*, only this is prison. I still can't tell if Ben is joking.

"This shit is straight out of a movie," I keep saying. "Ben, how could you leave your journal in the kitchen? This isn't your fucking house. This isn't your living room," I say, getting angry that he could be so careless. Still.

"Yeah, Mia. I know that now, okay? You don't have to keep saying it." His voice turns monotone.

"Ben, I'm actually scared for you. Do you think you're going to get hurt? Do you feel safe?"

"Mia, it's been two days, okay? It's been out for two days. If something were to happen, it probably would have already happened. Everything is fine. I'm just very anxious."

"Did you get it back?"

"What?"

"The journal!" I say.

"Yeah, one of the guys gave it back to me, but only after he showed the entire block. I'm just happy he gave it back."

"I'm honestly surprised he did," I say.

"I love you. I just wish you were here. When are you coming back?"

"April," I tell him.

"I wish you were here. I love you," he keeps saying.

"Me too," I say. "Don't be nervous."

"I'm not nervous. I'm anxious."

"That's the same thing."

"No, it's not."

"Okay, don't be anxious. It's going to be okay. Do you feel safe?"

"Yes, Mia. I'm fine. My anxiety is just going crazy right now."

"Okay, well, I love you. Everything is going to blow over. It's like a news scandal. You have to give people something else to talk about, and then it will all blow over."

"I can't even listen to you right now. My brain is going a mile a minute."

"Take a deep breath. You have to relax."

"You have one minute remaining," the stupid operator says. It's 9:14 already.

"I know. I love you. I'm fine."

"Okay. Don't be upset. Call me in the morning."

"What's going on? Is everything okay?"

"I'm in solitary. Don't ask any questions."

I have a million. "Confinement? Are you fucking kidding me? What happened?"

"I said I can't answer any questions."

I always forget the line is recorded.

"Are you okay?"

"Yes, I'm fine. I got punched in the face. It's all on camera."

You've got to be fucking kidding me.

"So why are you there?"

"I said I can't answer any questions. I'm fine though. Really, you don't have to worry. I have my cell again."

"Isn't it tiny? So, you're locked in there for the whole day? Aren't you going to go crazy? Can your mom get you out?"

"No, Mia. My mom can't get me out of this one. This is the SHU, not time-out."

"Ugh, I just don't understand. You shouldn't be there! Why are you there?"

The diary. It must be because of that fucking diary.

Why is my boyfriend in solitary confinement? Have I gone crazy? I feel claustrophobic just thinking about it.

"I'm going to be fine. I stocked up on books before I came in. My mom's going to call the lawyer, and everything's going to be fine."

Is it? I worry about what this will do to Ben's mental state. I'm on the verge of a panic attack just thinking about him in that place. I can't imagine actually living it.

"How long will you be in there? Like a day? A week? A month?"

"I don't know. We have to see. But I've done this before, remember?"

"What do you mean?"

"When I was at Walpole, they made us stay in our cell for twenty-three hours a day until they placed me here. Remember?"

"No, I didn't know that."

"I told you that."

"I forgot."

"Well, you don't need to worry. I'm going to be okay."

Ben tells me he has his tablet, so he can send emails and read e-books. Little luxuries in hell.

"I can't believe someone hit you like that. Did it hurt?"

"I can't talk about it," Ben says. "I think I'll be able to call you. Don't worry about me."

"Your mother is going to freak the fuck out." I think about the cocktail of pills Margot will need to stomach this.

"I just called her, and she's fine. She was at dinner with Jane."

Oh, how lovely.

"And she's not going insane right now?"

"No, I reassured her that it's going to be fine, and she said she would call Ed."

I can't imagine that Margot's fine. Knowing her, she's probably writing to the Department of Corrections right now to get Ben out of there.

"Okay. I love you. Please be careful."

"I will. I'll call you tomorrow."

I'm frightened for Ben. He emailed saying he might have to move prisons. The thought is daunting, as if he isn't far enough away already. I google "prisons in Massachusetts." There are a few options. Some place in Concord, another in Plymouth. My anxiety is escalating. I call his mother even though she'll probably make it worse.

She picks up the phone after one ring.

"Have you heard from him?" she says.

"He just emailed me."

I read her the part about him possibly transferring and that the situation seems to have escalated, but I reassure her that he feels safe. I can hear the concern in her voice. She's trying to calm me down, but I'm really not that unhinged. I just feel bad for Ben.

"Everything is going to be okay. It's like they told me in his Al-Anon meetings: this is out of our control. It's one day at a time. We can only change things we can control," she says.

"I know. It's just that I don't understand. He shouldn't be there. I'm worried about his safety. Why can't Ed get him out of there?"

"Ed can't do anything."

"But what if he has to go to another facility? Where will they take him? I thought he's at the best prison in the state?"

"Yeah, it's definitely a good place, but there are other options. There's Concord Max."

"Why would he go to a maximum prison?" I ask. "He's not a threat."

"Well, that's the thing I don't know. But there are a few other options. We just have to be patient and figure this out. I think he's in there for his safety right now."

Margot had gotten some intel from Ed. Once the guards found out the other inmates had read his diary, he called Ed, and the guards moved him to the SHU for his own protection. I get why Ben couldn't say anything now. I guess it's the lesser of two evils. It still sucks that he has to move, and I'm annoyed at how careless he was—but at least he's not hurt.

"I'm going to visit him this afternoon, but it's going to be through the glass, and we'll have to talk to him on one of those phones."

"At least you can see him."

"Yes, I'm going to have to motivate him to stay strong. I sent him an email last night, telling him how brave he is, that he can do this."

It sounds like Margot is trying to convince herself.

"Okay, well, tell him I love him and that I miss him so much."

"I know you do, and I will. I know you talk every day, and this is hard, but we're going to figure this out. We just have to take it one day at a time. You have an amazing love story. This is just a hurdle."

"Yeah, it's fucking crazy."

"But you know what? Whatever happens with you two, you'll always be best friends."

I want to believe her, but the burden of Ben's sentence is weighing on me, and it's getting harder to function with this living ghost. I feel guilty thinking about letting go. I know Ben will always want me in his life. He says it all the time.

But I know there will only ever be two options—with Ben, or without.

Ben's solitary cell is the size of a parking space. That's how he describes it. He lies on his back with his feet up the wall to get a good stretch. There's a tiny window with metal bars. His bed feels like a seesaw. Any time the guy in the cell next to his sits down, his moves up, like they're attached through the walls. I imagine he's sleeping on a slab of metal. He's been in the same pants since he got there four days ago and can only shower once a week. It's the same with the phone situation now. And he can only call when one of the corrections officers wheels around the phone. But thankfully, he's able to get Wi-Fi so he can still use his tablet to read, listen to podcasts, and watch old movies. I still can't wrap my head around the fact that he has Wi-Fi in the hole.

He's been listening to *How I Built This*, with the inventor of Spindrift, and another podcast called *Masters of Scale*, about how the guys from Airbnb struggled to pay their rent when starting their company. Ben has so many ideas. I hope all of this is inspiration for his next great one.

Ben is supposed to call tonight. I'm at a party at Sartiano's, clutching my phone. I haven't been out to celebrity-heavy media events like this in a while. The event is for an Italian winemaker. We're huddled in this stylish Soho restaurant that's undeniably beyond capacity. I invited Eva, who is always looking effortlessly chic.

"I'm so glad you came. I don't recognize anyone here," I tell her.

We're drinking rosé in February. Jonathan, a male publicist and the tallest person at the party, comes over to fill us in on the event's gossip. Eva and I gasp when we see Martha Stewart standing a stone's throw away.

When Jonathan leaves, I loop Eva in on Ben's situation. I didn't want to tell her, but I'll have to leave the table if he calls.

"So, you can't make this shit up, but did I tell you how Ben keeps this diary? A journal. He writes candidly about everything that's going on in prison. He's trying to write a book."

"Oh my god. That's amazing. He totally should. I mean he's got plenty of time," Eva says, a bit overexcited, the wine clearly hitting us both.

"Well, he was cooking in the communal kitchen and left the journal accidentally, and someone found it."

Eva looks at me, stunned.

"Shut the fuck up. No, who?"

"I don't know, one of the guys in there."

A gorgeously tall woman with dark brown hair and perfect eyebrows snakes her way into the crowd. She's in a leather jacket and the trendy clear-framed glasses everyone's wearing now. I gawk at her pink Prada satin slides.

"You know who that is, right?" Eva says in a hushed voice. She's usually not one to get starstruck. "That's Brooke Shields."

"Yeah, I know. She's gorgeous," I say.

"Should I tell her I'm obsessed with *Blue Lagoon*?" Eva says. We both laugh.

"Oh my god. Could you imagine?"

"So, anyway…" I try to get back on track. "One of the guys found it, and Ben panicked, because I mean, can you imagine what he wrote about everyone in there?"

"That's mortifying."

"Right, so anyway, I was concerned that he would get beat up over it."

"Did he? Oh no. I didn't even think about that. Will he be okay?" Eva asks.

"No, no he's fine, thank god. They just took the book, and they sent him…" I try my best to whisper solitary confinement so that Eva can hear me and so that Martha, inches away, won't think I'm talking about her sentence.

"No!" She cups her hand over her mouth.

"He's fine. It's just not an ideal living situation. Anyway, I didn't want to tell you, but he can't call me any time like he used to. Now he has this strict schedule, so I'll have to get up at dinner when he calls," I say, like it's a normal, annoying chore.

"Oh, of course. Don't worry about it. Just get it when he calls."

"It'll be fine. But fuck, can you believe it?"

We both take a long sip of our wine.

CHAPTER 23

AFTER NINETEEN DAYS, BEN FINALLY left solitary confinement. He just sent an email me from a new prison. I immediately open it. I've been living at my sister's place since the coronavirus outbreak and feel a bit like I'm in prison myself.

> Subject line: Canceled
>
> I'm sad that our visit is canceled. I wonder when they'll let people start coming back. Something tells me it won't be for a long time with everything going on. Thank god you still have a job. At least it gives you a sense of purpose.
>
> Now you know what I mean about life changing in a second.

It's weird to think Ben will never be at Franklin again. I'm filled with a strange sense of mourning and nostalgia. It's hard to explain, but I find myself missing it almost. That anxious anticipation of waiting hours in the waiting room. Those moments that made me question our whole relationship, why I was putting myself through all this suffering. *Why am I missing that horrible waiting room?*

The thought of having to adapt to another visiting room in another foreign place seems daunting. I think about how I'll never see the nice correction officer again, with her sunny demeanor beneath a shell of authority. I think about the inmate who took photos with the Canon, who was probably in for life. I feel lucky that I was able to sit so close to Ben and hold his hand for hours and hours, even though, for the most part, he was treated like dirt.

People are comparing their quarantines to prison on social media. I feel guilty about even complaining, but it still sucks. All of this sucks. I would have thought I'd have built a little more strength, but everything really does come in waves. I'm doing my best to stay on track with work, but my mind slows a lot, and I find myself triple-checking emails before I can finally press send. I wonder if it's OCD. Often, I look forward to 5 p.m., when it's socially acceptable to pour a glass of wine. The bottles are running low, but it's the only thing that takes the edge off. Does this make me an alcoholic? Does this make me weak? I don't care. I still do it anyway.

Instagram makes it all worse, but I can't stop scrolling. My eyes fill with tears over a colleague's post about her daughter's first birthday and how much joy she brings to her life. I cry because it feels like everyone else's life is still propelling forward while mine is stuck in neutral. It was already stagnant with Ben in prison, but now, I can't even see him. I want to feel that kind of joy again.

Maybe I'll email Ben. I keep allowing other people's happiness to steal my own. Ben says I need to fill these voids with work. Keep busy and work out, he says. When I look in the mirror, I don't see myself anymore. I see a skinny, sad person.

"Can you be an alcoholic without getting drunk?" is the last search I put into Google. It's been two days since I stopped drinking wine, and I'm already fiending for my next glass. Just to take the edge off. Just because life is so, so depressing right now. At least there's natural light pouring in. The trees make this confinement slightly more pleasant.

Ben says I shouldn't complain because I have a cushy job. He's right. He says you don't have to always be drunk to be an alcoholic. He sees characteristics of himself in me, but I can't tell if he's just manipulating. I hate the self-reflection that this quarantine is forcing on me.

Ben's mom called and asked a million fucking questions about his German homework. I did Ben's German homework, researched questions about its electoral system. *Am I really doing my boyfriend's prison homework?*

Do I regret Ben? Meeting him? My sadness turns to rage, and I can feel myself getting angry for no reason. I snapped at my mom. She's worried about me. She's never seen me this angry.

I am frantically sealing the edges of an aluminum tray of lasagna, packing to-go orders at the restaurant.

With pandemic restrictions and staff limited, my dad is desperate for help with customers and fielding to-go orders. By day, I'm writing news stories about the virus, interviewing nurses and doctors and first responders, and by night, I'm taking dinner orders, trying to get a fleet of masked customers out the door.

It's a busy time for my dad, which is good for business. He tells me that if I help him, he'll help me with a down payment on a new apartment, but neither of us can keep up with the demand, and the stress of the nonstop calls and orders isn't helping.

I'm carrying out a tray of lasagna to the back of a woman's Range Rover. I must not have sealed the lid tight enough because it comes pouring out. A bloodbath of red sauce, meat and cheese, lifeless on the driveway, and I'm panicked that my mistake cost my dad hours of labor.

Luckily, the woman, in a cropped jean and leather driving loafer, is understanding, coddling me that it's okay, that it was an accident. But my dad is livid at the sight of the wasted one-hundred-dollar tray, cursing that I should have been more careful.

"You know what, just go home," he tells me, shaking his head.

I'm so overwhelmed and angry at how he's treating me. How I've been working constantly and it's still not good enough. For anyone.

I think about how Ben once told me the only way I can get my dad to listen is to match his level of anger. So, I go into the kitchen and grab a plate and smash it until it shatters. Shards of glass litter the floor. My body is shocked at what I did. I feel guilty that he'll make the dishwasher clean up my mess. I've never acted out this way. It stuns my dad, because he's standing with both hands cupping his head. His eyes widen, and I can see his pain. Like he's been struggling his whole life. I know that if I leave, he won't have anyone to answer the phones. I want to apologize, but I'm too ashamed. I sprint out the door and run to the train station.

I brought my mail back from the city over the weekend; it had been accumulating since mid-March. There's a letter from Ben dated February 15. I wait days before opening it. I don't want to feel the pain of missing him. The envelope has a heart on it with the letters "B" and "M."

I've grown distant. Missing his calls, not on purpose, just not making it a priority to have my phone on me constantly like I used to. When I open the letter, I see the college-ruled paper is folded long-ways, with a magazine clipping. The only thing visible is a header that reads, "Don't Cry. We'll repair or clean it." It's an ad for a shoe repair. He must have written it the night after reprimanding me for spending fifty dollars to fix my boots. I got angry with him because it's my money, and none of this is his business.

Below it, there's a magazine cut out of a gorgeous home with a wraparound driveway and fall foliage. "One day we'll have one like it. In Boston or New York." I'm clinging to this paper house, hoping that one day this can be real. Ours. Having Ben to hold again, night after night. Us. Am I just naïve?

Conversations with Ben have gotten monotonous. Talking to him sometimes feels like a chore. He berates me for not answering his emails sooner. He just says I should be enjoying this time working from home when I share that I'm uneasy. He says maybe I am depressed. I am.

But he makes it worse sometimes. Every time I complain about how unhappy I am or express that I feel like something's missing, he pushes me to work harder. To fill my days with side projects. To make more money. To work out more. He casually rattles off models with bodies he loves. *Bella Hadid has the perfect body.* He has this way of making comments that make me feel like I will never be good enough, no matter how much I progress. There are always three other things I can be doing. I made a comment about how I'm not worrying about my student loans because of the COVID-19 allowances. Ben blew up and said I am childish for not being more proactive. But I'm saving money, more than I ever have. I've been working out every day. I finally carved out a side project to make more money. Of course, Ben says that if this job didn't fall in my lap, I wouldn't have it. I find the lecture hypocritical. His own negligence and lack of forward thinking are what landed him in prison in the first place. My emotions are getting more and more erratic. I feel so wound up. Even just sitting on the balcony makes me anxious.

"You're just angry because you hate your job and your boyfriend's in prison," my mom says. *Bingo, hon. You hit the nail on the head.*

I cry later thinking about just how right she is.

I want to scream when Ben tells me again and again to "toughen up." I know that he's right. I know that I don't have real-world problems. I still have a job. Everyone in my family is healthy. I'm healthy. I'm breathing without a respirator. I can leave my house.

But a subconscious rage continues to beat inside me, leaving painful bruises that only I can see. And I'm sick of being in pain. I don't want to feel like this anymore. I don't want to wait another three years for Ben. I want to be happy again.

Ben calls again to nag me about not mailing him letters. I answer all of his calls. All of his emails. I carry on relationships with all of his family. I did a goddamn Zoom Passover with twelve of his family members and didn't understand a word of the prayers.

I've done everything right. I still love the part of him that's good, more than anything, but I want my freedom. Ben doesn't understand that. I know if the tables were turned, there is no way he'd wait for me for this long. He's too impulsive, there's no way he would be content waiting for anything.

I don't remember the exact conversation. I told Ben I wanted some space to "do my own thing," which Ben interpreted as "fuck other guys."

Ben tells me no one will ever love me as much as he does. All of this feels abusive.

My body fills with rage.

Rage that I've put myself on autopilot to appease him.

Rage that he's exploited my good nature.

Rage that I've taken a passenger seat to his constant criticism.

Rage that I've allowed myself to endure all of this pain.

This is not love. It's control, and I will not let him derail me any more than he has.

Ben says he'll call me in a week. Instead, he emails me two days later.

> Subject: Four years
>
> Running into you four years ago was one of the greatest things that has ever happened to me. I will never forget how fortunate I was to spend time with and get

> to know someone as special as you. And our chemistry, well, it's undeniable. On our last phone call, I listened to you. I put a lot of thought into it over the last seven days (you know how I am with this stuff), and I've had these realizations. It is because of the deepest love that I have for you that I am unable to simply be friends with you.
>
> This is not the right time to worry about where I am or where you're at. I don't want to put you through any more interrogations or arguments. I don't want to question you about what you're doing. I don't want that kind of stress in my life right now, and I want you to be free.
>
> You need to move on so that you can find out what you're really looking for, and without question, so do I. This is the time when I really need to find myself, and you need to find yourself. Anything else is too difficult. You know that I care about you. I just want you to have a better life. However, more so, I need this time to focus on myself. That's why I'm not going to call you. It's a better time for us not to be a couple. Let's just take this time to grow.

Ben doesn't call me on my birthday. I visited him. I called him during his darkest times, and now, in mine, he's ignoring me on purpose. I can't get the hurt to stop. Then he emails again, telling me he regrets what he said. He sends me a bookmark he made me from *New York Magazine* clippings.

He keeps calling my cell phone, but I stop answering. I don't want to speak with him. I'm sick of the whiplash. His actions make me realize just how selfish he is. How cruel he can be.

I don't deserve to be treated like this. And I won't tolerate any more of his mind games.

I call Lauren.

"I finally ended it," I tell her. "For good this time."

"Mia, I'm proud of you," she tells me. I can hear her stepping outside the salon to talk.

"I know how hard these years have been. And it kills me to see you dull your shine because of him. You weren't yourself. You deserve to be happy. I've only ever wanted the best for you, and I always will," Lauren tells me.

I go on a Hinge date with someone named Matt. He's sweet and so normal. He picks me up in his Volvo from my sister's apartment. I'm still staying in Westchester.

I cannot get over how well the date goes, and when I get home, Matt says how nice a time he had. He wasn't expecting his first date since lockdown to have gone so well either. He doesn't kiss me, and Lauren convinces me it's because he likes and respects me.

"What did I do to deserve this?" I ask Lauren, savoring a piece of chocolate before bed.

Lauren looks at me, taken aback.

"Everything," she says.

The summer felt like a blur. I spent most of it in Matt's apartment in Astoria. He'd take his guitar off the wall and play Fleetwood Mac songs, and I sang for the first time in years while he fretted the strings. We never had an emotional connection, but his company shadowed my sadness. I cried in the passenger seat over the Queensboro Bridge when he took me home after we broke up. It's been almost exactly a month since I last spoke to Ben.

In his absence, I can see how much I relied on him for approval—to the point where I'd hear his voice instead of my own. My dependence on him was crippling. Even my family has noticed a difference. I'm not snapping as much. I have less rage.

But I still feel so alone.

My apartment is a dark mess. I took apart the bed and sold the headboard on Craigslist, so I'm sleeping on my mattress on the dirty hardwood floor. Melanie, my roommate, took the lamp, so there's one light for my whole room. Depressing is an understatement. I walk into the kitchen and hover over the fake marble countertop, the stickers peeling off. My refrigerator is the barest it's ever been. The magnet collection is stored away, and outlines from Spain and Argentina and Hawaii and Dubai linger. I pick at a cold, two-day-old rotisserie chicken, pulling back the dry skin like string cheese. I'm crying into the bag. I cannot wait to leave.

My lease is up, and I've been searching all over the tri-state area for an apartment. Nothing is in my price range. Nothing. I'm feeling defeated and displaced. I've never had my own place, and I desperately want something of my own so I can feel settled. So I can finally move forward.

I write down the words, "Just keep moving forward," on a piece of paper and tape it above my shitty folding Amazon desk. I have to move forward. I will get a new job I don't hate. I will get a new apartment. I will find love. I write down those three things in my planner. And I say them over and over again in my head. I've been living and working out of my bedroom. I look up at the mantra I taped up and start crying. I cry so much because I miss Ben, and because now I am completely alone.

Jared, the Tribeca doctor I've been fucking, is coming over soon. I take down the sign so that he doesn't think I'm having a mental breakdown. He's made it very clear that he's in residency and doesn't want a relationship. I still try to act happy and flirty to convince him to date me. He's always stressed, more stressed and anxious than I am, and I try to get him to relax with forced optimism. He has a buzz cut. He's short. But he's hot and muscular. And I love the feeling of his body on mine, even though I'm still so fucking sad when he leaves.

⚐

Ever since I let go of Ben, life has been a slow domino effect of good things.

I started an Instagram account called "The Relentless Reservationist," where I leave bite-sized reviews in less than one hundred words of restaurants around New York, fielding recommendations for followers. So far, three of my posts have gone viral.

⚐

I'm sitting in a courtyard, eye level with the Empire State Building across the East River. I can actually hear birds chirping. Birds, in New York City—well, Brooklyn technically. It's so serene on this patio in Williamsburg.

I'm waiting for Gabe. We met on a dating app. I ignored him after our first date, and he persistently followed up again and again, even though I delayed answering—and sometimes didn't at all. I didn't think he was my type, initially. He's handsome, but I thought he was quiet, too quiet for me, and I was in the middle of a move and distracted. But he still pursued me, and by March, I finally gave in and let him take me on a second date.

We picked an Italian restaurant. Wax dripped from the candles. I don't remember much of our conversation that night. Truly, I wasn't really that into him.

I rambled about how my lease was up at the end of the month and that I'd have to leave the city soon if I didn't find a place. I didn't want to leave.

"I really don't see you moving back to the suburbs," Gabe told me. He barely knew me but was so convinced that I still belonged here, that I would be miserable moving anywhere else.

He was right. I knew he was.

"Really? How do you know? You don't even know me," I said.

"I know," he said, so confidently. "I think you're just working with the wrong realtor. I know a guy. I can send you his contact information if you want." His voice is soothing.

I still wasn't convinced that I liked Gabe, so I did something I never really do: I ordered something I really, really wanted off the menu without looking at the price—veal francese.

And he must have enjoyed my company, because we went for drinks after. It was a dive bar, but I ordered a martini. He did the same. He told me about climbing Kilimanjaro. I could tell he was trying to impress me.

The next day, he sent me the name of the realtor. Later that weekend, I saw a true one-bedroom in my price range, and street-facing, so there was lots of light.

Gabe texted, wanting to hang out, but I was so stressed. My apartment was half packed, boxes everywhere. I was still not convinced that I liked him. But it was thoughtful for him to connect me with the realtor. I told him I could meet for an hour.

The realtor, Jeffrey, called to tell me he put in my offer.

"You made an offer?" Gabe asked, surprised that I called the realtor, and more so that I didn't tell him.

There's something calming about him. Apparently, he's very into energy and meditation. He says everything's about mindset, that I have to convince myself that I will get the apartment and the move will be done and over with soon.

He told me about a quote from a book called *Man's Search for Meaning* about how someone can take away everything you have except for the way you react to things. How we have control over how we choose to respond. I know I'd heard it before from Ben and didn't know how to respond. I think about how deeply I loved him, but how much of our relationship was rooted in suffering. In fear. My fear of letting go. Of being alone. How I convinced myself that I would never find anyone like Ben, someone who could deal with life's hardships. Someone who could protect me. But he never did.

I feel bad that I judged Gabe. I can see how strong he is. And how caring. And I'm so drawn to him. For the first time, I feel safe.

When I get home, I start crying. I feel so much relief. I can feel myself finally letting go of Ben.

Somehow, in the process of moving, Gabe and I get to know each other more.

He tells me he loves me. I feel it too. I tell him about Ben and the last four years of my life. I feel like I can be unfiltered with him. He listens without judgment. I feel a sense of relief I haven't had in a long time—maybe ever.

Letting go of Ben still has its ripple effects. Gabe and I are sitting on the beach, and suddenly, it feels like my whole head is shaking, like the sand beneath me is unsteady, like I'm having some type of seizure—only I'm not. Gabe assures me of that. He can tell I'm having a panic attack without calling it to my attention. He just holds my hand and helps me calm down. It passes.

I'm staring at bright yellow walls painted with imperfect strokes dried in sloppy streaks. I can't wait to paint. Everything needs to be updated, but I'm so content to finally have the keys. I bask in all its messy glory: the dated white Formica cabinets with cheap silver handles and the lack of working lights. But there's sunlight—so much sunlight—streaming through the windows into my living room.

I'm hit with a wave of self-awareness, knowing the light at the end of the tunnel was me.

I'm so happy to be home.

FREE FALL

I see the good in everyone. Seeing only the good means you can't ever get hurt. It's self-defense. It's also an agonizing way to live.

Seeing only the good in you almost destroyed me. I spent years living in my own solitary confinement. Your sentence became my sentence. Thankfully, that is no longer the case.

You'll be out soon. For five years, I pictured the day that you would walk free. I would be there waiting in the unpaved parking lot. I pictured you running out, smiling and crying. I pictured you in that gray V-neck sweater. The one you always looked so handsome in. The one that made you look like a human, not an inmate, not the number I still have memorized like a hot metal iron branded to the inside of my skull. I pictured jumping into your arms when you ran out of that hellish place, and I'd feel the happiest I'd ever felt, euphoric. Like my life could finally start. Like we could resume and make up for lost time.

But I also struggled imagining it ever coming to an end. It was hard to imagine a day when you would be free, and we'd be together. I couldn't imagine it because it wasn't meant for me. And now I'm finally free.

Being brave enough to lose you helped me become myself again. In the years we've spent apart, I began to perceive time differently. Suddenly, it's flying. I'm enjoying my life for the first time in years. I'm laughing again. I'm happy again.

I allowed myself to be whole again when I shed that double life, your sentence. Time took you. But it saved me.

ACKNOWLEDGMENTS

JED, MY ANGEL. FOR ALWAYS seeing me. For your unconditional love. For the deadline that got me to this finish line. For supporting my dreams endlessly. You are the strongest man I've ever known. I love you, my sweetheart.

Mom, for every sacrifice you made to give me the privilege of pursuing my dreams.

To my beautiful, selfless, strong, and devoted sister, Danielle, you are my whole heart. Your love carries me.

Dad, for instilling passion and determination in me through all that you do.

Endless gratitude for my editors at Regalo Press, Adriana Senior, Gretchen Young, Caitlin Burdette, Anthony Ziccardi, and the entire Post Hill Press team. Your support is the greatest gift of all. Thank you for championing this story.

To my agent, Elizabeth Bewley. For believing in me and supporting this project. I am forever grateful.

To the Sterling Lord team, thank you for the editorial support and for believing in me.

Berni Vann, for your enthusiasm about my novel and for your continued support.

ACKNOWLEDGMENTS

Laura Chasen, for being the first to read my earliest drafts. You are a truly compassionate editor. I couldn't have done this without you.

To my smart and encouraging editors, Shelly Ridenour, Hailey Eber, and Andy Tillett, for your constant support and for every opportunity.

To my *New York Post* family. It's a privilege to know you. I'm so grateful. Dana Kennedy, for telling me to keep going. Your words got me through the hard days.

Olivia, my rock. Thank you for everything.

Robert, my dearest friend.

Hanna Halperin, for your beautiful writing that inspires me, and for your insightful edits.

Gotham Writers Workshop, and to everyone who made me feel safe enough to share.

Larry, for helping me move forward.

Rachel, for everything.

To my readers, you are loved.

ABOUT THE AUTHOR

Photo Credit: Alexandra Genova

JEANETTE SETTEMBRE IS A JOURNALIST living in New York City. *Little Red Flags* is her first novel.

Praise for *The History We Carry*

"Margaret Whitford's compelling memoir—a reflection on her family history, her relationship with her mother, and trauma that spans generations—is clear-eyed, compassionate, and often startling in its insight and originality. I was engrossed from beginning to end."

—Clifford Thompson, author of *Jazz June: A Self-Portrait in Essays*

"Rarely have I finished a memoir understanding how our histories, both personal and generational, live and breathe within us in the present. By unearthing the complicated and poignant relationship she has with her mother, Margaret Whitford also powerfully speaks to the collective soul-searching so vitally necessary during these trying times. Written in elegant, luminous prose, this is a memoir that will stay with you long after the story is told."

—Ken Harvey, author of *The Book of Casey Adair*

"Despite Tolstoy's famous quote—families are generally neither happy nor unhappy—they are complicated, like Whitford's. This important memoir delves into sibling conflict, parental infidelity, and substance abuse. Overlying these familial tensions is geopolitical upheaval and the effects of successive world wars, almost unwanted family members themselves. *The History We Carry* seats them together at its literary table and gives each their due in courageous, precise, and ultimately both urgent and forgiving prose."

—Sue William Silverman, author of *Selected Misdemeanors: Essays at the Mercy of the Reader*

"An exhilarating mix of memoir and deep personal research, *The History We Carry* explores a mother's complex history and a daughter's lifelong struggle to understand and connect with her mother. In clear prose that never presents simple answers but rather digs to discover unknown truths and questions even her own long-held narratives, Margaret Whitford has written a robust story of love and trauma."

—Sheryl St. Germain, author of *50 Miles*

"All our parents live lives before we arrive, lives that come to bear on our own. In this new memoir, Margaret Whitford bravely ventures into her mother's past to better understand her own present and future. *The History We Carry* is a gorgeously written book about generational trauma and the intersections of love and grief. It's a stunning debut."

—Lee Martin, author of Pulitzer Prize finalist *The Bright Forever*